THE GIRLFLESH CASTLE

She heard movement in the outer room. The door opened a crack and she glimpsed a long narrow slice of a shadowy figure. She was being spied upon. A fresh thrill coursed through her as she squirmed in her bonds, shaking her head and making mewing sounds behind her tape gag that might have been pleading or indignant. After a moment the door was pulled to again.

There came faint rustles and foot shufflings and her heart thudded. After a minute the door opened all the way and a man stepped into the room.

He was tall and thin, swathed in a green hospital gown, mask and cap. The gap between cap and mask was filled by thick-rimmed glasses, through which dark eyes blinked in owlish wonder.

Vanessa squirmed appealingly, locking onto his gaze and widening her eyes in a show of despair or need – which were fast becoming the same thing for her. Please, please, she tried to say through her gag. If he could distinguish the words under the muffled squeaks that emerged on the other side he could interpret them in any way he chose.

The man circled her almost warily, taking in her naked form. Slowly he reached out and stroked her palpitating stomach. Vanessa stilled at his touch, lying motionless except for a shiver of anticipation, gazing up into his eyes with mute appeal. I'm surrendering myself to you, she thought. You can do what you want with me. I'm begging you to be gentle but don't expect you will be.

By the same author:

THE GIRLFLESH INSTITUTE

THE GIRLFLESH CASTLE

Adriana Arden

This book is a work of fiction.
In real life, make sure you practise safe, sane and consensual sex.

Published by Nexus 2008

Copyright © Adriana Arden 2008

Adriana Arden has asserted her right under the Copyright, Designs and Patents Act 1988 to be identified as the author of this work.

First published in Great Britain in 2008 by
Nexus
Virgin Books
Random House
20 Vauxhall Bridge Road
London SW1V 2SA

www.rbooks.co.uk

Addresses for companies within The Random House Group Limited can be found at: www.randomhouse.co.uk/offices.htm

The Random House Group Limited Reg. No. 954009

Distributed in the USA by Macmillan, 175 Fifth Avenue, New York, NY 10010, USA

A CIP catalogue record for this book is available from the British Library

ISBN 9780352345042

The Random House Group Limited supports The Forest Stewardship Council [FSC], the leading international forest certification organisation. All our titles that are printed on Greenpeace approved FSC certified paper carry the FSC logo. Our paper procurement policy can be found at www.rbooks.co.uk/environment

Mixed Sources
Product group from well-managed forests and other controlled sources
www.fsc.org Cert no. TF-COC-2139
© 1996 Forest Stewardship Council

Typeset by TW Typesetting, Plymouth, Devon
Printed and bound in Great Britain by CPI Bookmarque Ltd, Croydon CR0 4TD

2 4 6 8 10 9 7 5 3 1

nexus Symbols key

 Corporal Punishment

 Female Domination

 Institution

 Medical

 Period Setting

 Restraint/Bondage

 Rubber/Leather

 Spanking

 Transvestism

 Underwear

 Uniforms

One

Vanessa lay naked on the hospital bed.

Broad cuffs of thick clear plastic encircled her wrists and ankles. These were connected to rings bolted to the gleaming tubular metal side-rails of the bed by a few links of shining chain, pulling her arms out from her sides and spreading her legs wide. A length of crepe bandage had been wrapped mummy-like about her head and face, leaving only her nostrils and bright clear hazel eyes exposed. Over her mouth was a wide strip of flesh-tinted sticking plaster, through which the contours of her lips could be seen. From under the bandage dark fluffy hair tumbled over her bare shoulders. More bandages had been bound about her hands forming tight pale fingerless mittens.

Encircling her neck was a white enamelled collar, from the front of which hung a tethering ring. Discreetly stamped into the side of this metal band were the characters: VANESSA 19 WHITE.

Vanessa's milk-pale breasts, with their contrasting sharply defined swollen nipple-crowns, trembled slightly, while her stomach rose and fell in time with her excited breathing. Between her spread legs was a thick matt of pubic hair trimmed back at its heart to expose a deep in-rolling cleft that glistened wetly. A

1

small gold ring gleamed where it pierced her left labia minora.

Standing by her bed were a man and woman in the traditional costumes of doctor and nurse: he in a white coat with a stethoscope hung round his neck and she in a blue uniform, white cap and apron. He was middle-aged, bespectacled, pink-faced and balding, while she was petite, young and pretty, with a broad clip-belt about her waist that emphasised the swell of her hips. About her neck she wore a yellow metal collar with the characters: JULIE 5 CANARY stamped upon it.

The doctor was consulting the clipboard that held Vanessa's medical charts. After a moment he reached down and pinched her right nipple, stretching and twisting it sharply. Vanessa whimpered behind her bandage gag and squirmed at his touch, tugging at her restraining cuffs, the muscles of her well-toned body standing out. However, neither the doctor nor the nurse took any notice of her muted protests.

'Hmm ... pronounced swelling of the areola and hardness of the nipples,' the doctor said. His hand slid down across Vanessa's stomach to the mound of her sex and prised her labia apart. 'Also discharge from the vulva and marked erection of the clitoris ...' He pinched the hard nub of flesh in question firmly between thumb and forefinger, making Vanessa whimper afresh and jerk violently, rattling her chains. Her eyes bulged and began to fill with tears.

'Take her temperature again, Nurse,' the doctor commanded.

'At once, Doctor,' the nurse said meekly.

She touched a control pad by the head of the bed. With a subdued hum the lower halves of the bedside rails began to lift upwards, hingeing about the middle

2

of the bed and pulling Vanessa's legs with them. In a few seconds her legs were raised high over her upper body and she had been folded into a right angle. The swell of her sex pouch and the pucker of her anus were now displayed between the taut curves of her buttocks.

From an instrument tray on the bedside locker the nurse took up a long thick thermometer and slid it up the greased sheath of Vanessa's rectum. Vanessa shivered as the hard rod penetrated her, squeezing it tightly. The remainder of the thermometer jutted out and upward from her bottom cleft, twitching slightly.

The doctor's eyes were riveted upon it and he licked his lips. By now his forehead glistened with sweat while a prominent bulge grew midway down the front of his coat.

After half a minute the nurse pulled the thermometer from Vanessa's bottom and showed it to the doctor.

'Ah ... yes ... well above normal,' he said knowingly.

'What's your diagnosis, Doctor?' the nurse asked breathlessly.

'It's a clear case of sexual overheating leading to potentially dangerous slackness of the vagina,' he declared. 'She needs cooling down and tightening up. Fetch a freezing pack at once!'

Vanessa's stomach fluttered and she moaned and shook her head. Again they ignored her.

'Yes, Doctor,' the nurse said obediently.

She slipped though a gap in the floor-to-ceiling curtains that surrounded Vanessa's bed and hurried off. Meanwhile the doctor took up a pair of latex gloves from the tray and pulled them on, snapping them into place and smoothing the wrinkles carefully out of the fingers. Then he stood over Vanessa's doubled-over body and smiled down at her through the wide gap between her raised legs.

'Don't worry, my dear, I'll fix you up.' He stroked her sex and dipped his rubber-sheathed fingers into her wet cleft. 'Sluts like you need this sort of treatment regularly or else you leak everywhere. Look at the stain your pussy's leaving on the sheets.' She squirmed and tried to pull her knees together. He gave the tight bulge of her bottom a warning slap. 'Now you know there's no point in struggling. Of course it's going to hurt a bit but it's all for your own good. You have to be cruel to be kind . . .'

The nurse returned with a folded rubber sheet and a fresh instrument tray that she set down on the locker. She spread the rubber sheet out on the bed and slid it under Vanessa's raised haunches. She pulled the cover off the tray to reveal a frosted and steaming bowl of ice cubes, a large stainless steel clamp with curving jaws and a clear plastic ball with a ring handle.

'The equipment is ready, Doctor,' she reported.

The doctor licked his lips, took up a lozenge of ice, prised open the mouth of Vanessa's vagina and thrust it up her passage as far as he could reach. Vanessa gasped at the sudden icy chill that blossomed deep inside her. The doctor took up another cube and pushed it into her trembling sheath after the first. Vanessa moaned and squirmed and shook her head.

'Hold her still!' the doctor commanded.

The nurse reached over and pinned down Vanessa's hips.

'This has to be done,' the doctor said as with trembling fingers he thrust another slug of ice into her. 'We've got to get you tightened up!'

He was sweating now and his eyes were misty and round with lust. Ignoring Vanessa's struggles he thrust another ten cubes up inside her before he was satisfied. Holding the last one in place with his thumb where it jutted out from her lovemouth he snapped the clamp about her inner labia, pinching the flesh petals together and closing her passage over its chilly contents.

The nurse released her hold on Vanessa's hips. Vanessa wailed from behind her strapping gag and wriggled her rump desperately over the rubber sheet, feeling the numbing cold growing between her legs and spreading through her belly. Melted water was dripping from her ice-packed vagina but she could not shake off the clamp.

'Her rectum as well I think,' the doctor said with an undisguised grin of delight.

Vanessa screwed up her eyes as he forced a further half dozen ice cubes through the tight greased pucker of her anal sphincter into the warm tunnel of her rectum. When he was done he pushed the plug-ball into her bumhole, sealing it tight so only its ring handle showed. Then he stood back, admiring the results of his efforts.

By now Vanessa was gurgling and shivering, her fingers clenching and clawing, straining her legs against the cuffs that held her ankles over her head, lifting her bottom off the mat as she wriggled about. Melted water was trickling freely from both her orifices but she could not expel the ice cubes packed inside her, held in place by plug and clamp. She felt her clitoris shrivelling even as her nipples swelled to India-rubber hardness.

There was a squeal from the nurse. The doctor had pulled her roughly back against his chest, pushed one hand under the bib of her apron through the closure of her uniform blouse and had his hand clamped about her left breast, which he was cupping and squeezing. She gave a little shudder. 'Oh . . . doctor! Not here . . .' she protested feebly.

'Be quiet and observe the patient!' he commanded.

With his free hand he tore her apron ties free and ripped open the poppers of her uniform front. She was bra-less and her naked glossy rounded breasts capped by pert pink nipples spilled out. Clasping them with both hands he pinched and kneaded her globes while rubbing his crotch fiercely against the taut fabric covering her bottom. As he mauled her the nurse sighed and rolled her eyes up, catching her bottom lip between her white teeth, while before them Vanessa whimpered and writhed about as her passages inexorably closed up about their plugs of ice. She squirmed and twisted, setting her breasts jiggling and heaving, tugging at her cuffs. But the bands of plastic were too thick and tough and would not yield.

There was no escaping her torment. She would suffer for the pleasure of this perverted doctor. But then that was what she was here for . . .

By now a red flush was spreading on the doctor's face and his eyes were shining lustfully as his fondling of the nurse grew more agitated. Abruptly he pushed her away. 'She's ready . . . open her up!'

With her breasts still hanging out of her uniform front the nurse scrambled to obey. She unsnapped the clamp from Vanessa's by now numbed and purple-mottled labia and yanked out the plug from her tight-pinched anus. With a groan Vanessa tried to squeeze her knees together. Twin streams of water mingled with half-melted ice cubes bubbled and gushed from her frozen passages onto the rubber sheet.

Meanwhile the doctor was tearing open his white coat and unzipping his flies. 'Must check the treatment has been successful,' he grunted as his thick hard cock sprang free.

The nurse gathered up the sodden rubber sheet and pulled it aside as, with desperate clumsy haste, the doctor clambered onto the bed and almost threw himself between Vanessa's spread and elevated legs. With frantic stabs his cock found the cold, wet and tight-clenched mouth of her vagina and forced its way in. Vanessa gave a gag-muffled shriek as her shrunken passage was violently opened up by his thrusting cock. It was almost like losing her maidenhead again. The sudden heat and friction of his hot cock in her chilled insides was shocking even as it brought the life back to her. It was painful . . . but it was the kind of pain she craved.

He rubbed his pink face over her pliant breasts, nipping at her hard nipples even as his hips rose and fell between her legs and he pumped away madly inside her, heedless of doing any damage to her tender passage, making the bed shake. Blood flowed back into her clit in a frightening pulsing tingling rush, bringing with it acute sensation and awareness. It swelled and budded and filled out, as though straining to touch the shaft wet with her juices sliding past it. That the doctor was completely unattractive to her had nothing to do with the intensity of her response to having his cock inside her. Such things she had found were quite beyond her control. He had called her a slut and, though that was a cruel word, in her heart she knew it was true.

Then he was growling and grunting and thudding into her and hot sperm was pulsing inside her and she was clenching at him with her unnaturally tightened vaginal sheath and the liquid knot in her loins burst and suddenly there was no more pain, only the

7

exultant release of a shattering orgasm. Freed from all concern her mind spun ecstatically . . .

The previous morning Vanessa had steered her red VW between the high wrought-iron security gates of the Alves Clinic that nestled in the folds of the Surrey downs.

Beyond was a driveway winding between mature trees and thick shrubberies to the front of the main clinic building. This was a nineteen-thirties modern construction of three storeys, with a flat roof, white rendered walls and tall windows. The ends of its twin wings were bowed where the roof cantilevered out over open balconies. One truly modern alteration, Vanessa noticed, was that the windows were all of mirrored glass. No doubt it could be justified on the grounds of energy efficiency, but it also effectively concealed whatever lay within.

Vanessa parked in a bay at the end of a line of cars the least of which was five times the value of hers. The clinic evidently had wealthy patrons, but then she knew it offered a rather exclusive service.

She climbed out of her car and smoothed down her white cotton two-piece jacket and short skirt. The shell top under the jacket was also white, as were her wedge-heeled open-toed sandals. Only the scarf about her neck was black. This complemented the black silk band of the white fedora she took up off the passenger seat and put on at a jaunty angle. Tucked into the side of the hatband was a card bearing the neatly printed word: PRESS.

Gathering up a digital notepad recorder and camera she locked her car and followed the signs to the main entrance of the clinic. On the plaque beside the doorway, in smaller letters below the clinic name, it said: A SHILLER COMPANY. Seeing the name gave her a happy shiver, reminding her that she was a part of something secret and wonderful.

Within was a cool tastefully fitted lobby. A pair of solid-looking doors opened off from it, one marked PRIVATE and the other CLINIC, both fitted with pad and key card security locks. To one side a middle-aged man was seated amongst the carefully tended greenery of a waiting area, flicking through a brochure. Opposite was an efficient-looking and immaculately dressed red-haired woman seated behind a glass-topped desk. Unsure of the status of the waiting man and aware that certain illusions had to be maintained, Vanessa crossed over to the desk and said formally:

'Good morning, I'm Vanessa Buckingham from *Datumline*. I have an appointment with your manager, Miss Mayken ...' Then she bent forward, briefly pulled her scarf aside to reveal the slim metal collar locked about her neck and added quietly: 'Vanessa Nineteen White.'

She had just announced herself to be numbered and collared corporate property. It should have been disgusting and shameful but instead she felt only pride.

The receptionist returned her greeting formally. 'Good morning, Miss Buckingham. Yes, we're expecting you.' Then she smiled and added softly: 'You're *GN*'s new reporter, aren't you? I've read your articles. They're very good.'

Vanessa found herself blushing. She had become a most unlikely celebrity in a very private world. 'Thank you, I'm glad you liked them.'

In a businesslike tone once more the receptionist said: 'I'll let Miss Mayken know you're here.' She picked up a phone, spoke into it briefly and then said: 'Miss Mayken will be with you shortly. Do take a seat.'

'Thank you.' Vanessa sat down opposite the desk a little aside from the waiting man.

The CLINIC door opened and a man in a white coat came out. He greeted the waiting man and escorted him though the same doorway, using a key card to re-enter.

With just the two of them in the lobby the receptionist took the opportunity openly to look Vanessa up and down in a calculating manner. Normally such an obvious show of interest might have been thought impolite, but the rules of etiquette were different here. The receptionist was not wearing a collar and Vanessa was. She was free to look at Vanessa as long and hard as she liked. Vanessa felt the familiar stirring in her loins and seemingly unconsciously parted her legs and brushed down her skirt. The air caressed her panty-less pubes and she saw the receptionist grinning. Not so long ago she would never even have dreamed of displaying herself so blatantly to a stranger, even a pretty one like the redheaded receptionist. Now it gave her a delicious thrill.

The door marked PRIVATE opened and a woman emerged. She was a trim blonde perhaps in her early forties, dressed casually in a loose top and ankle-length skirt. A key card hung on a cord about her neck.

She offered her hand to Vanessa. 'Miss Buckingham, a pleasure, I'm Gillian Mayken . . . do come this way . . .'

Using her key card she led Vanessa back through the door into a small vestibule closed at its far end by another solid-looking door marked STAFF ONLY. Miss Mayken checked that the first door had swung closed and latched shut before she opened the inner one onto a corridor that crossed the bottom of a flight of stairs. Vanessa approved her caution. It would not do to let an outsider glimpse what lay beyond.

The sign on the inside of the door gave some hint of this. It read: NO LEASHED SLAVES BEYOND THIS POINT! And: ARE YOU DRESSED?

Beside the doorway was a row of hooks from which hung several leather and chain leashes.

'Remove your scarf,' Miss Mayken said briskly.

Vanessa obeyed and Miss Mayken clipped a red leather leash to her collar ring. Vanessa's heart gave a little flutter. She was leashed like a dog and in the control of a perfect stranger. But then Miss Mayken had the right. She worked for the clinic that in turn was owned by the Shiller company while Vanessa was merely a chattel, if a proud one, of the same company. This woman could do more or less what she liked with her. A warm exciting wetness began to seep between Vanessa's pubic lips.

Miss Mayken led Vanessa down the corridor and through a door into a comfortable office. Through its shaded window was a view out across well-tended lawns and flowerbeds, backed by a screen of tall trees. Still holding Vanessa's leash Miss Mayken sat down in an easy chair to one side of the desk and pointed to a small round mat on the floor. Vanessa knelt on it facing her, resting back on her heels, parting her knees and letting her skirt ride up her thighs.

Examining Vanessa with interest Miss Mayken said: 'So, you're the *Girlflesh News*'s famous new slave reporter.'

Vanessa blushed once again. 'I'm not sure about the "famous", Mistress, but I am a company slave and I do write for *GN* . . . and *Datumline*, of course, when they want articles for public distribution.'

'How versatile of you. And you're a white-collar

11

girl. We don't see one of the Director's favourites very often.'

'We go where the Director sends us, Mistress,' Vanessa said simply. 'For the moment she wants me to continue working on *GN* just like any other reporter. Zara Fulton, my Mistress Editor, thought an insider's view of the clinic's work would interest our core readership, especially those chains who haven't served here before.'

'And I suppose you want to do interviews and take photographs and that sort of thing.'

'And to serve as a clinic girl for a few days, if that's no trouble, Mistress.'

'Like any other chain girl?'

'Of course, Mistress. I expect no favours because of the colour of my collar. My Mistress Editor would be furious if she thought you'd been soft on me. Also it would be like lying to my readers if I hadn't experienced what I wrote about first-hand.'

'Naturally I'd like our work at the clinic to be appreciated, but you understand the need for total discretion, especially where it comes to pictures?'

'I've reported from private house parties where they'd hired Shiller girls to entertain, Mistress. I'm most careful to use no material that could identify an individual client. Mistress Zara double-checks and she'd tan my backside raw if I was stupid enough to let anything like that through.'

'I'm pleased to hear it. But in any case I'd rather our clients did not see anyone wandering around with a camera. We offer them official photo or video records of their stay by prior arrangement, but insist they do not bring in their own cameras for the peace of mind of their fellow guests. Aside from the fear of blackmail, should a single image of one of our clients in a compromising position become public, even by

12

chance, then it could be a disaster. So I would prefer you limited photography to times and places when clients are absent. Of course we can always pose some of the girls for you to show the facilities and equipment in use.'

'I understand, Mistress. And what about the staff? It's their story as well.'

'I'll sound them out about it.'

'Thank you, Mistress. And of course you'll see the article and any images before they're published. It's the Shiller company magazine, Mistress, not some muckraking tabloid. The Director wants to celebrate quality and honest service in everything bearing the Shiller brand name – girls included. That's more important to her than anything.'

Miss Mayken's manner seemed to soften. She leaned forward and asked hesitantly: 'I read your articles on the initiation and graduating ceremonies for Cherry Chain. I've never been to one of those affairs. Were the Director's speeches really as, well . . . as heartfelt as you make them sound?'

'Even more so, Mistress,' Vanessa said sincerely, feeling a lump rise in her throat even as she spoke. 'The ceremonies were like nothing I'd ever seen before. You had to be there. You can't really understand what it means to be a Shiller chain girl otherwise. I'm sure, if you make a request to the Director, you'd be invited to the next one.'

Miss Mayken nodded slowly and said with a smile: 'I think I will.'

Vanessa felt the mood lighten. She held up her recorder. 'May I start by interviewing you, Mistress? It won't take long. Just some general background material.'

Sitting back in her chair, Miss Mayken said: 'Go on then.'

Vanessa set the recorder going. 'Interview for *GN* with Gillian Mayken, Manager of Alves Clinic . . . First, Mistress, can you tell me what sort of service you offer here?'

Miss Mayken smiled. 'I suppose you'd call it "Doctors and Nurses" for adults. We provide a realistic medical setting for certain select clients to indulge their fantasies through role-playing with grown women. There's a general ward, private suites, waiting and examination rooms and an operating theatre in which clients can practise a variety of simple medical procedures. Usually the clients take on the roles of doctors with staffs of chain girl "nurses" to assist them where necessary. The nurses are allowed a little more freedom than the patients, as they may have to play dominant as well as submissive roles.'

'What sort of medical procedures, Mistress?'

'It varies with the client. It might be mock anaesthesia, internal examinations and irrigation, insertions of various devices, minor injections or the use of vacuum and electrical stimulation. We employ a genuine medical consultant to ensure it's all suitably painful but safe.'

'Do the clients usually have an idea of what fantasy they want to play out from the start, Mistress?'

'About half do, I'd say. We usually manage to accommodate their wishes. To inspire the rest we have a brochure of suggestive scenarios. They're especially useful for shy or first-time clients.'

'Do you have many of those, Mistress?'

'Quite a few, actually. You don't think all masters start out sure enough of themselves to properly dominate a submissive first time, do you?'

The idea surprised Vanessa. 'I suppose not, Mistress. I'd never thought about it.'

'You wouldn't have met any in Shiller's employment, but they do exist. And they sometimes need a little encouragement in the same way natural submissives need to be trained to become proper chain girls. They know what they want to do but they need to be introduced gradually so they can refine their technique and build up their confidence. So we provide easy scenarios for them as practice which don't require too much interaction, such as . . .' She paused and raised a questioning eyebrow. 'I wonder . . . you did say you wanted to be treated just like the other girls. Hands-on experience. I mean the clients' hands on you, of course.'

Vanessa felt a shiver even as her lower stomach began to knot in delicious anticipation. 'Yes, Mistress.'

'Well, we've a new client arriving shortly. I was going to suggest he starts with our deserted surgery scenario. An empty waiting room opens onto an examination room. Our client can peep in. He sees a single occupant: a gagged and naked woman strapped down and arranged for a gynaecological procedure. Hanging by the door is a surgical mask, cap and gown to put on as a disguise. The mask gives him confidence. Now he can do anything he wants to her and she'll never know who was responsible. He enters the room. There's a surgical tray beside her with some implements in it he can use on her if he likes . . . Pull up your skirt and show me your pussy!'

The last words were snapped out in commanding tones. Automatically Vanessa obeyed. Miss Mayken looked closely at Vanessa's bared pubic delta with its damp curls and chuckled.

'You're wet.'

'Yes, Mistress.'

'Did that little fantasy excite you?'

Vanessa felt her cheeks warming. 'Yes, Mistress.'

'Would you like to help bring it to life?'

'Yes please, Mistress.'

'You're a slutty masochist, aren't you?'

Vanessa lowered her head while smiling in shameful delight.

'I am, Mistress.'

'I think you'll fit in here very well . . .'

Vanessa tugged against the broad rubber straps that bound her to the padded vinyl of an examination couch, but of course they did not yield.

Her nipples were hard cones of pulsing flesh while a familiar churning filled her stomach, a counterpoint to the burning tingle deep within her loins that was a combination of fear and sexual need. It was a sensation she had become used to over the past few months, when she had gone from denial and resistance to unashamed craving. Had she become an addict to submission and degradation or, after twenty-two years of life, had she simply found her normal state of being? Did it matter any more?

She was in a replica of a medical examination room with equipment cabinets arrayed around the walls and illuminated by a single long high strip window of frosted glass. She was naked, except for her collar and a broad strip of adhesive strapping that covered her mouth. Her arms were pulled up above her head and held against the top of the couch by rubber cuffs. Another strap was pulled tight across her stomach. The hinged stirrup arms of gleaming steel mounted on the bottom of the couch were folded outwards so as to form virtually a straight line. Rubber cuffs about her knees and ankles bound her to them, forcing her legs to spread wide in a position of the most extreme exposure and blatant invitation. The prominent mound of her vulva hung over the foot of the couch. Under its cap of dark curls its pink mouth gaped wetly.

A sheet of paper couch roll had thoughtfully been placed under her bottom. A dark stain was growing on it where the discharge from her vagina had trickled down through her buttock cleft. She was perfectly open and helpless, trembling with anticipation, marvelling at how she had come to be here but not wanting it any other way.

She heard movement in the outer room. The door opened a crack and she glimpsed a long narrow slice of a shadowy figure. She was being spied upon. A fresh thrill coursed through her as she squirmed in her bonds, shaking her head and making mewing sounds behind her tape gag that might have been pleading or indignant. After a moment the door was pulled to again.

There came faint rustles and foot shufflings and her heart thudded. After a minute the door opened all the way and a man stepped into the room.

He was tall and thin, swathed in a green hospital gown, mask and cap. The gap between cap and mask was filled by thick-rimmed glasses, through which dark eyes blinked in owlish wonder.

Vanessa squirmed appealingly, locking onto his gaze and widening her eyes in a show of despair or need – which were fast becoming the same thing for her. Please, please, she tried to say through her gag. If he could distinguish the words under the muffled squeaks that emerged on the other side he could interpret them in any way he chose.

The man circled her almost warily, taking in her naked form. Slowly he reached out and stroked her palpitating stomach. Vanessa stilled at his touch, lying motionless except for a shiver of anticipation, gazing up into his eyes with mute appeal. I'm surrendering myself to you, she thought. You can do what you want with me. I'm begging you to be gentle but don't expect you will be.

His hands moved up to her breasts, cupping and squeezing the hot pliant mounds. His fingers closed about her straining nipples, testing their hardness, rolling them between thumb and forefinger. Vanessa groaned. His fingers tightened, pinching and twisting her hard teats. Vanessa gave a whimper of pain, her eyes misting with tears. Was that a smile she saw behind his mask?

With growing confidence he thrust a hand down between her widespread thighs and dug his fingers into her cleft, stirring and stretching her sexmouth. Vanessa shuddered and rolled her eyes as he rubbed against her erect clitoris. He took his hand away and examined the sticky wet smear she had deposited upon it. He had her shamelessly aroused, her vulva engorged and vulva gaping wide, begging to be filled.

He moved round until he was standing between her spread legs and then knelt down so his eyes were level with her groin. Carefully he prised apart her labia, examining their complex folds, looking down into the hot dark tunnel of her vagina. Could he smell her need? It was filling the room by now. He dipped a curious finger into the tight pucker of her anus and she squeezed tight about his digit. Was this his first penetration of a bound slave girl? She had greased her anus as she did every morning so it had slid in easily. Would he use her that way? She hoped he liked the feel of her.

The man rose once more and began examining the contents of the instrument tray set out beside her couch. Vanessa twisted her head round, straining to see what he was looking at. Was he going to do this properly? No girl displayed like she was could expect to escape without being punished. It was what she was here for. It would make what followed so much better. What a pain slut she'd become.

He'd picked up a length of translucent yellow rubber tubing and was clumsily wrapping one end about his hand. Oh yes, that would make a good whip . . .

Taking up position in front of her once more he drew back his arm. Vanessa screwed up her eyes in joyful anticipation. Nothing happened. She opened them again. He was standing there blinking uncertainly. No! She gurgled and whined, straining at her straps and trying to lift her hips in frantic enticement. But he only lowered his whip arm. He was losing his nerve. He really was a beginner at this game. But he couldn't leave her in agony like this. He needed a push to deliver the first blow . . . but what?

So in desperation she peed on him.

It was a fine strong jet, fountaining out cleanly from between her parted labia and splattering across the front of his gown. For a moment he was too stunned to react, staggering back slightly while gaping at the steaming stain. Then he looked at her and spoke the only words she ever heard him utter: 'You dirty bitch . . .!'

And he swung the rubber tube hard.

It hissed through the air and cut across her soft inner thighs and the mound of her sex.

Yes! Vanessa cried triumphantly in her head as the blow seared through her.

For the first time he heard the sweet sound of a lash on female flesh, saw a girl convulse under his hand, heard her gag-muffled yelp of pain. There would be no stopping him now.

There wasn't.

He lashed her unmercifully, laying the tube across her from every angle, even cutting straight up and down so it parted her pubic hair, spread her pussy lips and dug into her furrow, curling up into her bum cleft or across her stomach. And she sobbed and screamed and writhed until she was teetering on the verge of such an orgasm as only a masochistic submissive could know.

Then he dropped the tubing, tore open his sodden gown, ripped his flies wide to free his straining erection and rammed it into her.

When Vanessa opened her eyes again the man was gone. Her inner thighs simmered and stung and her vagina ached as though it had been host to a road drill. Cold sweat was drying on her and the couch roll under her bottom was sodden with urine, her juices and his sperm, but she felt wonderful. Miss Mayken was standing by the side of the couch, smiling down at her.

'That was very well done, Vanessa,' she said, idly tracing the contours of her right nipple, which automatically began to swell at her touch. 'Peeing on him at the crucial moment was inspired. I suspect watersports will play a key role in his fantasies from now on. You may have shaped his future as a dominant. You're really quite special . . .'

Miss Mayken lowered the head end of the couch, laying Vanessa flat. Then she pulled the plaster off Vanessa's mouth with a sharp jerk that left her lips stinging. Undoing her long skirt Miss Mayken laid it across a chair and then tied the trailing ends of her top about her waist. She wore no underwear and the shaven mound of her vulva stood out prominently. Climbing onto the couch she straddled Vanessa's chest, her buttocks brushing the tips of her nipples, and then shuffled forward and spread her knees until she could press her sex into Vanessa's face.

Without needing to be told Vanessa began to lap at her soft-scented cleft.

Miss Mayken smiled down at her and stroked her hair.

'I can see now why you're a white-collar girl. I envy the Director owning you. But you mustn't waste your time on interviews while you're with us. You'll get your story serving the clients with the other girls. I think I'll put you on the general ward first . . .'

For a couple of minutes the 'doctor' lay slumped between Vanessa's up-stretched legs recovering his breath, while 'nurse' Julie stood patiently by the bedside. Then he levered himself off Vanessa, pulling out of the clinging clutches of her vagina, and clambered off the bed. His shiny softening cock was dangling from his flies, his face was red and sweat-stained and his spectacles were awry, but he looked immensely pleased with himself.

Vanessa, knowing that she had given satisfaction, lay still enjoying her reward of post-orgasmic bliss. It troubled her not at all that she was being used as a sex-toy and plaything there to be humiliated and abused, because that was her natural place in this ultimate game of doctors and nurses. Just a few months ago she would have dismissed such a response as perverse madness, but a lot had happened since then . . .

Julie 5, her uniform front still hanging open exposing her breasts, played her part by asking breathily: 'Is she cured, doctor?'

'What? Oh . . . yes, completely.'

'Oh, you're wonderful, Doctor,' she said adoringly. 'May I clean you up?'

He nodded. She went down on her knees before him, took his limp cock into her mouth and began to lick all traces of his sperm and Vanessa's juices from his shaft. The doctor sighed and sat back against the side of the bed.

As Julie dutifully sucked and licked, Vanessa saw his shaft begin to stiffen once more. After a minute he grasped a handful of hair at the back of Julie's head and pulled her closer to him. Her cheeks bulged as his revitalised cock filled her mouth and a blush spread over her face but she kept on slurping and sucking. Suddenly his hips jerked and he rammed hard, making Julie's throat bulge as his cock slid down her gullet. Julie choked, gasping for breath and gulping rapidly, still sucking for all she was worth. Then he sagged, limp and utterly spent. Julie licked him clean once more and slowly he pulled out of her mouth, trailing strings of sperm and saliva from her lips.

Breathing raggedly he stuffed his now shrivelled penis back into his trousers, straightened his coat and said vaguely: 'Right . . . Nurse . . . Ah, I think that will be all for now . . . Tidy up here . . .'

He fumbled for the gap in the curtain and staggered unsteadily out of the cubicle.

Julie wiped her lips and turned to grin at Vanessa. A slight sheen of sweat glistened between her breasts. 'I'm not allowed to lick you out unless a guest orders me, but I wanted to know what you tasted like,' she said.

Shiller-trained girls are wonderful, Vanessa thought happily, and I'm so proud to be one of them.

Two

Vanessa watched as Julie 5 neatly gathered up and packed away the contents of the freezing pack. Then she took down a device that had been clipped to the wall next to the bedside basin. It resembled a garden hose spray gun but with a transparent plastic cup fitted about the barrel from which extended a flexible rubber nozzle with interchangeable tips. Instead of a single hose it trailed behind it a bundle of three of different colours, all of which connected to sockets in the wall. Vanessa had a device like it in her bathroom at home, as every company girl should.

Julie inserted the tube into Vanessa's vagina until the cup pressed firmly against her skin and pulled the trigger. A douche of warm water flushed her passage clean of sperm and spent juices, flowing back into the cup where it was sucked away down a vacuum tube. Julie changed the tube tip and slid it into Vanessa's anus, which she flushed out in the same way. Then she pumped a plunger with her thumb, sending a spurt of lubricating jelly up into her rectum. A Shiller girl's rear passage was always kept clean, fresh and greased. The next client might require the use of it.

Filling the basin with warm water, Julie sponged Vanessa down, towelled her dry and combed her hair where it spilled out from under her bandages.

Vanessa luxuriated under her careful attention, feeling deliciously pampered.

Julie operated the bed controls. The upper halves of the side-rails to which her wrists were cuffed now rotated, dragging her arms up level with her raised legs and lifting her bottom clear of the bed. As she hung there Julie changed the sheets under her for fresh ones, then lowered her down again until she was reclining with her arms by her sides, upper body slightly raised and legs spread to the sides of the bed.

The last thing she did was to peel back the plaster over Vanessa's mouth. She fed her some water and then bent over, the nipples of her still bared breasts brushing Vanessa's own, and kissed her passionately, to which Vanessa responded in kind.

When their lips finally separated Julie said: 'Sorry, I just had to do that.'

'I'm not,' Vanessa said with a smile.

'I know you've got a special girl of your own in Cherry Chain and I'm not trying to get between you.'

Vanessa frowned. 'With a single kiss – even if it was seriously hot? I know Kashika does a lot more than just kiss her chain sisters, let alone what she does when she's serving clients. She won't expect me to be any different when I'm working. As company slaves we've performed just about every sex-act imaginable with masters, mistresses and each other. How can we have any body jealousy left in us?'

Julie looked troubled. 'I just didn't want you to get the wrong idea. Your own colour sisters are like a family and the rest is just earning a living being our natural horny slavish selves. That's not the same as having a personal one-to-one thing with another girl. That's private and I'm not trying to go there.'

Only a Shiller-trained slave could bother about such things, Vanessa thought. That's what comes of having such an ethically minded company Director. Aloud she said: 'I know what you mean. But don't let it worry you. I'll tell Kashika how nice you've been to me and she'll understand.'

Julie brightened. 'Thanks. I had to do it in case I don't get another chance.' She lowered her eyes shyly. 'I mean you are white collar and *GN*'s famous slave reporter.'

'I'm just a Shiller girl serving as ordered,' Vanessa protested.

Julie briefly put a finger over her lips to silence her. 'No, you're something more than that, I can tell. And now I can say I kissed you and it was great. Will you put that in your article?'

'I'll say you were my ministering angel,' Vanessa promised.

'We swap over with Sapphire Chain in four days so they get their chance to play nurses. Will you still be here? You could look after me while I'm cuffed to a bed.'

'Sorry, my Mistress Editor wants me home before then. But when you get back to B3 and Kashika is free as well, maybe we can get together.'

Julie grinned hugely. 'I'll look forward to it.' She glanced at the fob watch pinned to her uniform. 'But I can't pretend the doctor might be coming back any longer. I've got to put you on show again . . .'

She replaced the plaster, refastened her uniform and then pulled the curtains back from around the bed revealing the rest of the mock medical ward.

It was a large long room situated on the first floor of the clinic. Its mirrored and blind-hung windows dimmed the outside daylight.

The bed curtains ran on the inside of floor-to-ceiling glass partitions, accessed via close-fitting sliding doors, that enclosed each bed in its own cubicle.

The curtains provided visual privacy and the glass aural isolation when clients were using the girls. Once the clients had finished with them the curtains were of course drawn back since chain girls neither expected nor received any concessions to modesty.

The partition glass was perfectly clear and Vanessa could see that currently five of the other beds were curtained indicating clients were within. A couple of the remaining beds were empty, suggesting their occupants had been taken to examination rooms or the surgery. Naked Sapphire Chain girls wearing blue collars occupied the rest of the beds, all restrained, gagged and bandaged in one way or another. More yellow-collared Canary girls dressed as nurses bustled about between them.

Julie gathered up the soiled sheets and freezing pack gear, smiled once more at Vanessa, slid back the door of the cubicle and left her for whoever next cared to indulge their fantasy.

As she waited Vanessa tried to take in all that was going on around her, starting to compose her article in her head. Clearly she was not going to be allowed much time to take proper notes and conduct formal interviews so she had to remember it all. She could always research background facts and figures and take a few photos before she left. Perhaps working with impressions gathered on the job was the best way in any case. It was how a chain girl would experience serving in the clinic and chain girls were her primary readership . . .

The bizarre perversity of what she did suddenly struck her, as it had on occasions during the past few months, with the force almost of a physical blow. She wrote for *Girlflesh News*, the secret in-house magazine of the Shiller company who literally dealt in girlflesh as they might any other goods or services, seeking

out, training, organising and supplying willing submissives to stock places such as this clinic. She was
fairly certain it was the only magazine in the world
written primarily for slave girls to read. At first, when
she had been in denial of her own secret nature, the
very concept of it had sickened her. But then she got
to know FG Shiller, the remarkable Director of the
company that bore her name and the inspiration
behind its secret business of ethical slave trading in
the twenty-first century. Shiller in turn had helped
Vanessa on a journey of self-discovery and coming to
terms with her own nature. Now she was prouder
than she cared to admit at being *GN*'s only true slave
reporter and paradoxically felt freer in chains than
she ever had as a supposedly modern, equal and
emancipated woman. In fact freedom was very important to her. She had learned that everybody
should have the right to be free ... including the
freedom, when they so chose, not to be.

Her thoughts were interrupted by the appearance
of a Sapphire girl being brought back into the ward
by a couple of nurses.

The clinic's 'patients' were naturally not allowed
the freedom of walking where they chose or the
dignity of a simple wheelchair when they had to be
moved to another room for specialist attention. To
reinforce their sense of absolute dependence they
were taken out and returned to their beds while being
secured at all times. So they were transported in
devices she heard the nurses refer to as 'Alves frames'.

These were open rectangles of heavy-gauge tubular
metal large enough to fit over a girl lying with her
hands by her sides. The inner rims of the frames were
fitted with an array of rubber straps for securing
purposes. The frames were set on swivel-wheeled
bases by way of a pivoting 'L' shaped post connected

to one side of the frame by a horizontal rotating mount. This allowed the frame to be adjusted from flat to upright so it could be slid over a bed, balanced by its cantilevered wheels. A gas piston in the mounting post then raised and lowered the frame as required.

Vanessa thought the name entirely appropriate. The frames' function was to restrain, contain and display them, just like the clinic did.

The girl was being wheeled along upright in her frame, held there by a web of straps from neck to ankles. Her eyes were red with tears that had streaked her cheeks and run over her gag bandage, while her breasts, jutting out from between her straps, were blotched, the nipples swollen and encircled by scarlet and purple rings. On her face was that strange look of triumphal exhaustion that Vanessa had seen on other slave girls, and on occasions in reflections of her own face. It told of a submissive nature being tested to the limits and having found ultimate pleasure in the depths of her suffering.

The nurses positioned her frame by one of the empty beds, flipped the frame and the girl imprisoned within backwards until she lay flat, slid her over the bed and lowered her onto the sheets. They freed her straps one by one from the frame and re-cuffed her to the sides of the bed. As her legs were spread Vanessa saw the cleft of her vagina was also red and swollen. She wondered what 'treatment' she had undergone. Perhaps she would find out for herself first-hand.

Vanessa's thoughts were interrupted when a middle-aged woman dressed in a dark blue sister's uniform entered her cubicle and drew the curtains. She was carrying a bedpan with a towel draped across it. If she'd been a member of the clinic staff she would not have bothered to draw the curtains to save

Vanessa's blushes, but if she wanted to keep this private it meant she was probably a client. There was no reason why they all had to dress as doctors.

Playing safe, Vanessa dropped back into the character of an unwilling patient and began pulling at her cuffs, letting her eyes go wide in apprehension and making pleading noises behind her gag. *I'm a helpless prisoner in some mad sex-clinic*, she thought, embracing the fantasy with secret delight. *Please let me go . . .*

'None of that, girl,' the 'Sister' said briskly. I've just come to put you on the pan. Mustn't get constipated or risk wetting the bed . . .'

She operated the bed controls. The lower section of the side-railing to which her ankles were cuffed contracted, pulling her feet back along the bed and forcing her knees to bend upward even as her thighs spread wider. Then the upper section pivoted, lifting her arms up into the air and pulling her into an enforced squatting position. The sister caught hold of a pinch of Vanessa's pubic hair and tugged, forcing her to raise her hips so she could slide the bedpan under her bottom.

'Now you do your business for me, girl. I want to see plenty of pee and poo come out of you.' She looked Vanessa's stretched body up and down and licked her lips as her gaze lingered on her pussy and the exposed pucker of her anus beneath it. 'I've got to check you're staying healthy . . .'

Vanessa squirmed awkwardly, letting the induced shame fill her mind. How degrading to perform such an intimate act in these circumstances before a stranger. She shook her head and whimpered.

The sister slapped the insides of Vanessa's thighs. 'I said I want to see you piss and shit! Now!'

Vanessa hung her head and obeyed, voiding her bowels into the pan. The sister watched in undisguised fascination as her sphincters opened and the wastes spurted and plopped from her. When Vanessa had squeezed out the last drop and gobbet she said: 'Well done. You see, that wasn't so hard, was it? And I can tell you're a perfectly healthy girl.'

With meticulous care she wiped Vanessa's orifices clean with toilet paper, lingering a little as her fingers trailed through her cleft. Then she covered the pan, drew back the curtains and left.

Is that it, Vanessa wondered?

Seeing Vanessa suspended squatting over her bed, one of the Canary nurses came in and used the douche gun to wash her out internally and re-grease her. Then she gave her some water and returned her to her normal reclining position ready for the next client. As she was being tended to Vanessa saw the sister, carrying a freshly washed bedpan, methodically making her way round every girl in the ward.

Just how weird had that been? A little degradation and a few light smacks with a dash of coprophilia thrown in for good measure. Presumably that satisfied the woman's fantasy, even if it hadn't done anything for Vanessa apart from deliver a small degree of pleasurable humiliation. In fact the woman's evident obsession with excreta had been a little spooky. But then a list of her own pleasures would earn Vanessa a pretty high rating on the 'philia fetish scale herself, and a lot of people would think what she enjoyed was unusual if not downright sick by 'normal' standards.

How strange that a man who gave her a lashing and then screwed her because it gave him pleasure should give her such a high, whereas this woman, who had only slapped her lightly and then merely watched as she relieved herself, did not. Would she have enjoyed it more if the woman had treated her more harshly and stimulated her first? Perhaps it was not what she did so much as what she didn't do.

Vanessa decided what mattered ultimately was she had responded in a way that had apparently pleased the client, albeit a weird one. That was all that should concern a Shiller girl when serving another. She might mention the incident in her article as a test of her own tolerance and understanding and a warning to her readers to look for satisfaction even in unexpected ways. Part of the pleasure in being a willing slave was surrendering to the desires of others, whatever they might be. Masochistic, erotomaniac, exhibitionistic bondage fetishists should be the last people to pass judgement.

It really was true that it took all sorts, Vanessa thought philosophically. And in here I'm at the mercy of every one of them . . .

A doctor came into her cubicle wearing a facemask. Another shy client, Vanessa wondered, or one simply keen to remain anonymous even from the other guests?

Without saying a word he drew the curtains and then operated the bed controls. The headrest under her pillow folded flat, laying Vanessa down. Then the points where Vanessa's wrists were cuffed to the top halves of the bedrails extended, dragging her arms along the bed and over her head, pulling her taut. The left-hand set of side-rails then slid across the bed even as the right-hand set swung upwards in an arc over them, carried on arms that rotated about pivot joints set in the bed's foot and head frames. In a few seconds they had swapped places. The effect was to roll Vanessa over onto her front. He pulled the pillow out from under her face, pushed stiff fingers into her vaginal passage and lifted, jacking her bottom up, and slid the pillow in under her hips.

31

She'd been squirming about as he positioned her but now he smacked her raised bottom sharply.

'Hold still, slut!' She froze. 'I want to test the tightness of your anus,' he continued brusquely. 'Whatever I do you stay as tight as you can, understood?'

Vanessa nodded. What a good thing she'd had the ice treatment earlier. Had the 'doctors' been conferring?

The doctor pulled down his trousers, clambered onto the bed and rammed the head of his cock into her bottom cleft and into the ring of muscle guarding the way to her rectum. Vanessa clenched her buttocks, resisting as she'd been ordered while he pounded away like a battering ram. She'd have such bruises! He wanted the pleasure of forcing his way in . . . which, thanks to the grease around her hole, he was doing. She could not keep him out . . . not that she wanted to . . . *ahhh!*

With a muffled squeal she was broached, his rod forcing its way inside her. Then he began violently to sodomise her.

He was big and hard, his thrusts making the bed shake and forcing grunts of pain out of her as he bore down. Her passage distended painfully with each thrust, testing its elasticity and resilience, and his weight flattened her breasts into the mattress and left her gasping for breath. She was being used without any regard for her comfort. But it was the kind of discomfort and intimate pain she had come to crave and it mingled with the pleasure of being filled by a living cock. That its owner was utterly anonymous only added to the thrill. Seepage from her pussy began to make a wet patch on the sheet under her hips. If only he didn't finish too quickly.

She just made it, jerking her hips and squeezing

desperately, milking his cock as it sprayed hot sperm deep into her rectum. *Oh, yes, that was good . . .*

He collapsed over her, pressing her deeper into the mattress, and for a minute he lay still. Then he said softly in her ear: 'Did I say you could cum? You moved your hips when I told you to hold still. That wasn't part of the treatment. You'll have to be punished for that . . .' He levered himself up, pulling his cock from her rear with a slight pop and climbed off the bed.

Vanessa tensed, her stomach knotting, fearful of what he might do, feeling guilty for having disobeyed the letter of his instructions even as she suspected he would have found some fault in her anyway. He was just looking for any excuse to punish her.

She twisted her head round to see he'd taken a small slim plastic case from his pocket. He flipped it open to reveal the coloured ends of a dozen hypodermic needles, without tubes and plungers. Vanessa whimpered, buried her head in the sheets and screwed up her eyes.

Slowly and carefully he sank each needle into the soft smooth fleshy swell of her buttocks, forming a ring in the centre of both her trembling hemispheres. He did not push them in very deep, perhaps a centimetre or so, but how they stung! She could feel the free ends of the ones already stuck in her bobbing slightly as she flinched from the next insertion. Vanessa clenched her teeth, wishing she had a bit or ball-gag in her mouth to bite on. They were such comforts at times like this. If only this part had come first. Pain and then sex or pain with sex, yes, that fired her up, but pain after without any stimulation was the hardest to take.

But not impossible, she reminded herself. This was another test of her submissive ideals. She was a

Shiller girl and she was bound and naked and she could still feel sperm oozing out of her anus. That was what she lived for. This pain was not the end but merely foreplay for her next user. The liquid heat of anticipation began to flow back into her loins. So she moaned and whimpered pitifully, satisfying her abuser, and savoured her discomfort.

When the needle rings were completed on her buttocks he made one final addition to the artistry he had performed on her backside to complete her shaming. He took a daffodil from the vase by her bed and thrust the thick sappy stalk up her still-distended anus, leaving the bright yellow flower head jutting out from its fleshy cleft. It was sexual gardening, Vanessa thought as he drew back the curtains and left her for all to see. A flower planted in an earthy hole he had opened up with his dibber and fertilised with his own seed.

Vanessa remained on display, much to her discomfort and the amusement of the other doctors, for an hour until Julie 5 came in. She removed the daffodil and the needles, placing furtive kisses on her sore cheeks as she did so. Then she applied some soothing cream, turned Vanessa over onto her back once more, flushed out and wiped her down.

As she worked on her, Julie whispered encouragingly: 'The clients have to leave the ward by nine and then you and the Sapphires can rest. We're still fair game, though. The clients staying overnight have the keys to the nurses' rooms. Then it's our turn to get gang-banged in our beds!'

While she was feeding her supper, Julie said something that moved Vanessa deeply. 'I think it's great how you're ready to let yourself get screwed like the rest of us. You haven't just taken pictures of us getting fucked and then done a few interviews. The others think the same. I used to think white-collar girls were a bit superior, you know, but not you. Reading your stuff in *GN* makes us feel more connected and worthwhile, somehow. At times, when I have doubts about living like this, that helps a lot.'

Fortunately a mouthful of food prevented Vanessa from responding at that moment but she had to fight back a tear. What they read in *GN* really meant so much to them. Though they loved their strange way of life it was secretive and not something they could share beyond their chain sisters and company workers. How many had family or friends in the outside world they could never tell? There would always be that nagging sense of shame for what they were. Perhaps *GN* helped give them a greater sense of unity, knowing that other members of the company could learn what it truly felt like to be a slave?

Whatever the reason, Vanessa silently resolved never again to be tempted to do it the easy way. Hands-on would always mean hands-on. Do it for real first and only then write about it.

When supper was done Julie paused as she was about to place a fresh strapping over Vanessa's mouth, glanced round quickly, and then stole another kiss.

'I really hope we can meet up again.'

Vanessa felt a lump in her throat. No other slaves could be this considerate of each other. They were all family, bond-sisters. That's what made them unique.

The ward closed and the 'doctors' finally departed. The Canary girl nursing staff cleaned up and then dimmed the lights and left the 'patients' to sleep. Despite having spent most of the day in bed they were exhausted by the 'treatments' and 'examinations' they had undergone and badly needed the rest. They would be woken the next morning at seven and the ward would open for the first 'doctor's rounds' at eight. Though their gags were removed overnight, the bandages on their hands stayed and naturally they remained cuffed to their beds. But sleeping in restraints came as second nature to Shiller girls and bothered them very little.

Not being able to play with themselves was more of a frustration. Those girls who still had an excess of sluttish need in them even after their exertions of the day could not bleed it off. It would just have to be stored up for the clients to release the next day. Vanessa found being forced to sleep alone even more of a burden. She longed to sleep with Kashika in her arms. Julie 5 would have been a very acceptable temporary substitute but she was also denied her. Vanessa had learned that being a slave and loving another slave also meant surrendering such choices to others. Still, it made those times when they could be together all the more intense.

She went to sleep thinking of Kashika's lovely body curled up against hers. And to think only a few months ago she had not even suspected she could lust for another woman. How her life had been transformed . . .

A pair of respectable-looking middle-aged men in white coats, referring to each other with mock solemnity as 'Doctor Foster' and 'Doctor Gloucester', visited Vanessa next morning. They gave her a long examination, involving much poking and prodding in every orifice, and then conferred with each other very loudly in Vanessa's hearing.

'Loose in the limbs but hot in the slot, Gloucester,' said Foster.

'Quite so, Foster,' Gloucester agreed, 'aggravating her rounded heels which give her the tendency to fall on her back with her legs open.'

'A sad case but what's to be done?'

'Casts and traction, perhaps?'

'It's her only chance of ever getting straightened out.' Foster snapped his fingers at the Canary nurse who had been attending them dutifully. 'Take her to the casting room at once. Meanwhile have traction stands set up in here and put out a number three tray.'

'At once, Doctor.'

Five minutes later Vanessa was being rolled down a corridor inside an Alves frame propelled by a pair of nurses while Foster and Gloucester strode along behind, each man bearing himself with an air of profound importance. The frame was turned sideways to its direction of motion and Vanessa was very aware of how she must look; raised up high on the frame base and suspended within the oblong of tubular metal by her straps like a fly trapped in a web. They passed several doctors, nurses and clinic staff along the way who looked her naked body over with interest as they went by. Her sense of helpless exposure was acute and very arousing. But were they really going to go through with the messy business of putting casts on her?

The casting room turned out to be perfectly clean without a single roll of plaster bandage to be seen. About a large central table were racks of shelves containing a selection of ready-made and foam-lined medical-blue resin casts in different shapes and sizes. They were split into sections that only needed taping together. Each cast had metal rings embedded in its sides and ends.

The doctors supervised as Vanessa was laid out flat

on the table and the frame straps were swapped for cuffs linked to wire ropes and crank handles. She was pulled tight and spreadeagled.

'Now,' Foster said, rubbing his hands and turning to the racks of casts. 'I'd say she'll take mediums, but what types shall we have?'

'I think straight extensions for the limbs with maximum immobility, but leaving the torso uncovered,' Gloucester suggested.

'It would certainly be a pity to cover her torso. Such pretty tits . . . But what about a neck brace?'

'Good idea. And a facemask for increased constraint?'

'Shame to cover her face. I like to see 'em crumple up and cry.'

'Her eyes will still be able to roll about. And look, there's a tinted one here with a tongue clamp.'

'Well, that's different. Girls have got to learn to curb their tongues.'

'Right, then, let's get her fitted out . . .'

Gleefully the pair fitted the casts onto Vanessa's limbs while the two nurses stood by holding repair-tape dispensers. They cut and handed the doctors lengths of tape as required that were bound about the sections of the casts, sealing them tight. Vanessa's legs were encased from ankles to mid-thighs and her arms from wrists to shoulders. A high flared brace, covering her from collarbones to chin, was closed about her neck. The bandages were unwound from her head and the tape pulled from her lips, but they were replaced with a mask of rigid blue-tinted plastic that fitted tightly over her face, with holes only over her eyes, nostrils and an O-shaped mouth. It was held in place by five broad straps passing round the back of her head in pairs below and above her ears and singly across her crown. An adjustable metal clamp was fitted across the mouth hole. Her tongue was pulled through this and the clamp jaws closed about it, so that its pink tip protruded from the plastic hole.

Vanessa felt the compression of the mask on her face forcing it into near immobility. Now even her range of expressions was being limited. Her tongue was held so she could not speak. All she could do was plead mutely with her eyes for them to be kind to her while secretly hoping they would not.

'Now let's get her into traction,' Foster said.

Being wheeled back to the ward in her frame she savoured her new restraints. The tight constriction of the padded casts held her limbs rigidly straight and the neck-brace made it impossible to turn her head, leaving her hardly more flexible than a shop-window dummy. She swayed in her straps so stiffly it almost seemed as though she was standing to attention. And what were they going to do with her when after she was put into traction? Her pussy pulsed hot and wet in anticipation.

Metal posts supporting pulley blocks, weights and wire cords had been fitted to the corners of her bed. She was placed between them and the snaplink ends of the cords were hooked to the rings in the ends of her casts. Then the weights were hung on the dangling cord ends. Vanessa's immobile limbs were pulled out wide and lifted off the bed until they were elevated to about forty-five degrees. And there she hung, splayed wide and inviting, exposed and helpless. The blue casts enclosing her limbs, neck and face made them seem disconnected and artificial, focusing the eye on the pale bare living flesh of her torso. The red of her swollen nipples, rising and falling with her trembling breasts and the dark pink glistening gash of her sex, open to any who looked up at her from the foot of the bed, stood out clearly.

Foster and Gloucester admired their handiwork for a minute, then Foster said to one of the Canary nurses: 'Bring Nurse Julie here . . .'

Vanessa stiffened. What were they doing?

In a minute Julie 5 entered the cubicle. She flashed a quick glance at Vanessa's stretched and splayed body, then said meekly to Foster: 'You sent for me, Doctor?'

Foster and Gloucester adopted stern expressions.

'It has come to our attention, Nurse,' Gloucester said with ponderous solemnity, 'that you have been having improper relations with this patient!'

'You have been taking a suspiciously long time attending her needs and on one occasion you were observed actually kissing her,' Foster explained. 'That was not in her treatment schedule.'

'Well, Nurse, what have you got to say for yourself?' Gloucester demanded.

Julie adopted a suitably shamed and contrite expression, biting her lip and hanging her head. 'I'm sorry, Doctor. I couldn't help myself.'

'Naturally this sort of unprofessional behaviour cannot be tolerated,' said Gloucester.

'You must both be severely punished,' said Foster with undisguised relish. 'Take off your clothes . . .'

Julie looked convincingly horrified. 'Oh, Doctor, I couldn't. Please don't make me . . .'

'Strip!' Gloucester thundered.

Miserably Julie obeyed.

Vanessa had already seen Julie's pretty breasts and now the rest of her was revealed. She had a lovely curvy body with rounded buttocks and a small severely trimmed triangle of golden hair above her deep cleft. With her uniform lying about her ankles Julie stood before them dressed only in her cap, a picture of shame with blushing cheeks, ineffectually trying to hide herself from their gaze.

Foster uncovered an equipment tray that had been placed on the bedside locker. By rolling her eyes sideways Vanessa could just see it contained a large double-ended dildo, encircled in the middle by a disc of rubber. One side of the disc was plain while the other was studded with sharp metal studs. There was also a pair of spanking paddles with flat rubber blades and bulbous phallus handles.

'Plug the smooth side up your cunt and the other into her,' Foster commanded Julie. 'We'll spank you until we see her cry and then orgasm. The harder you try the easier and quicker it'll be.'

With trembling hands, Julie took up the dildo, spread her legs and fed one end up inside herself until the rubber pad was pressed against her mound while the doctors looked on grinning. Then she climbed onto the bed and edged forward, the rubber shaft bobbing ahead of her, until she was kneeling between Vanessa's splayed and raised legs. Her hands rested on either side of the captive girl's chest and she looked down into the wide eyes staring up out of the mask.

Sorry, Julie mouthed as she lined up the tip of the dildo with Vanessa's gaping pussy mouth. Vanessa tried to force a smile under her mask to show she knew Julie was just obeying orders, as any good company slave should. Pleasing their masters of the moment was all that mattered. Julie thrust into her. Vanessa's mound bulged as her passage was filled and then the sharp studs ground into her soft vulval flesh.

Vanessa's eyes bulged and a distorted scream issued from her tongue-clamped mouth. Her inner lips, peeled back by the thickness of the shaft between them, felt like they were being used for pincushions.

Swish, smack!

41

Foster and Gloucester had taken up position on either side of the bed and were swiping the paddles across Julie's bobbing bottom. Julie yelped but kept on thrusting, making Vanessa whimper in turn.

Through her own rapidly misting eyes Vanessa saw Julie's eyes begin to glisten. Well, the doctor's had their tears already. Now to turn the pain into pleasure like good slave girls should, savouring the smack of rubber on resilient bottom flesh, sharp girlish gasps and groans, the sucking of rubber shafts within clinging wet passages, the musky scent of arousal, the heat of two bodies intertwined, breasts grinding together, hard nipples trailing through each other's soft billows and metal studs digging into sticky flesh lips. The two men sweated away wielding paddles while watching suffering slave girls perform thinking this was all for their pleasure, when secretly Vanessa knew it was almost exactly the reverse. Under those circumstances a climax was not a distant goal but a rapidly approaching inevitability.

Vanessa bucked and jerked as far as her casts and traction cables allowed, setting the weights swinging as she clenched at the rubber shaft inside her. Julie dipped her head and kissed the clamped tip of her tongue as she also went into spasm. Their sweaty bodies rubbed frantically together and then subsided into blissful stillness.

But now the doctors needed their release.

Foster managed to clamber onto the bed first. Tearing open his flies he dragged Julie's unresisting legs wide, prised apart her buttocks and rammed his cock into her greased bottom hole. Vanessa groaned as his weight joined that of Julie on top of her. But such was his passion that it was not there for long before he came with a gasp of triumph.

He had hardly finished spouting before Gloucester, who had already exposed his stiff shaft in anticipation and was red in the face with need, dragged him out of the way and took his place. Tearing the dildo out of the twin passages it was filling with a double plop, he rammed between Vanessa's sore lovelips and spent himself within her hot passage.

We've given satisfaction, Vanessa thought with pride.

Vanessa was left in her casts all day. Several more clients, attracted by her inviting posture, novel immobility and the red blaze of her pubic lips, took advantage of her. Occasionally she saw Julie bustling about performing her duties. She moved a little stiffly but there was a barely suppressed grin on her face. As she passed she flashed Vanessa a quick smile.

Briefly Vanessa allowed herself to daydream about having Julie and Kashika both trying to please her at the same time. And if she wished it need not be just a dream. She shivered. Was all this adoration going to her head?

That night her casts were removed and she was able to bend her limbs once more, as far as her cuffs allowed. She'd recommend casts to any girl but they did make you stiff afterward, she thought ruefully.

Next morning the nurses put her into a frame before the first doctor stepped onto the ward.

'You've been booked for the operating theatre,' one whispered as they wheeled her off. 'First on the list . . .'

The operating theatre was a dark room with a narrow heavy padded and black vinyl-covered table in its centre, brilliantly illuminated by a cluster of overhead spotlights. The table was fitted with hinged extension arms, also padded. Two were set at right angles to its top and two made a 'V' from off its foot. Beside the table was a monitor screen and machine on a stand. It had switches and dials on its front and transparent air hoses extending from its back. An array of clear plastic cups and what looked like inverted test tubes of different sizes, all with valve connections on their tops and flared bases, were set out beside the device. There was also a tube of petroleum jelly and a spanking paddle.

Vanessa was laid on the table and spread out, her arms extended straight from her shoulders and her legs parted at ninety degrees. Black rubber straps were fastened over her wrists, elbows, in a cross over her chest between her breasts, over her midriff, about her thighs, knees and ankles, pulling her firmly down into the padding. Her bandage gag was pulled off and a clear plastic dummy gag was pushed between her teeth.

Then the nurses left the room. For a moment Vanessa though she was alone. Then a man in cap, mask and gown stepped out of the shadows. His hands were encased in latex gloves and he held them in front of him like a surgeon about to operate. The light glinted off familiar spectacles. He was the first-time master she had served in the examination room the day she had arrived at the clinic. Her stomach did a little flip-flop. She'd peed on this man . . .

Once again the man, her 'surgeon', went about his work in silence. Squeezing out some petroleum jelly from the tube he rubbed it thickly over her breasts and pubic mound until they glistened. Then he plugged a hose from the machine into the valve on top of a small tube. He pressed the tube against her breast over her right nipple so that its flared mouth fitted snugly. He flipped a switch on the machine and turned a dial. A pump hummed as it began to suck the air out of the tube enclosing her nipple.

Vanessa gave a squeak as her flesh tingled and her nipple bulged upward. The stinging became more intense and the band of flesh about the tube rim felt as though it was being stretched and squeezed. Her swollen nipple was going deep pink and the stinging had become hot and cold needles jabbing into her.

The surgeon turned off the pump, closed the valve on top of the tube and unplugged the hose, leaving the tube stuck on her breast like a tiny lighthouse perched on a mound of rock. Trapped inside, her nipple burned and stung as it slowly went from pink to purple. Vanessa moaned in dismay. The surgeon took up another small tube and repeated the process on her left nipple. It was just as painful. By the time he was done, Vanessa's eyes were wet with tears and she had two throbbing purple nipples trapped in tubes that swayed and trembled as her chest rose and fell.

Then he moved round to her legs. Vanessa squirmed and gurgled in futile protest. He pulled out and adjusted something from under the table and then turned on the monitor screen. Vanessa twisted her head to one side and saw a close-up view of her vagina, shiny with grease and her own arousal. She was on CCTV. Plugging in a smaller tube to the airline, the surgeon prised open her labia and fitted the tube over the swell of her hooded clitoris and then began to suck the air out. Vanessa bit on her gag and whimpered. On the screen her clitoris, bulging red and wet and flushed with blood was drawn out of its hood and crept slowly up the tube, engorged beyond anything she'd ever known before. Then the surgeon locked the valve and pulled the hose off, leaving the tube with her most sensitive organ bulging within it jutting out from her by now steaming cleft.

Vanessa thought there was no more he could do, but she was wrong. To her horror he selected a much larger, squatter plastic tube the size of a small basin and plugged that into the pump. He fitted the dome over her right breast, wriggling it tight while still leaving it clear of the tube already capping her nipple. Then he turned on the pump. Vanessa sobbed and moaned. Her whole breast felt as though it was being sucked up the dome sides, swelling and stinging and tingling and going pink and then purple before her eyes. The surgeon closed the valve and pulled off the airline, leaving her breast encased like a taxidermy specimen under a glass dome in a museum. Fitting another large tube over her left breast he repeated the process.

Then he took up a shallower dome with a contoured lip and a flask attached to its valve and moved between her legs again. She craned her neck, peering down at him between her stinging, pulsing, vacuum-domed breasts and then turned to the monitor. *No!*

He fitted the dome over her vulva, its curves following the lines of her delta and cupping its pouting swell and the small tube over her unnaturally swollen clit. The pump began to suck air out of the dome. Vanessa felt her labia sting and become puffy while eerily the air was drawn out of her front passage. The suction began to affect her bladder and she felt the pressure building up on her sphincter, the other side of which was being drained of air through her urethra. Suddenly she could not hold back and her hot pee spurted into the dome, filling it with mist and trickling down the insides as condensation.

The surgeon chuckled at her disgrace. Was this his revenge for peeing on him?

The pump continued drawing out air and her fast-evaporating pee was sucked out of the dome and condensed into the flask beyond the valve, keeping the airline clear. The dome cleared and her vulva bulged further, turning pink and purple and stinging ferociously. She felt the external pressure building on her lower stomach as her vaginal passage pricked and burned and was squeezed tight. He was going to suck her insides out!

The surgeon stopped the pump, closed the valve and unplugged the hose. Vanessa groaned in relief, though the pain had not gone away. He picked up the spanking paddle and stood back, silently watching her sob and squirm as the feeling drained out of her breasts and vulva, fading to a vague sense of compression and spreading numbness.

Fear filled her. How numb could she get? She wailed behind her gag, pleading with her eyes.

Suddenly he stepped forward and began cracking open the valves. Air hissed into the breast tubes and pubic dome. He yanked them off and did the same to the smaller tubes over her clit and nipples.

For a few seconds she felt warmth about her tormented glands and a huge sense of relief. The surgeon parted his coat to expose his erection, moved between her legs and pushed his cockhead under her swollen projecting clit and between her purple labia. As he forced his way up her numbed passage, blood began to flow slowly back into the cold flesh of her breasts and vulva. Drawing back his arm he began to smack the purple mounds of her breasts even as he thrust his cock deeper into her.

Vanessa shrieked as his cock seemed to burn inside her and her cold breasts bounced sluggishly, the imprint of the paddle lingering as darker marks on their surface. Then the returning blood began to surge and with it came pain. She clenched her fists and writhed in her straps as blood throbbed and pins and needles became burning pins and needles as sensation returned with a vengeance.

He was raining blows forehand and back across her breasts and nipples, battering the blood back into them and filling them with burning, pulsing life. Her clit was filling with pain and gross overstimulation. It was swollen and utterly exposed. His pubic bone was grinding against it, crushing it with every thrust. It was impossible to feel more. She was bursting!

She convulsed and came and fainted.

Her breasts and vagina stung all day as she lay strapped to her ward bed, the lingering suction tube marks on her vulva and breasts turning by stages back to pink speckled with purple within still-pale rings. Her clitoris remained unnaturally swollen and prominent, pulsing and throbbing. It was painful when other clients used her. She caught Julie 5 giving her concerned glances as she passed by.

That night in the darkness gnawing doubt assailed her as it had occasionally during these last few months when she slept alone.

Was this all madness? Why did she subject herself to such pain and humiliation from total strangers and put herself at the mercy of sadists on an industrial basis? Was it sick to enjoy it? All right, so she was a masochist and submissive but she didn't have to broadcast it. She could find a master or mistress to serve and keep it private and lead an outwardly normal life. *GN* could find a new reporter . . .

And Kashika? Would she leave Shillers to be with her? She was dedicated to the slave life. And she did admire the Director so . . .

Damn, fuck and damn . . .

She was woken from exhausted sleep by a hand being placed over her mouth. It was still dark and silent in the ward. Lips brushing her ear whispered: 'It's me, from reception the other day. Call me Red. This is the last chance I've got to have you. It's all right, I'll do all the work ...'

Vanessa felt the bedhead lowered, a gown rustle to the floor and then a warm bare scented body reverse-straddled hers. Even as soft thighs slid past her cheeks she felt breasts flatten onto her stomach and lips brush her pubic bush. A warm bare wet cleft settled over her face and automatically she nuzzled into it and began to lick.

In turn a tongue delved into her sore cleft, kissing her clit tenderly. Red said: 'You really suffer for your work, don't you? I so much respect that. In fact all you chain girls amaze me. I could not do what you do. You're the best ...'

Red's tongue slipped in deeper and Vanessa sighed, filled with sudden contentment.

Perhaps all of it was worthwhile. The company gave her what she could not find alone: a caring family who above all understood what she was.

Vanessa was still feeling on top of the world as she drove home late the next afternoon.

Once more she was respectably dressed with a scarf hiding her collar. Outwardly she was a normal woman but at heart she knew she was and always would be a Shiller slave. The suction marks on her breasts and vulva had faded, leaving only a lingering tingle. No doubt there would be other marks to replace those in due course but she would bear them with pride like her chain sisters. Belonging felt wonderful.

She'd spent the day doing interviews, taking some background pictures to set the scene for her article and along the way managing to pose Julie for a photo while sneaking a goodbye kiss. But her story would be built first and foremost about what she had experienced first-hand. That's what her readers expected from their own slave reporter.

Her mood had been further lifted when she checked her phone messages before setting off and found one that said simply: WAITING FOR YOU, K. Before Vanessa had left for the clinic Kashika had said she hoped to be allowed time away to welcome her back. And there was no welcome more passionate than that given by her slave girl lover.

Vanessa got caught up in the evening traffic and it was gone half-six when she parked round the back of the slightly shabby nineteen-thirties block of flats in Richmond, on the third floor of which she lived. She climbed the stairs with a spring in her step and latch-keyed herself into the small hallway of her flat.

'I'm home, lover,' she said cheerfully as she went through into the sitting room.

Kashika was waiting for her . . . naked and bound to a chair, a strip of silver tape over her mouth and a look of terror in her lovely eyes. Before Vanessa could react, shadowy figures closed in from either side and grabbed her arms. Some small hard device was jabbed into her side; there was a crackle of electricity, a searing jolt of pain and then blackness.

Three

The first thing Vanessa saw when she opened her eyes again was Kashika. She felt weak, nauseous and horribly confused and the sight of someone so lovely and reassuring was a balm to her addled senses.

'Kashika' meant 'Shining One' and she was a rare and striking blend of Scandinavian and Indian. Mellow golden hair contrasted with her coffee-tinted skin, her face was almond-shaped and very beautiful. She had finely shaped neat breasts with dark nipples and a full deep cleft capped with curls the colour of dark honey with golden highlights. Her groin was so well displayed because her thighs were splayed wide and legs crooked, with her feet pulled round the back of the front legs of the dining chair she was sitting in. Silver tape bound her ankles. About her neck was a red metal collar inscribed: KASHIKA 5 CHERRY.

Then Vanessa noticed the fear showing in Kashika's face and shook her own throbbing head, trying to think clearly. She realised that she had also been stripped down to her collar. She was kneeling unsteadily on the carpet, being supported by somebody grasping a handful of her hair. There was tape over her own mouth and about her wrists, binding them behind her back. Her side stung where she had

51

been zapped and there was a tingling and twitchy tremble in her limbs.

The curtains were drawn and the light was dim, but she could now see two other men, apart from the one who had hold of her. They were dressed alike in black; jeans, zip-jackets, gloves and balaclavas, exposing only their eyes. One had a phone earpiece strapped over his head and was speaking into the microphone:

'. . . yeah, we've got the second one. No problem . . .' He glanced at Vanessa. 'She's coming round now. The flat's secure. The Indian girlfriend, Kashika, was preparing a dinner for two when we took her. No other visitors expected so we can work from here as planned until you've got her to play ball. You want us to go on with stage two . . .? Right, we'll set things up like you said. Give us ten minutes . . .' He motioned to his companions. 'Get them into the bedroom.' He picked up a large holdall that had been resting in one corner.

The man who had hold of Vanessa's hair pulled her to her feet and then bent her forward, forcing her to stumble along with him towards the bedroom. As he did so he looked her over and said: 'They must have really pissed him off to deserve this. And why's this one got a collar on as well? "Vanessa nineteen white" it says. What the fuck's that meant to mean?'

'We're not getting paid to ask questions,' the man with the headphone said tersely.

'I think they're a couple of hot dykes who like to play pervy games with each other,' said the third man, tilting Kashika's chair back and dragging it after Vanessa. 'See, they've both got the same rings in their cunt lips.'

'You a pair of lezzies, then?' the man holding her

52

asked Vanessa rhetorically. 'Ever had a proper man inside you?'

'You'll have one soon enough,' the third man promised as they dragged the girls through the door into the bedroom.

'Shut your mouths and do your job,' the phone-man said.

The realisation penetrated the sick fear and confusion clogging Vanessa's thoughts that this was no ordinary break-in or robbery. She and Kashika had been deliberately targeted. The men had captured Kashika and then waited for her to return to the flat. They must have been watching for some time to establish their routine and know Kashika would be there to welcome her. But the men didn't know anything about their collars or what they signified. They were being controlled by whoever was on the other end of the phone. Somebody who wanted something badly enough from them to go to extreme lengths to get it . . .

Kashika's chair was set down beside the bed and Vanessa was forced onto her knees beside her. Kashika twisted her head round to look at Vanessa. Her eyes were wide and fearful, but her cheeks bunched as she forced a smile against the resistance of her tape gag. Vanessa smiled back as bravely as she could. Whatever the men intended doing it could not break the bond between them.

Unzipping the holdall, the phone-man took out a laptop that he set on the dressing table, aligning the eye of its inbuilt camera with the bed. The laptop screen came to life. It showed a graphic image of a single unblinking malevolent red eye that seemed to be staring right through them, taking in every detail of their naked bound bodies. Kashika whimpered and turned her head aside while Vanessa forced herself to stare back defiantly. Who would hide behind such an intimidating image?

The phone-man tapped his earpiece and listened for a moment, then said:

'Strap her to the bed on her back and put the other one on top of her . . .'

The two other men lifted Vanessa onto the bed. Instinctively she kicked and struggled until one of the men slapped her on both cheeks hard enough to bring tears to her eyes, quelling her feeble show of resistance. From the holdall the phone-man took out a bundle of padded bondage cuffs, some paired and some trailing lengths of rope, and gave them to his companions. They buckled the single cuffs about Vanessa's ankles and then dragged her legs wide, tying the ropes to the posts at the foot of the bed. Then, flicking open switchblades, they cut the tape from her wrists, replacing it with more cuffs, pulled her arms wide and secured them to the head of the bed.

Vanessa tugged at her bonds but the cuffs were secure. She was helpless in a way she had not known for a long time and desperately frightened. This was not the delicious fear she had known in the clinic at the hands of an approved client but the gut-wrenching fear of unknown terror. She raged at her impotence, but what could she do?

Then Vanessa saw her own reflection, spreadeagled, red-eyed and desperate. It was in a large picture mirror with a natural wood frame that hung on the wall opposite the foot of the bed. The mirror was hung at such an angle out from the wall that anybody in the bed could see herself reflected in it. Yes, there was one slight chance, but for it to work she must play for time any way she could.

They cut Kashika free from the chair, cuffed her wrists behind her and then buckled single cuffs about her upper arms. The trailing ropes were tied between her arms and then up under the back of her collar and down about her wrists, forming a rope handle. Using this Kashika was hauled onto the bed and dropped on top of Vanessa's spreadeagled body.

Kashika squirmed desperately as they touched, rubbing her cheek against her lover's, her deep eyes briefly filled with joy. Despite Vanessa's fear it felt wonderful to have Kashika's warm body pressed against hers, her pale breasts flattening against Kashika's more pointed cones, their pubic bushes mingling, inhaling the scent of her once more. Nothing could take that away from them.

The men were looking down at them and laughing. 'They look like they're having fun,' observed number two.

'I said they were dykes,' said three. 'What about making them fuck each other first?' he asked the phone-man.

They were getting seriously distracted, Vanessa realised, and like most men would in the circumstances they were starting to let their cocks rule their heads. Could she make use of that? She began squeaking and nodding frantically. Kashika caught on and copied her, adding pleading moans and a suggestive wiggle of her hips. They must have looked both comic and pitiful in their sudden desire to enthral their captors, but it was their only weapon. The men chuckled cruelly once more.

'See, they want to put on a show for us,' number two said mockingly.

The phone-man bent over the bed and pushed Kashika to one side so he could look Vanessa square in the face. 'You want to say something?' he asked.

She nodded again eagerly, trying to put as much suggestive passion as she could into her eyes and the muffled sounds issuing through her gag. She thought: *Come on I'm hot! Why not try me? We can't escape. You've got nothing to lose ...*

He touched his headphone and listened for a moment, then said into the microphone: 'Maybe she can give you what you want without ... I know what I'm being paid to do but it can't do any harm to ... right ...' He held the tip of his switchblade to her right nipple, which was shamelessly and defiantly erect. 'You know what'll happen if you try to scream or do anything stupid?'

She nodded.

He pulled the tape back from her lips far enough for her to speak.

'We can please you, all of you,' she said in a rush. 'We are lesbians but we also like men. And you wouldn't believe how perverted we are! You want to watch us fuck and we'll do it any way you want. We're really good. And we've got incredible sex toys in that cupboard. You can try them out on us and –'

The phone-man cocked his head as though listening and then pressed the tip of his knife a little harder against her nipple. 'That's not what he wants to hear. He wants you to do a job for him or else your girlfriend gets hurt. Say yes and it'll save her a lot of grief and after the job's done you both go free.'

Vanessa shivered. So that was why they had arranged them together like this. Whatever they did to Kashika she would have to witness every intimate detail while face to face with her. And the purpose was not simple sadism but to force her to cooperate in some scheme. Of course she would do anything to herself to spare Kashika, but she could not simply agree blindly to undertake some nameless 'job', even if she did trust the three men, and whoever was employing them, to keep their word. How did she know they really would be set free afterward? Her eyes flicked sideways to Kashika who shook her head slightly. She hoped that meant she understood.

Spinning her response out as much as she dared, she said: 'I don't want Kashika hurt, of course I don't ... but I have to know what this job is before I can promise anything. You can't expect me just to say yes. Can you tell me more about –'

'This is getting nowhere!' A harsh electronically distorted voice had come from the laptop speakers, causing the men to flinch. The glowing pupil at the centre of the eye pulsed in time with the words, making the image seem eerily alive. 'Don't waste any more time being kind to that slut! She doesn't deserve it. Shut her up and get on with the job I paid you for! I'll talk to her again after she's seen what you do to her girlfriend. It doesn't matter how much you mark her. Maybe then this one will be more cooperative ...'

Kashika was trembling. The phone-man shrugged and pressed the tape back over Vanessa's lips. 'Sorry. Any other time and I'd have taken you up on that offer, but like he said we've been paid to do a job and I always deliver. Nothing personal ...'

They buckled a long strap about their waists and pulled it tight. Kashika could squirm about on top of Vanessa but she could not pull free. Then they spread her legs and cuffed and tied her ankles to the insides of Vanessa's own widespread feet. Over Kashika's shoulder Vanessa could see in the mirror the perfect smooth brown double swell of her buttocks above the 'V' of her own thighs. Framed between them the plump clefts of their pussies seemed to be kissing.

The phone-man took a couple of leather tawse straps mounted on wooden handles from his bag and handed them to his companions, who slapped them experimentally across their gloved palms. 'We're going to use these on your girlfriend's arse the first time round,' the phone-man told Vanessa. 'If you don't do what he says, or if you doublecross him, then we have another go using these . . .' He took out another pair of straps with metal studs in them.

Vanessa flinched at the sight of them while Kashika whimpered. They'd tear Kashika's flesh to pieces. The man behind the eye on the screen must know she could never let them use something so cruel. The first use of the plain tawse would prove they meant business while the threat of the studded versions would keep her in line. Why hadn't she agreed earlier? Now it was too late and Kashika was going to get a beating. She looked into Kashika's eyes in desperate anguish, only to see fear mastered by calm resolution. She was so brave! She would survive this. And all the time they spent on beating her improved their chances.

The two men took up positions on either side of the bed, lined up on Kashika's upraised bottom and began their merciless task.

The swish and crack of leather on flesh filled the bedroom. Kashika jerked with every blow, grinding her body against Vanessa's as her face contorted in pain and her eyes filled with tears. And Vanessa had to look into her eyes and share her pain, while in the mirror she could see maroon stripes multiplying across her buttocks and merging into spreading blooms of hot tanned flesh.

Vanessa hated the cruelty, callousness and motives behind what was being forced upon her lover, and yet, despite her very real fear of what might happen next, she was at the same time helplessly aroused. Her nipples were hard and pressing into Kashika's breasts and her pussy was wet with the friction against

Kashika's mound. And Kashika was responding the same way! Vanessa could feel the heat in her and the wetness from her cleft seeping into hers. Bless their perverse sluttish natures for being their greatest strength!

The men did not know any better, did not understand what it meant to wear Shiller collars. They were only given to natural masochists and submissives who knew how to turn pain into pleasure and embraced suffering. The man behind the eye on the screen was misguided. He could imagine no other way of getting what he wanted from them except to employ sexual sadism. Perhaps he was getting off on it, in which case more fool he! Kashika could survive what ordinary women could not. She was strong in a way he could not dream of! Even now through her tears Vanessa saw the faraway look of one being transported by the pain to a special place ordinary people could not understand. Perhaps they expected immediate surrender, but instead they were simply wasting more time.

Suddenly the voice of the eye rasped: 'You two! You wanted to have them earlier, well now's your chance. You can both fuck the Indian girl. One up her fanny and the other her arsehole so it hurts. Make that one underneath know you mean it! If she doesn't cooperate after I've talked to her you can have her as well while she watches her girlfriend get her arse lashed to shreds!'

The men dropped their tawse straps and fought to be first while the phone-man looked on with what Vanessa sensed was dismay. His mysterious paymaster was usurping his authority before his eyes. This was not going as planned.

Number two won the struggle. With a triumphant 'You can have her bum . . .' he tore open his flies, knelt between Kashika's splayed legs and rammed his stiff cock up her cleft. Kashika gave a muffled grunt and her tear-reddened eyes went wide. Vanessa gasped as his weight bore down on Kashika and then herself. His masked face loomed over Kashika's shoulder, eyes hollow with lust as he pumped into her.

Another mistake, Vanessa thought with silent triumph as she saw Kashika's eyes roll up. A hard cock was the reward after the foreplay of pain. It was meant to humiliate and degrade, but to a Shiller girl that was the normal way of things. It was not a shameful thing to her. The man behind the eye was getting carried away with their humiliation when he could have employed the threat of real brutal sexless torture to get what he wanted faster. She didn't think a woman would have made that mistake. Never mix business with pleasure.

His thrusting cock was making Kashika's vulva bulge, grinding her erect clit deeper into Vanessa's own cleft. What wonderful twisted delight, she thought. Now she was getting seriously excited as well. *Bring it on, bring it on . . .*

The man grunted and came inside Kashika, then slumped forward over her, his sudden dead weight driving the breath from Vanessa's lungs. But she did not have to endure it for long. His companion hauled him aside and took his place between their spread legs.

'Up her arse!' the angry distorted voice rasped from the laptop. 'I want to hear her pain!'

The man prised Kashika's sore buttocks apart and rammed his prick into the dusky hole between them with brutal force. Kashika gave a squeak of pain as he forced her tight passage open. Vanessa knew he would find it a clean, hot, tight, ready-greased welcoming haven, used to entertaining rampant penises. Kashika had been trained to respond to lust in any form with passion. She could not help it, and neither could Vanessa.

She felt man two's sperm dribbling from Kashika's pussy onto her own as the repeated impacts of the sodomite's thrusts against Kashika's haunches were grinding them together. It was filthy but exciting. Their bodies were now lubricated by a sticky sheen of sweat. *Forget this is for real; pretend it's a game*, Vanessa thought. *Turn it on its head. Defy them by enjoying it.*

Even as man three gasped and spent inside Kashika's rectum, filling it with his sperm, Vanessa and Kashika bucked and squirmed with passionate muffled moans of delight. The man pulled out of Kashika's behind, his cock trailing sticky threads over her thighs, but nothing could stop them now. *Here's your show!* Vanessa thought wildly as lust burst inside her.

'They've bloody well both cum!' she heard the phone-man exclaim quietly.

'What the fuck are they?' number two said with incredulous admiration.

We're Shiller girls, Vanessa thought proudly.

'I said you were to hurt her!' the screen voice blared out, cutting through the respectful pause. Hatred and frustration was clear even through the harsh artificial distortion. 'Take the Indian away and wire this one up! I'll deal with her myself!'

Kashika's limp body was unstrapped and hauled off Vanessa, who lay sweat-streaked and exhausted on the bed. She had one last anguished sight of her lover as men two and three dragged her back though to the sitting room then she was gone. *We've done our best*, she thought.

61

Meanwhile the phone-man took more equipment out of the holdall.

There was a small metal-cased box fitted with multi-pin sockets that he placed at the foot of the bed between Vanessa's spread feet. Uncoiling an extension cable he found a wall socket and plugged the box into the mains. A red light lit up on the box. Vanessa shivered at the sight, feeling new dread steal over her.

He took out a bondage bridle with a split rubber bit. Fastened to the cheek rings of the bridle was a plastic box with a socket fitting and a miniature gas cartridge.

Tubes from the cartridge fed into the bit. Tearing the tape from Vanessa's lips he buckled the bridle about her head. She clamped her mouth shut, resisting the bit. Anything to waste a few seconds more. He drew his knife again and pressed it meaningfully against her right nipple.

'You've shown you've got nerve, girl, but don't waste my time,' he said grimly.

Vanessa opened her mouth.

He forced her tongue through the slot in the bit. It seemed loosely fitted and she found she could still move her tongue about a little. She could probably even talk. Then he twisted a valve on the gas cartridge. There was a hiss as rubber bladders on the top and bottom of the bit suddenly inflated, filling her mouth and holding her tongue firm. She was very effectively gagged once more.

Next from the holdall was a dildo with its rubber-sheathed sides studded with metal contacts. It had a pair of spring clamps fitted to its base that also housed a socket fitting. He forced this into her vagina and closed the base clamps about her inner labia, holding it firmly in place. Vanessa whimpered. The clamps had spiked teeth.

He took out a bundle of cables. Two connected the bridle and dildo to the control box. Two more had crocodile clips on the ends. These he clamped about her nipples and the other ends he plugged into the box. Then he carefully plumped up her pillow, raising her head so she could look down the length of her wired-up body to the control box. Bringing over the laptop he mounted it on top of the control box and used the last cable to link the two. A green bulb lit up on the box front.

'It's working,' said the voice behind the eye. 'Now get out and don't come back until I call you . . .'

With a last, almost regretful look back at Vanessa, the phone-man closed the door.

For a moment there was silence as Vanessa stared at the eye on the screen, fighting to control her fear. Then the bladders round her bit deflated with a hiss, leaving her tongue relatively free.

'I've been waiting for this moment for months, you deceiving bitch!' the voice spat out. The eye faded from the screen to reveal the head and shoulders of a thickset man in his late fifties, with grizzled hair, a heavy jaw, and a cigar in one hand.

The last time Vanessa had seen that face it had also been peering at her from a TV screen. It had been in the conference room of the *Daily Globe*, the paper he owned and she had once worked for. He had set her the task of going undercover to expose Shiller's secret business activities. What she had not known at the time was that he secretly ran a far less ethical slave business of his own and wanted incriminating evidence to blackmail Shiller's, not expose it. But after she had discovered her own slavish nature and been converted to Shiller's ways and returned a negative report, he had revealed the thug and bully beneath the bluff public façade. Knowing at last where her loyalties lay she had resigned on the spot with the suggestion that he screwed himself . . .

'Harvey-fucking-Rochester!' she said with contempt, her words slurred by the bit clamped about her tongue.

Her bit inflated. Lights flashed on the front of the control box. Burning pain stabbed though her nipples. Her back arched and the balloon bit plugging her mouth absorbed a shriek of pain.

'That's Sir Harvey, to you, Buckingham, and don't you forget it!' he snarled, his voice no longer distorted except by natural anger.

The current ceased to flow and her bit deflated, leaving her breathing raggedly. Her nipples stung and throbbed and felt like they had been scorched, but they looked undamaged.

She sobbed: 'You don't deserve any title except bastard of the year you . . . mmffhh . . . eeekk!'

Her mouth had filled and the current hammered through her again. When it was over she was left trembling and fearful she would suffer some real harm. On the other hand, while he was punishing her for not flattering his ego, more time was passing. But did she have the courage to keep this up? Fortunately Rochester had things to say for himself.

'You went over to Shiller even though you were working for me!' he growled. 'I had you watched until I was sure. Seeing that Indian girl come calling, seeing the collars you tried to hide. Then I knew you'd sold out. I should have employed somebody with some guts, not a slut who'd open her legs at the sight of a collar. This is what you get for siding with Shiller against me!'

This time it was the dildo, sending jolt after searing jolt tearing through her vagina. Spikes of electricity seemed to be stabbing through her. Cruelly stimulated, the muscles of her sheath went into spasm, clenching about the dildo as though embracing its searing pain. Her hips jerked and thudded on the bed uncontrollably.

Then the current ceased and she sagged, whimpering and twitching fitfully. Her gag deflated. Rochester's triumphant laughter assailed her ears.

'Nobody crosses me, understand!'

Vanessa knew she had to play up to him at the same time as stringing him along. To do so meant digging deep into her masochistic side to find the pleasure in what he was doing to her. Forget who he was. She was chained to a bed with an electric dildo up her fanny and crocodile clips on her nipples. The remote-controlled bridle gag was neat, muffling her screams so as not to alert the neighbours and denying her the power of speech at his whim. He was a client who wanted to see her broken and humbled, to enjoy playing the master. This was what she enjoyed . . . but she had to put up a show of resistance.

'When you gave me the job you forgot to mention you were also in the slave business!' she retorted feebly then whimpered when the clamps about her labia seemed to sink electric teeth into her tender flesh lips.

'Call me "Sir", you cheating slut!' Rochester snarled. 'So we're both in the girlflesh business? What's the difference?'

'Because the Director honestly cares about us, while to you we're just pieces of meat, you misogynistic bastard . . . mmffhh . . .'

He sent a jolt through her nipples and then up her vagina, back and forth. And while she bucked and writhed and jerked on her chains Rochester thundered: 'Shiller's a freak and I'm going to bring her down! And you're going to help, you treacherous little slut . . .'

Vanessa surrendered to the pain. It was all stimulation and was so terrible it was wonderful. It was an electric screw, the biggest one ever, and she was going to cum in his face and he wouldn't know! There was a starburst inside her, drenching the dildo with her juices. The raw thrill of it was too much and her bladder cut loose, pumping urine over the sheets between her legs. *Yes!* For a few seconds the pain was wrapped in joy. Then, twitching and sobbing, she sank back onto the steaming sheets, her chest heaving, utterly spent, letting darkness close about her even as Rochester was shouting: 'Don't you dare faint on me! Don't you dare . . .'

She was roused by a slap on the cheek. The earphone man stood over her. Beyond him the red eye floated on the laptop screen again. Her nipples and vagina throbbed in agony as though they had been burned. The cold, urine-stained sheet clung to her bottom and thighs.

'She's coming round,' he said. 'If you want to get something out of her next time don't shock her so hard.'

'When I want your advice I'll ask for it,' Rochester's disguised voice grated. 'Now get back outside until I call you.'

Cold-eyed, the phone-man left the room. Rochester's image replaced the eye on the screen. 'Not so arrogant now, are you, lying there in your own piss,' he chortled in his own voice, gloating at Vanessa's dishevelled body. 'I'd like to see you whipped until you bleed for betraying me, but I don't want to leave any marks for tomorrow. Because tomorrow you're going to finish the job you started.'

Desperately she gathered her senses to play her part. She was not sure she had the courage to face another shock like the last, but it had bought some more time. Hopefully it was enough. She dare not risk pushing him to bring Kashika back in to face the studded belts. Now she had to start giving ground. Would he believe her capitulation? Yes, because he believed in his own supreme power. She had to let the fear show on her face and give him a small token of surrender. She was crushed, broken, beaten. He was her master . . .

'How?' she asked feebly.

A warning jolt coursed through her nipples making her yelp.

'How . . . Sir Harvey?' she corrected herself humbly.

His face creased into a smile. 'That's better. Now you know what I can do to you and your friend you're going to be a good girl and do everything I say, aren't you?'

'Yes, Sir Harvey,' she said miserably.

He appeared to relax a little, enjoying her surrender. 'So Shiller gave you a white collar. I know that means you're a privileged slave and can go pretty much where you please. And you've even found yourself a slut girlfriend from Shiller's stock. That was a mistake. When I saw the two of you together I knew I had a handle on you, because having a lover meant you had something to lose. Do I have to get them back in and whip her arse raw, or will you obey me to the letter?'

And now I know you never let anybody get as close as we are, Vanessa thought contemptuously, while aloud she said wretchedly: 'I'll obey, Sir Harvey.'

'You will, if you don't want her hurt. Now this is what's going to happen. When it's dark my men will take your precious girlfriend away to a safe place . . .' he smiled coldly '. . . just in case you were thinking of trying to organise some sort of rescue. When you go in to Shiller's tomorrow you tell them she's sick and resting back here. That'll give you maybe three days to finish the job I gave you: get incriminating evidence on Shiller's slave business! Enough to destroy her! You're a white-collar, which means Shiller trusts you. I've seen you're still playing at being a reporter and carry a camera. You can get pictures of Shiller with slave girls or any guests with their slaves – famous faces, preferably. I know they call in to dine there.'

Vanessa protested: 'But Sir Harvey, I can't be seen taking any pictures of clients. I only photograph slave girls in training.'

'You won't be using that clunking camera, girl, you'll use this . . .' His image was briefly replaced by a still photo of a metal and plastic device about the size and shape of a torch battery with studded sides and a curved arm extending from its underside like an inverted periscope with a tiny lens on its tip.

His grinning image returned. 'I call it a pussycam. Squeeze and click. Put that cunt of yours to good use at last. But be sure to trim back your bush. I don't want anything obscured by your short-and-curlies.' He sounded almost jolly now, confident and in control. 'My men will leave it with you with full operating instructions. I assume you'll have no problems inserting it yourself. If you need motivating, think of your girlfriend. While you're at work my men will be keeping her amused. Maybe I'll plug her in like you are now and see how prettily she screams. That's what'll happen unless you bring me back what I want. Every night you'll come back here and download what you've got to an address I'll give you. If it's good I'll have her freed. If you don't deliver you'll never see her again. I've got places a pretty tart like her can be put to work. Any questions . . . or do I have her brought back in here for a proper lashing?'

At that moment from the other side of the door came a muffled thud, and the sound of a man's cry cut off in the middle, followed by the rush of booted feet.

Vanessa raised her voice to cover the commotion. 'There's one thing you haven't thought of, Sir Harvey.'

He scowled. 'What?'

'How perverted Shiller girls like us are. Do you know I even have a mirror on my bedroom wall with a micro-camera in it, so that Miss Kyle, our trainer back at HQ, can look in when Kashika is staying over to make sure we're being good slave girls in bed –'

The door burst open to reveal a Shiller security guard holding a batten.

Rochester's face clouded into a mask of rage as realisation dawned.

'You bitch!'

He stabbed at an unseen button in front of him. Vanessa's body arched as the full force of the current the transformer box could deliver pounded her nipples and vagina. As her scream dammed up behind her gag bit there was a pop and crackle as the laptop fused.

Then the pain died and she flopped back limp and trembling on the bed again. The security man was standing over her looking concerned. In his hand was the end of the power cable he'd ripped from the wall socket.

'OK, girl, you're safe now . . .'

Vanessa tried to smile and then, accompanied by the only sense of true shame she'd felt all day, she fainted for the second time.

Four

Half an hour later, Rochester's agents and their devices had been removed from the flat. They would face neither courts nor police since, officially, none of this had happened. Respectable city companies did not trade in slave girls so there could be none for other business rivals to attempt to kidnap and coerce for the purposes of industrial espionage. The men themselves did not even know who had hired them.

Rochester had been very careful that way. None of the men had heard his undisguised voice or seen his face on the screen. The laptop had been fused by an internal self-destruct charge and its memory destroyed, leaving no traceable connection to him. None of the special devices they had used bore any useful identifying serial numbers.

But the men would not escape unpunished. As they were escorted away the head of the Shiller security team mentioned dumping them naked in the middle of Epping forest as a gentle warning not to interfere with their girls again.

A company doctor, quite used to attending naked women wearing only slave collars, had accompanied the rescue squad. He checked Vanessa and Kashika over and declared they had suffered no lasting ill effects from their ordeal. Physically it was not much worse than what a strict client might have inflicted. Their mental scars might take longer to heal. The best treatment for those was their own love and the knowledge that they were safe in the company's care once more.

Now Vanessa and Kashika sat on the end of the bed, arms about each other. Vanessa still felt sore and dizzy from Rochester's device and secretly embarrassed about that second faint, even if it had only been for a few seconds.

They were facing the mirror camera so Director Shiller could look at them. Her voice came from the concealed speakers Miss Kyle sometimes used to encourage them in bed. It was a steady, assured voice with a faint trace of accent, and currently full of concern. Just listening to it made Vanessa feel better.

'Two of my security staff will stay the night,' Shiller said, 'though I don't think it's likely Rochester will try anything again. You can come in tomorrow when you feel stronger. There'll be an escort, just in case. We'll talk further then.'

'Thank you, Director,' Vanessa said.

'This is the second time you've become caught up in the war between Rochester and myself, Vanessa. I'm sorry for what you've suffered.'

'Rejecting him months ago was my choice, Director. Seeing him again like this for real, when he wasn't even trying to put on his rough-diamond self-made man act, made me glad I did. He's a real . . .' she hesitated, knowing the Director disapproved of crude language in any circumstances. 'He's a twenty-four carat bastard.'

'Yes, I think that fairly sums him up,' Shiller agreed. 'But that does not diminish my own concern. When Miss Kyle alerted me to what was happening I felt I had let you both down.'

'It wasn't your fault, Director,' Vanessa protested.

'When you gave yourself to the service of my company your safety and well-being became my responsibility. We value our girlflesh as a most prized commodity, unlike Rochester who sees you only as merchandise to be exploited and manipulated. It was a callous thing to do, but sadly entirely in character. Two birds with one stone, as he would say. Not just taking revenge upon you but trying to undermine my reputation with damning evidence of my secret business. Unfortunately I have no suitable evidence with which to fight back.'

'I can testify against him for what he did to me, Director,' Vanessa said. 'That should ruin him.'

'It would be your word against his, Vanessa. You would be making an unbelievable accusation without any hard evidence to back it up. Note how careful he was not even to let Kashika see him. In any case neither of us can admit the circumstances in which this event took place. No, this war will continue until one or the other of us gains decisive evidence against the other and forces capitulation.'

'He mustn't be allowed to win, Director!' Kashika said fearfully. 'I could never be a slave to anybody else . . . or trust them like I do you. Vanessa has told me about Rochester. He's . . . he's evil!'

'I hope it will not come to that,' Shiller assured her. 'I would dissolve my girlflesh business rather than let you fall under his control. But he's a ruthless and capable rival. As you've seen today he's very careful never to leave any traces behind. He even operates his own girlflesh trade at arm's length.'

'He said he had a place he could have taken Kashika if I hadn't cooperated,' Vanessa said. 'Is that what he meant, Director?'

'Yes. He has several slave facilities. Real slaves, I'm

afraid: conditioned to serve. Even if girls go in willingly they find they cannot leave. The locations change regularly. I have on occasions launched private raids on them and freed the girls there, but I cannot close the whole network and there is never hard evidence linking him to them. One day perhaps he'll make a mistake and then . . . But enough of this. You must rest. I shall see you both tomorrow in my office at ten. Goodnight . . . and well done, Vanessa.'

'I just kept him talking as long as I could, Director.'

'Sometimes the right words at the right time can be very important.'

Vanessa and Kashika had a long hot soapy shower together, helping to wash away the lingering traces of their ordeal, both physical and mental. Vanessa used her douche gun to flush Kashika's passages both front and rear free of sperm, then applied some ointment the doctor had left to her sore bottom. In turn Kashika worked the cream deep into Vanessa's still smarting vagina. They began to giggle in sheer relief as they went about this intimate task. It was reassuring to touch each other.

Moving about the flat they were naturally conscious of the presence of the two Shiller security men. After repairing the chain on the front door that Rochester's men had cut when they broke into the flat after tasering Kashika, they had settled down in front of the television. In theory the guards were at liberty to make use of Vanessa and Kashika, being collared company slaves, as they wished. But clearly feeling sympathy for what they had been through they gave them no more than admiring glances.

For their part Vanessa realised they had not thought of dressing after their ordeal. It was natural, and exciting, to be naked in front of company employees in private. She compared the feeling to the fear Rochester's men had inspired in her. It was right that these men, wearing the company logo, should be able to look at their bodies. Was it as though they were 'family'? In this context the word had somewhat incestuous implications, but it did convey the essence of what Vanessa felt. It complemented the sense of 'sisterhood' she knew existed within and between the slave chains. Fundamentally it just felt good to belong to something so strange and wonderful. She'd never let Rochester destroy it.

She and Kashika tidied up, changed the bedding, put the sheets in the wash and then cuddled up in Vanessa's bed together. They didn't attempt any love play at first but just held onto each other and talked, with Kashika assuming the slavish and adoring demeanour that she adopted when they were alone which made Vanessa feel both foolishly proud and rich beyond measure.

'This was not how I planned this evening, Mistress,' Kashika said. 'I had such a lovely meal started. I suppose I might be able to rescue some of it.'

'This wasn't exactly how I imagined it going either,' Vanessa said ruefully. 'I was going to tell you about the clinic and a great girl there that you've got to meet. But what matters is we're all right now.' She paused then added: 'I want to say, if it had come to it, I'd have got Rochester his pictures. I couldn't stand the thought of losing you.'

'Oh! You must never put me before the company, Mistress,' Kashika said fervently. 'Think of all the other girls it would have hurt.'

'I can't help it. I feel guilty enough as it is.'

'Why, Mistress?' Kashika said in surprise.

'Because by being my lover you became a target for Rochester to try to use against me. Hurting you was part of his revenge. I'm so sorry I got you mixed up in all this.'

Kashika kissed her. 'Never feel sorry for that, Mistress. He's the enemy of both of us and the company.'

'But he would never have singled you out like this if it hadn't been for me.'

'If it hadn't been you and me it would have been somebody else, Mistress. But you stopped him here and now so maybe you saved two other people from harm. We have to make a stand for what is right, even if it means we get hurt. I knew you were trying to buy us time. If it had been necessary for me to take that beating with the studded straps to buy us more I would have.'

Now it was Vanessa's turn to kiss her. 'I knew you were strong. Now I think you're also braver than I am. But I'm still sorry your lovely bottom got marked.'

'It's still there for you to spank, Mistress,' Kashika giggled. 'I'd happily bear any marks you put on it. But that's my private pleasure. I think we also have a bigger duty to some ideals whatever the cost. I don't mean going out and destroying something just because we don't like it, but defending a way of life we have chosen voluntarily that does nobody else any harm. The company gives women like us a safe home and allows us to be ourselves as . . .' she chuckled lightly '. . . happy slaves. And our service pleases other people and perhaps stops them turning to true helpless slaves for pleasure. I think that's worth fighting for, don't you, Mistress?'

Vanessa kissed her again. 'It is. And I'm going to write up what you just said in *GN*. We're going to fight Rochester and all his kind who want to make us into something mean and dirty!' Now it was her turn to chuckle. 'We're going to fight for the right to bear the collars and chains of our choice!'

By the next morning the Shiller guards evidently thought they had recovered from their ordeal and normal master/slave relations were resumed. Waking Vanessa and Kashika they demanded to be fed. They also found slave chains from Vanessa's store and put hobbles on them.

After cooking the men breakfast, Vanessa and Kashika were ordered to eat their own meal off bowls and without utensils on the floor in one corner of the small kitchen. They neatly nibbled and lapped up the food with their bottoms raised and heads down, presenting their masters with a pretty view of their pubic clefts pouting from between their thighs, which was the proper way for slaves to dine in the presence of free people.

When they had finished the men opened their flies and required the girls to service their erections, which they did on hands and knees, enjoying a dessert of hot sperm. It seemed perfectly normal and natural to Vanessa and it put yesterday evening into context. Their submission was appreciated. It had value. The men knew what they could and could not demand. It meant she and Kashika were happy slaves once again.

After breakfast Vanessa and Kashika went through the normal slavish ritual of meticulously cleaning and greasing their nether orifices ready for any new use that might be required of them. Then they dressed in street clothes and left the flat. The Shiller guards followed at a discreet distance and shadowed Vanessa's car on the drive into the centre of London.

There was no sign of anything out of the ordinary, but Vanessa knew it was only a temporary reprieve. The knives were out now. Somewhere Rochester was nursing his frustration and anger and plotting some new scheme to bring the house of Shiller down.

Shiller's London headquarters occupied a custom-built modern tower block overlooking the Thames. Outwardly it was the prestigious home of a respectable and prosperous company, yet within it concealed secrets that would have astonished its neighbours.

Shadowed by their guards' car, Vanessa entered the tower's private underground car park, passed through a double set of security gates and wound her way down to the second basement level where she finally drew up beside an odd assortment of cars, vans and light lorries. Here Vanessa and Kashika waved goodbye to their guards. Vanessa used a key card and pad code to open the doors to a spacious goods lift. On the lift control panel the lowest button was marked 'B2', the level they were on. Vanessa pressed it three times. The doors closed and the lift descended.

Vanessa felt the familiar thrill of entering a secret, privileged world. She saw the same look on Kashika's face. Was it like coming home? A little. Perhaps it resembled more closely being taken to Santa's Grotto as a child, for there really was a wonderland awaiting them.

The doors opened and they stepped out into fresh warmth and soft light. The arching vaulted concrete roof overhead was painted in sky blue and skilfully lit by uplighters, making it seem higher than it was. On each side of the lifts a row of three timber chalets were tucked in under the false sky. The lift well was at the crossroads of long broad corridors, lined by tubs and planters of shrubs, each bathed in light from racks of mini-spotlights. The corridors ran between rectangular structures with concrete block walls painted in different colours and lower than the vaulted roof. Around the lift the floor was of woodblocks but the corridors were carpeted with thick, dark-blue rubber matting. A murmur of purposeful activity filled the place. It was an entire secret subterranean level in the middle of London hidden from public knowledge. It was where Shiller slaves were trained and housed.

With the slap and shuffle of bare feet and jingle of chains a dozen naked women came down the corridor towards them, escorted by a man and woman in nondescript grey overalls. The women were secured in a three-by-four grid by chains crossing between their collars, which were all green. Their wrists were chained behind their backs, their mouths all bulged with green ball-gags, their naked breasts jiggled in time with their shuffling steps and their eyes were bright with anticipation and very alive. Vanessa and Kashika stepped aside as the chain of girls were herded past them into the lift. They smelt the perfume wafting from their naked bodies combined with the musk of female arousal. The doors closed and the lift ascended to level B2, where Vanessa knew the girls would be loaded into one of those assorted vans or lorries that would carry them off to serve in one of Shiller's subsidiary slave facilities.

Vanessa and Kashika exchanged smiles. It was nice to be back.

They made their way to one of the blocky structures forming one side of the central alley that ran down the middle of the long axis of the level. Going down on their hands and knees they crawled through a low doorway guarded by a mesh gate. A short tunnel and a second gate led to a lobby with both slave-size gates and ordinary doors leading off it. Behind a glass-topped desk sat a large red-faced man in a security guard's uniform. Still on their hands and knees, Vanessa and Kashika shuffled over to him and respectfully kissed the polished toes of his boots.

'Kashika Cherry and Miss Buckingham,' he exclaimed, 'I heard you had a spot of trouble last night.' His evident genuine concern was only partly concealed behind his understatement.

'We did, Master Jarvis,' Vanessa said. 'But we're all right now. The Director said we were to see her about it at ten.'

'Well, go through and get yourself decent, then,' he said briskly. 'You don't want to keep her waiting . . .'

They shuffled through into a room lined with metal lockers, where they stripped off their clothes and stowed them away. Vanessa kept only her key card, hooked to her collar by a light chain, her press hat and sandals. Kashika wore only her collar. By the standards of this strange underworld they were now 'decently' dressed.

They went down on their hands and knees and crawled back out into the lobby. Miss Kyle was waiting for them.

She was a coolly beautiful dark-eyed brunette, a little older than Vanessa, with flawless pale skin. She was dressed in her normal costume, for a slave girl trainer in B3, of thigh-length black leather boots and a dark body stocking, which moulded itself to her body like a second skin. From a belt encircling her trim waist hung a cane and a coiled whip. It was Miss Kyle who had broken Vanessa in during her first day in B3. Vanessa was sure Mister Jarvis had told her they were here.

They shuffled forward and kissed her boots while her eye flicked over them with professional concern, noting the marks on their bodies. 'I had to see you to make sure you were all right,' she said, her normally pouting lips pinched in concern and anger.

'We're fine, Miss Kyle,' Vanessa said. 'Just a bit sore.'

'I don't mean your bodies, Vanessa. I know what you both can take and I know bruises heal. I meant in your minds. I was afraid it might make you doubt your calling.'

'No, Miss Kyle,' Vanessa assured her.

'I'm still a Shiller girl, Miss Kyle,' Kashika said simply.

Miss Kyle looked relieved. 'That's what I wanted to know.'

'Thank you for raising the alarm, Miss Kyle,' Vanessa said.

Miss Kyle smiled grimly. 'Luckily I checked the mirror early, knowing the pair of you might have jumped into bed before eating. For a moment I wasn't sure if it was something you had arranged privately. Then I saw you looking at the mirror and read it all in your face and alerted security. I kept watching in case they threatened you with serious harm, in which case I would have used the speakers to try to frighten them off.'

'They might have taken us with them before the security team got there, Miss Kyle,' Kashika said. 'Vanessa at least, so Rochester could have his revenge.'

'That's why I held back. Anyway, you're safe now. And I want to say how proud I am of the wonderful display of suffering you put on.'

'Thank you, Miss Kyle,' Vanessa said. 'But I was just playing for time by trying to keep them screwing us as long as possible.'

'That was the best thing you could do. You used your greatest weapons: your bodies and your sluttish natures, just as I would have hoped. Well done.'

Kissing both Miss Kyle and Mister Jarvis's boots again, they left the way they'd come. Vanessa felt a warm glow inside her. It was good to know how much they were appreciated.

Back in the lift Vanessa pressed the button for the top floor. Kashika looked both impressed at Vanessa's confidence in sending the lift up to the summit of the tower, yet also apprehensive.

'I've never been to the Director's personal office before,' she admitted as they ascended. 'Is it like the other girls say?'

'It's special,' Vanessa agreed. 'Nothing far out, just very . . . individual. After a while you realise it suits the Director exactly and you couldn't imagine her working anywhere else. Just do everything I do. She won't bite.'

'But she's so masterful. I feel I should be down on my knees all the time.'

'Me too. And you will be. But she cares for us, remember that.'

Kashika hesitated, then asked: 'Have you ever served her?'

It was something that had been troubling Vanessa ever since the Director had honoured her by making her a white-collar girl a few months earlier. 'No, I haven't. I haven't actually seen her that often since my probation month. Most of the time I work in the *GN* office and take orders from my editor. I mean I really want to please the Director so much . . .' she added hastily: '. . . it's nothing like how I feel about you, lover; you know that. That's private and personal. But I also want to be able to please her.'

'I understand,' Kashika said with a smile. 'She's just so powerful and dominating you couldn't not want to. It's natural. I mean in a way we all belong to her. We're Shiller company girls. She's our mistress. Our owner.'

Vanessa felt a thrill at Kashika's matter-of-fact words, feeling a flutter in her stomach. It was true that the Director was in effect their absolute master. She could have any of the girls down in B3 she wanted and they would die to please her. But she confined her personal pleasures to her own elite retinue of white-collar girls. True, Vanessa wore a white collar but there was one other difference between them and her. Her fingers slid down to the gold ring piercing the lip of her left inner labia. The other white girls had three rings, one in their other lip and one through the hood of their clitorises.

All girls who graduated from basic slave training down in B3 received one ring. Vanessa had got hers for defying Rochester and not revealing Shiller's secrets to him. Perhaps she had to earn two more rings before the Director decided she was fit to serve. They were not a symbol of beauty or passion but a reward for character and ability. Well, she must simply be patient. The Director respected honesty and diligent work. If she stuck to those principles she might be judged worthy some day.

In the meantime she was young and healthy, she had an incredible job and was blessed with Kashika's love. Who could want for more?

The lift opened onto an airy foyer looking out onto a lush roof garden. A double row of glass-topped desks ran down each side of the room bearing computer terminals. Seated before each, legs held casually parted, was a naked woman in a white collar, slave chains and ankle hobbles.

Vanessa led Kashika through the room, between the secretarial rows of parted legs and exposed pubic deltas, to a large frosted-glass double door at the far end. She knocked and then went down onto her hands and knees. Kashika quickly copied her.

The doors slid open and they shuffled through. The doors were actuated by a pair of hooded blue-collar slave girls, but not by using their hands. Vanessa noted their method of attachment to the doors had changed since she'd last visited the Director's private office.

Both girls stood faced inward, backs pressed against the doors, their hands cuffed behind them. They stood with their legs spread to accommodate the upward curving door handles that extended between them. The handles ended in spiked balls that nestled firmly in their clefts, spreading their soft pink lips wide. Vanessa imagined it would be quite painful to shuffle sideways, dragging the weight of half a door however smoothly it slid on its runners. She was not surprised to see, however, that their sexes were wet with excitement and their nipples straining hard. Naturally. They were company girls privileged to operate the Director's own private door.

The office also looked out onto the rooftop garden. Between the large windows was a living sculpture.

Strung between two posts mounted at each end of a plinth was a spider-web of stainless steel ribbons. Caught in the web and stretched taut and wide was a girl in a pink collar. Steel bands were strapped over her eyes and mouth, they encircled and squeezed her breasts and teased her pouting vulva. She was there completely at the whim of anybody free to do so to be admired, touched and fondled; the contrast between her soft pliant flesh and the unyielding metal to be enjoyed.

83

Vanessa recalled seeing a girl similarly displayed on her first frightening, wonderful day in the Shiller building, where shock had piled on shock. At the time she had been appalled anybody could do such a thing and denied utterly that a girl could enjoy such exposure. Now she understood how the girl felt and was not surprised to see her vagina was engorged and had dripped onto the plinth. Any girl chosen to decorate the Director's office would be immensely proud. Vanessa would have swapped places with her in a second.

FG Shiller, the founder and director of Shiller plc, sat behind a large leather-topped desk, which was bare except for a single slim screen and keyboard. She was a slender, still attractive woman in perhaps her mid-fifties, with a strong straight nose, piercing bright blue eyes and short well-groomed hair crowning a narrow, intelligent, unlined face. She was the darkest thing in the room in her dark-blue business suit and seemingly the least unusual, yet she filled it with her quiet dominating presence.

'You wished to see us, Director,' Vanessa said.

The Director smiled. 'Yes. Come up here, both of you.'

A pair of backless stools stood in front of the desk. Vanessa shuffled forward and used one stool to climb up onto the desk and sat back on her heels in a display posture with arms folded behind her back and thighs spread. Kashika gracefully copied her, positioning herself on the other side of the computer.

The Director looked them over closely. 'No ill effects from your unfortunate experience?'

'A slight headache, Director,' Vanessa said. 'Nothing that won't pass.'

'Just a sore bottom, Director,' Kashika said meekly, her eyes wide with wonder and delight at being face to face with the Director.

'Good. You've both been very brave.'

Vanessa bit her lip but she had to say it. 'Director, I must confess . . . if it came to it, deciding between Kashika and the company, I . . . would have got what Rochester wanted. Kashika would have been braver, but I would have spied for him . . . been a traitor to you.' She hung her head. 'I'm so sorry.'

Shiller shook her head. 'Don't be, Vanessa. You are only human and Kashika is your friend and lover. It's not a choice any of us should have to make. What you felt was not wrong and no sign of disloyalty. Don't concern yourself about it any more.'

Vanessa felt relieved. 'Thank you, Director.'

'Now, I want to sample your responses so I can decide how this incident should best be handled. If Rochester was having you watched it's possible he's had other girls or members of staff followed, in which case he might try the same method to induce them to spy for him. Of course few would be as well placed as you, Vanessa, to obtain incriminating evidence. But if he has miniature cameras capable of being carried within body cavities then we must be on our guard. I may have to order scans and closer body searches for girls who have been out of the building unescorted, but I don't want to lower the girls' morale or make them feel they have lost any of my trust. How would the two of you feel about submitting to such searches?'

'The girls will always do what you say, Director,' Kashika said fervently. 'If it's necessary they'll understand.'

'Thank you for your confidence, Kashika.' Shiller said gravely. 'And what about you, Vanessa?'

Vanessa said slowly: 'I think you should make any new searches a ritual. Make it a new slave routine, something the girls are taught. To keep the staff on their toes maybe you can have dummy cameras hidden and prizes for finding them.'

'Now that's an interesting idea,' the Director mused. 'I said before that you had a certain independence of mind.'

Vanessa felt a wonderful sense of warmth at her praise. 'Thank you, Director.'

'Now, what do you think the consequences will be if Rochester's attempt on you is made public amongst the girls? I do not wish to alarm them but they should also be forewarned, especially if new security measures are introduced.'

'It wouldn't surprise them, Director,' Kashika said. 'I think every girl here has heard something about how Rochester tried to use Vanessa before. I've told the story to all my chain sisters.'

'If it was up to me I'd tell it all, Director,' Vanessa said. 'Gather them all together like you do for a chain graduation and explain what happened. That would make any new security measures easier to understand. It's all about being honest with the girls. There's no pretence about being a company slave. It's admitting what we are. Don't start holding anything back from them now . . .' She felt a lump forming in her throat. 'I know that's what won me over, that's what makes this place so different from anything Rochester can have!'

Kashika was nodding, moist-eyed.

Shiller smiled. 'You have confirmed my own thoughts. I won't defeat Rochester by lying to my own girls. If I spoke to the girls this afternoon, say, would that give you time to write up what happened as a special single-sheet edition of *Girlflesh News* so it can be handed out afterwards? We can also send copies to our other facilities nationwide for the chains there to read. They can go out with the details of the new security measures. Then every girl will understand what's required of her.'

'Of course, Director,' Vanessa said. 'I can get started as soon as I get back to my office and talk to Mistress Zara.'

'Then off you go. And you can tell your chain sisters there'll be an announcement this afternoon, Kashika, but say no more until then.'

'Yes, Director,' they said, and then scrambled down from the desk and shuffled to the door.

Vanessa got off at the fifth floor while Kashika continued on down to B3. Hurrying through to the offices of the Shiller house magazines she remembered the first time she had passed along these corridors just a few months before, though it seemed to belong to another life. She had been wearing a plain steel collar and slave chains and had been sick with fear and almost paralysed at being naked in front of ordinary office workers. But then she had been trying to overthrow the company so perhaps the humiliation was deserved.

As a reporter working for the *Daily Globe* on the special assignment Rochester had given her to uncover Shiller secrets, she had managed to gain entry to level B3 and found to her horror slave trading taking place on a commercial scale. But before she could relay her discovery she had been apprehended. Shiller had talked her into a bargain, enforced by intimate electronic monitoring, that she would not reveal their secrets for a month. During that time she would work, supposedly still undercover, on the house magazines and be free to interview the slave girls and decide at first-hand if they really were natural submissives serving the company voluntarily. And she had discovered the truth, not only about the company but herself. And she had met Kashika and become a loyal company slave. And now rushing to her office naked except for a hat, collar and sandals was simply part of everyday life. But it was a life under threat once more from the same force that had unwittingly introduced her to it.

Zara Fulton, her editor, was a tall, attractive, full-busted woman in her mid-forties with a mass of dark wavy hair and narrow blue-grey eyes. She swivelled round in her chair as Vanessa entered her office.

Taking off her hat Vanessa went down on her knees and shuffled over to Zara, who drew up her red skirt to expose her panty-less crotch. Vanessa bent and kissed the moist scented vertical smile between her thighs, then sat back on her heels and said formally: 'Good Morning, Mistress Editor.'

'Good Morning, Vanessa. I hear you've been having quite an adventure.' Her words were offhand but there was genuine concern beneath them.

'Yes, Mistress Editor. And now the Director wants me to write it up . . .' She explained about the special edition.

Zara looked thoughtful, then said: 'You get started. Personal angle obviously, but don't let it get in the way of the facts. They'll speak for themselves, no need to sensationalise. Come to me with what you've got in an hour and we'll go over it. How many girls are in the building at the moment? Say we run off a hundred and fifty copies to be sure. If the Director is going to talk to the girls we should cover that as well. Hmm . . . I'll call her and suggest we have your copy ready to run but hold off printing it until we can add a transcript of her speech to it as the lead. We can still have them ready for distributing inside an hour.'

'I think that's a good idea, Mistress Editor.'

Zara smiled. 'Well, that's what they pay me for. Now get writing . . .'

Vanessa had her story ready inside the hour. She had to take a mental step back to recount the events as accurately as possible. Reliving the fear was not pleasant. Zara read it over with approval, though she wore a scowl by the end.

'You and Kashika had a nasty time.'

'It wasn't so much what they did as the fear of what might come next,' Vanessa admitted. 'But when I found out it was Rochester behind it, that made me angry and I think that helped.'

'Yes, I think anger's the best response to that man. But he's fooling himself if he thinks he can beat the Director. When he falls I'm going to be there cheering!'

Zara had hated Rochester since before Vanessa had become mixed up in the secret rivalry between the two companies. She seemed to hold even more enmity towards him than the Director. Vanessa wondered if it was something personal. Perhaps she'd find out one day.

'I'll add a brief editorial to put it all in context and then we're ready to go,' Zara continued. 'I'll cover the Director's address. She wants you and Kashika up on the podium with her.'

The thought of being in the spotlight suddenly made Vanessa feel absurdly nervous. Then the absurdity of her response struck her. A naked sex-slave feeling shy!

At lunchtime she had a visitor to her desk. It was Sandra, a pretty, slim, white-collar girl with shaven pubes and a ponytail of blonde hair. She had attended Vanessa during that first frightening, confusing, life-changing day she had served as a sex-slave.

She hugged and kissed Vanessa. 'I heard what happened. Was it terrible?'

'The Director told me to write it up so everybody knows the facts. You'll be able to read all about it in a few hours.'

'And Harvey Rochester was responsible?'

'Yes.'

'He's not given up attacking us?'

'It doesn't look like it.'

Sandra was normally confident and composed far beyond her years but suddenly she appeared very young and vulnerable. 'He mustn't destroy Shiller's. It's the only life I know!'

That afternoon level B3 came alive and Vanessa could see it for what it was: a tiny secret underground village of slave girls.

The girls came in from where they had been serving on other floors of the tower, excused from training regimes, taking time out from play or rest, attending before being shipped off to work in an outlying facility or entertain at some country house party. They flowed along the broad central corridor, known of course as the 'High Street', in a many-hued tide of flesh, bare but for multicoloured collars and personal adornments of ribbons, bangles and assorted footwear ranging from sandals to high-heels. The sudden announcement of an unscheduled personal address by the Director had caused puzzled excitement and there was much curious chatter as they filed in through the gates of the yard at the end of the High Street.

This was where new slaves were trained and where their ceremonies of welcome and graduation were

held, making it convenient for today's address. Slave
hutches, kennels, posts and racks were arrayed about
its perimeter.

Vanessa watched the girls form into a semi-circle
about the low podium that had been set up to one side
of the yard. Trapped as it was under the false sky, she
could feel the heat of their bodies, the scent of bare
flesh and twenty different perfumes, mingled with the
natural exudation of female lubrication that emanated
from lovemouths that had been trained to express
arousal freely and without shame. It was a strange and
undeniably erotic sight made even more wonderful
because Vanessa knew each girl was present of her
own free will. But now that freedom was threatened.

She knelt beside Kashika on the podium. With
them were the six regular slave girl trainers, all
individually dressed according to personal taste.
Apart from Miss Kyle there was muscular black
Mister Winston in black leather knee boots and
matching thong, slender blonde Miss Scott in a black
pvc bikini, Mister McGarry in leather trousers and
harness top, blonde athletic Mister Tyler in shorts
and singlet and Mister Hirsch in calf-length boots
and brief leather pouch.

Despite their very different styles, today all the
trainers wore set faces. They knew what had happened, of course. The quirky thought struck Vanessa
that if Rochester triumphed they'd be out of a job.
What would they do then? Did they have ordinary
lives, interests and occupations? She'd only ever seen
them handling the girls. It was hard to imagine they
could ever be ordinary people. Shiller gave a home
and purpose to more than just natural-born submissives.

Shiller appeared and made her way up to the
podium. The buzz of conversation faded. Perhaps the

smallest, most sombrely dressed person there, she still commanded instant respect and attention.

'I've had you gathered here because of an incident that occurred yesterday evening, involving Vanessa Nineteen White and Kashika Five Cherry. You will be able to read the full details in a special edition of *Girlflesh News* that will be distributed very shortly, but essentially it involved a new attempt by Sir Harvey Rochester to obtain images of you together with prestigious clients, and thereby subvert this company's girlflesh trade.'

A murmur of alarm rippled though the ranks of girls. Vanessa actually saw normally perkily erect nipples shrinking in dismay.

Shiller raised her hands in a calming gesture. 'However, I'm glad to say, due to the bravery of the girls involved and swift action by our security team, that the attempt failed. There is no immediate danger. But you will understand that security must be tightened to prevent any further attempts at infiltration. This will involve thorough body searches of all girls entering or leaving the building for personal visits unescorted.'

At this point Shiller suddenly smiled almost mischievously with a twinkle in her eye, yet somehow without losing any sense of dignity. Vanessa felt the mood immediately lighten.

'Now, I suspect most of you have no objection to your orifices being deeply probed by the more robust members of our security staff and may indeed find the experience enjoyable ...' there was a ripple of laughter '... but I wanted you to be in no doubt that this in any way reflects a lack of confidence in you or your discretion. I trust you always to maintain this company's standards of quality and service whatever may come. I promise I will do everything in my power to defeat Rochester, but there is a very real possibility that he will try again, perhaps by some other means. All I ask is for your continued vigilance and understanding, the precious gift of your bodies and the boundless delight you take in submission. Together we will prevail!'

A wave of applause filled the yard, girls and trainers as one. Even as she joined in Vanessa felt the lump return to her throat. Were slaves anywhere praised so highly by their Mistress? Only Shiller slaves. Surely something so unique could not be allowed to fail!

Five

Ten days passed after Shiller's speech in the training yard. Vanessa thought of it as an interlude while she waited for either Shiller or Rochester to make the next decisive move. Meanwhile life continued normally down in B3, or at least what was accepted as normal in such a strange place.

The chain girls, who had read Vanessa's account in the *GN* special edition with avid interest, were all deeply sympathetic. Every time she went down to B3 she received an embarrassing amount of attention and many barely veiled submissive offers of pleasure from off-duty girls that she had to politely decline. It was all very flattering and made her feel like a slave girl champion, bravely defying Rochester on their behalf. Shiller was doing so all the time, of course, but the machinations and manoeuvres of big business were remote, whereas they could identify personally with a girl strapped to a bed having her nipples and pussy zapped.

Some of their enquiries concerning her responses to that incident verged on the clinically intimate, and she became involved in debates over the merits of electrical versus physical torture. It was not what had been done to her and Kashika but who had done it and for what purpose that won their sympathy. That was what they found both frightening and indefensible. The helplessness, pain and sexual stimulation she had undergone, taken in isolation, were something else entirely. In other circumstances they could be the source both of personal pleasure and entertainment to the tormentor.

Her candid admission that the pain had driven her to wet herself was another point of interest, at least to other slave girls. There was widespread admission that the act of peeing when aroused could be exciting and might even trigger an orgasm. They all seemed to have tails about clients who had forced it upon them at various times. The joys of lying in cooling pee on a bed divided opinion, and the value of a rubber sheet or a fabric one were hotly debated. They were all agreed, however, that a remote-controlled inflatable bit-gag was a neat idea.

Only slave girls could turn such an incident on its head like that, Vanessa thought with pride, and only Shiller girls could discuss it so openly. She might suggest to Zara that a forum for such matters be opened in *GN*.

Vanessa wrote up her piece on the clinic for the next regular issue of *GN*, though she thought it might be a little anticlimactic compared to her dramatic exclusive. Still the clinic's work deserved to be documented and it would interest girls about to serve there. It should be that sort of story she wrote all the time, she thought resentfully, not revelations of clandestine assaults and warning of threats to their very way of life.

Another of these pieces was coverage of the new security measures. The practical consequence was a simple device, made of scaffolding poles, of two upright posts in front of a horizontal bar, being set up by the B3 lift doors. All girls entering or leaving the level in street clothes would have to be searched and scanned for electronic devices. Mister Jarvis and the other changing room and dormitory guards were also empowered to make extra locker checks of clothes and possessions. Vanessa recorded these changes and added a personal plea for the girls to accept them.

That the new measures were accepted without resentment or an apparent drop in morale was partly due to Shiller's decision to trust the girls with the truth and partly the self-discipline that existed in B3. This was not the kind of discipline enforced by chains and whips, but the sort that grew out of the sense of community and shared purpose that all the chain sisters felt. The new ritual that accompanied the process reinforced this mood. Kashika came up with a rhyme to go with it, which was reprinted in *GN*, much to her delight.

'Please lift our skirts and lower our knicks,
Search pussy, tits and derrière.
With welcoming mouths we Shiller chicks,
Show we have nothing to declare.'

The girls bent over the frame, grasped the uprights and spread their legs in a submissive accessible posture, but they were not restrained. Hair, if long and normally tied up, was left loose. They then begged to be searched, some of them chanting Kashika's rhyme. A scanner was run over them, their mouths, hair and cleavage were checked and their vagina and rectum probed. By encouraging the girls to ask for the search it made it seem less of an imposition. Shiller had taken up Vanessa's suggestion and every once in a while a selected girl would be given a dummy camera or other object to attempt to smuggle out. So far none had succeeded.

But Vanessa was only too aware that Rochester had not given up. He'd had a taste of personal revenge but once again he'd been cheated of his ultimate goal of destroying Shiller and taking over her girlflesh business. He might, with some justification, blame Vanessa for this latest failure and hate her even more, and he was a powerful and vindictive man. It was not a pleasant thought.

Vanessa did not return to her flat except accompanied by a security guard to check her post and see all was well. She spent her days in the office and nights down in level B3. She would have loved to share a dormitory with Kashika and the Cherry Chain girls, but instead she was passed around between the trainers and stayed in their chalets.

Having spent years training slave girls, dominance came as second nature to them and they bore an unquestioning air of authority that required total obedience in return. They made use of Vanessa in their individual ways and she was perfectly content to serve them, relishing her surrender of choice.

It felt right that she serve as often as possible like an ordinary chain girl. It was also the perfect antidote to any danger of her quasi-celebrity status amongst the girls going to her head and would help maintain her empathy with them and keep her writing focused on their viewpoint. These were the people who had trained Kashika and Cherry Chain only a few months ago. Vanessa had not undergone any formal slave training and had learnt by example and necessity as she went along, discovering her own secret pain-slut submissive nature along the way. Of course she didn't need to be restrained at night to keep her from trying to escape any more than other Shiller chain girls, but it was unthinkable to stay in the building as a free woman. It was no good having the submissive instinct if it was not regularly exercised. Besides, it made her feel safe. The highlights stood out in her mind long afterward . . .

Mister Hirsch used her rear as a footstool while he watched a DVD of a classic black and white western. She was bound face down on her knees with her arms pulled back under her and cuffed to a short bar that also secured her ankles. A strap went round both her elbows and knees, pulling them inward. This pushed her bottom up high with her sexmouth pouting between her thighs. She was placed so this aspect faced him as he lounged back in a big club chair. He was naked except for a pair of highly-tooled leather boots complete with spurs that he rested on her bottom. The peak of her posterior supported the lower calves of his boots, so the spurs overhung and just brushed the curve of her lower back. As the film progressed, however, he began to shift his feet and run the spurs back and forth across the taut swell of her buttocks, or else probe her cleft with the silver toecaps of his boots. By the time the film was done she was desperate for his cock, which he duly obliged by feeding into her sopping cleft.

Miss Scott had her dress in a maid's cap and pinny and made her scrub floors, clean and polish her chalet until it was spotless. The slightest fault was rewarded by a swipe of a cane across the upper slopes of her breasts while she knelt meekly with hands folded behind her. She was then taken to the shower and made to scrub her mistress's back and bottom. As she was kneeling engaged in this activity Miss Scott turned about, pushed Vanessa's head down and peed over her. As the hot water flowed though her hair and dripped off her nose Vanessa felt a deep and entirely appropriate blush of shameful delight at being reminded of her place so simply. The wonderful unfairness struck her that when she was forced to wet herself in bondage and under duress she was demeaned and yet when a Mistress peed over her she was still demeaned.

Mister McGarry used her, literally, as a living lamp-stand stood by his chair. He impaled her anally on a steel rod that rose from a solid round base plate and then bound her with a dozen straps, working up her body until she was fixed rigidly to the post. Her arms were bent and twisted outwards, forearms strapped to upper arms and then in turn strapped to the sides of her chest. Straps even went over her fingers, bending them outward and leaving her hands palm-up and level with her shoulders. A final strap went over her mouth forming a gag. He brought out four thick stubby red candles set in holders made of thick metal foil, like cake cases. Two of the bases were level and two cut at forty-five degrees. With double-sided tape he stuck the two level candles to the palms of her hands and the two with angled bases to the upper slopes of her breasts, so that they stood vertical. Then he lit them, put on some soft background music, dimmed the room lights so the light from her candles shone out, sat in the chair beside her, picked up a book and read by the light of her candles; the ones on her breasts trembled slightly as she breathed.

Soon the candles grew warm and trickles of hot wax began to run into her hands, flowing between her fingers and dripping onto her thighs, and down and around her breasts. The wax melted and flowed so easily, Vanessa suspected it must be unusually soft. These rivulets dripped off her nipples or joined and trickled down through her cleavage. They flowed over her stomach, into her navel and even reached the edge of her pubic bush before finally hardening. The candles rapidly burned down to mere stubs and their metal bases grew hotter, but she could do nothing to put them out. Only when she was frightened she might be scorched and was making little whining sounds did Mister McGarry seem to notice. He put down his book, got up, blew the candles out, turned off the music and electric light and left her alone in the sitting room all night streaked in hardening candle wax.

Mister Tyler did not play such subtle games. Laying her on her back across his bed he bent and spread her, pulling her forearms and shins together so that her elbows were pressed against her knees and wrists next to ankles, and buckled sleeve restrainers about them. Threading ropes through rings in the ends of the sleeves he pulled her wide so she opened her body to him. Tying the rope off to the top and bottom of his bed she lay with her bottom hanging over the edge, her anal ring pouting and her vulva bulging invitingly. He stood over her, sliding his rock-hard penis first up her vagina and then her anus, all the while slapping her breasts with a rubber paddle, making them bounce and tremble and flop back until they took on an even rosy blush.

Miss Kyle was a complete contrast. She bound Vanessa with black rubber adhesive tape, strapping her arms to her sides and leaving only narrow strips of bare flesh between the winding coils. Pads of cotton wool went over her eyes and into her mouth and were taped in place. When she had been turned virtually into a rubber mummy, Miss Kyle laid her down in her bed and climbed in beside her. For an hour Miss Kyle's expert fingers toyed with Vanessa, caressing her breasts, teasing her nipples, slipping into the close humid cleft between her thighs and tickling her pulsating clitoris. The imprisoning strapping seemed to contain Vanessa's growing arousal, trapping it within her like steam in a pressure cooker, until finally she bucked and arched and orgasmed wildly.

Mister Winston was the principal trainer in B3's ponygirl stables, a part of the complex Vanessa tended to avoid. Perhaps it was because it was almost the first thing she had seen months earlier when she had infiltrated level B3 as Rochester's unwitting spy. The image of girls harnessed and kept in a stable like animals had at the time shocked her deeply. Even though now she knew the girls had been there entirely voluntarily the irrational aversion lingered. Perhaps it was the costumes they wore. They were not merely harnessed like ponies and used to pull carts, they had been given horses' heads. These were artfully sculpted equine masks moulded out of translucent plastic. While admitting they were very clever and striking, Vanessa had always thought they diminished the humanity of the girls in a disturbing way that mere slavery did not.

Perhaps Mister Winston knew about her feelings, because when it came time to serve in his chalet he ensured she confronted them, literally, head-on.

First he bound her on her hands and knees over a small low stool mounted on rocking chair runners so she was in an ideal position to be taken from behind. There was a large mirror set in front of her in which she could see her reflection. He wanted to watch her face as he mounted her, she thought. Then he brought out a pony mask and fitted it over her head. She whimpered as it enclosed her but he took no notice. The neck of the mask reached from her chin to sternum, encasing her own neck and collar, with rings embedded in the plastic to serve as new hitching points. Its horse-like snout complete with flared nostrils extended out from her natural jawline. It had an integral rubber bit that pushed between her teeth, trapping her tongue, while long, fluted forward-facing ears rose from the sides. They channelled sounds down to her ears in a strangely acute manner. Mister Winston pulled her hair through slots in the top and back of the mask, so that it hung down over her shoulders like a flowing mane.

She saw herself in the mirror; she had become a strange chimerical creature, the flesh-tinted, pliant mask merging with her flesh. Her breasts hung down beneath a horse's snout. God, she looked so weird! Her human features were blurred and absorbed by the plastic, making it seem more alive.

Mister Winston patted and stroked her head as she had seen him do to his charges in the stables, calming them like you would a flighty animal. Then he went down on his knees behind her, prised apart her buttocks and pushed his shaft up into the hot greased pit of her anus. He was big and she gasped as he filled her rectum, but it felt good. Her groan of delight issued from the mouth of the mask as a slobbering snort. He began to pump into her and set her moving back and forth like a rocking horse. He was riding her. She was his pony, his mount. They were master and slave, that's what mattered. He smacked her flanks and she clenched harder with her internal muscles. Her breasts swayed and jiggled and she tossed her head and snorted and whinnied with delight. Now she understood. All this time the trainers had been teaching her the most important lesson a slave girl could learn: complete acceptance of a master's will. A slave girl could be turned into anything a master wished. When she truly accepted that, she was a perfect slave.

* * *

Staying overnight meant Vanessa could observe for the first time the full sequence of slave girl activity in B3 and the Shiller Building above.

She saw chain girls going up to clean at night and coming down again in the small hours. They were surely the most beautiful, and certainly the most naked, army of 'Mrs Mops' ever assembled. Hair tied back and rubber-gloved, clad in their slave chains, they diligently vacuumed, swept and polished. After all, there was no point in having a captive labour force if it was not used to the full. The duty was regularly rotated so it did not become onerous and it served not only as good physical exercise but also as a reminder of the mundane world of simple labour they were privileged to have escaped.

Privileged? Vanessa had wondered about that word when it had come into her mind when observing the small army of cleaning girls and contemplating writing a brief article on night life in the Shiller building for *GN*. She decided it was not inappropriate. She suspected many non-submissive women facing years of drudgery and grind cleaning offices would, if given an insight into the lives of Shiller girls, actually envy them.

Of course that sort of reasoning was what drove some to the miseries and danger of prostitution and worse. It only went to show how lucky the chain girls were living the life their true natures craved. They must never forget that.

The arrival of night also brought an almost magical physical transformation to level B3. As evening in the city above drew in, the lamps that lit the false sky slowly dimmed to a deep blue night glow and the air conditioning shifted to a cooler cycle. Wall lamps came on to provide pools of brighter light replicating street and house lights and colourful strings of bulbs garlanded about the larger trees and shrubs lit up. Now it became quite easy to imagine they really were in a tiny village of narrow alleys.

It was at this time of day, when the Cherry Chain girls were free of their duties, that Vanessa joined them as they went for a run round the exercise track that encircled the entire level. She'd come to know all the Cherry girls well since her first assignment for *GN*, which had been to cover their initiation and basic training, while at the same time she had gone through her own strange process of self-examination and inner awakening. That, together with her love for Kashika, meant they regarded her rather like their own personal reporter and friend in high places.

The running track was lined with more shrubs and small trees, overhanging it in places, which were also illuminated. Clad only in their collars and trainers and feeling the cool air flow over their naked bodies, they jogged through leafy archways hung about with coloured stars, knowing a freedom denied to those who had to pound along the streets above.

The 'Mall' was a corridor running parallel to the High Street in the manner of a mews. It was fronted by a double row of small cell-like rooms, each with large low windows sheltered by striped awnings and a single recessed doorway. The windows were in fact one-way mirrors, seen from the inside. Some of these mirrors were raised and stands put out to display small goods such as books, papers and magazines, fruits and sweets, perfumes and cosmetics, ribbons, footwear and jewellery that off-duty girls could buy. It was almost like a small shopping street above ground except for the naked women on both sides of the counter. Between the shops the cells served different purposes, though in a manner of speaking they also offered goods and services. Some were curtained and could be used by one or more slave girls wanting privacy, while others had girls enticingly on display bound to various restraining devices for use by members of staff from the offices above.

One day Vanessa was walking along the Mall arm in arm with Kashika, who had a rest day, when a familiar figure in a yellow collar threw herself at Vanessa from the mill of girls and hugged her. It was Julie 5 Canary.

'I read your story,' Julie exclaimed when she finally allowed Vanessa to breathe. 'God, to think when you went home from the clinic you walked right into that! My chain only got back this morning. I had to see you and say how sorry I was . . .'

Vanessa formally introduced Kashika and the two girls hugged and kissed with a ready passion as only uninhibited Shiller-trained slaves could: mouth to mouth, nipples to nipples and a hand reaching round to slip between the other's buttocks. For a moment Vanessa worried there might be some sign of jealousy between them, though it seemed rare amongst Shiller girls. Perhaps living such an utterly open life with almost no privacy helped, or that most sexual urges were satisfied by their work without any need for subterfuge or deceit. The kiss certainly was no mere politeness. You must learn a lot about somebody when you get that close, she thought.

When the two girls broke the clinch their cheeks were flushed and their eyes sparkled happily. Julie slid her hand through Vanessa's free arm and they walked on together around the corner towards the High Street.

'Vanessa's told me how well you looked after her in the clinic,' Kashika said to Julie. 'Thank you.'

'That was easy,' Julie assured her. 'Not like the crappy time you had. How are you doing?' She sounded genuinely concerned.

'The strapping and the screwing weren't that bad, it was being in the other room not knowing what he was doing to Vanessa. I'd have my bum whipped raw rather than go through that again. But I knew she had a plan and I was ready to play along. I was sure it would work out all right. She always knows what she's doing.'

'I know what you mean. She's so strong-willed.'

'I love that,' Kashika said with simple sincerity.

'That's what makes her so special,' Julie said. 'We can all see it, but she can't.'

'I know, isn't it strange?' Kashika agreed.

'Hallo! I am listening to all this,' Vanessa said, beginning to feel embarrassed. They apparently ignored her.

'I mean she has to be special to have faced up to Rochester twice and got away with it,' Julie said.

'I don't think I could have done that,' Kashika said.

'Me neither. But she tries to act just like the rest of us, even though she's so much more masterful.'

'Yes, that's another thing that makes being with her so exciting.'

Playfully Vanessa took hold of a handful each of their hair and made them look at her. 'Shut up both of you!' she said with a chuckle. 'You're making it sound like I've done something incredible, but I just told a bully what I thought of him and prevaricated until rescue came along, that's all.'

They were both looking at her with adoring eyes.

'Yes,' Kashika said quietly, 'but that took courage. He's a powerful man but twice you've talked back to him like an equal, stood up to him and tricked him.

If you hadn't kept him and his man talking for so long they might have taken me away before the security squad arrived.'

'And you came even when he was torturing you,' Julie said. 'That's something we all hope we could do, but you were so casual when you wrote about it, when it must all have been terrifying and you were more concerned about Kashika than yourself. That's what all of us admire about you.'

'Which is why we'd do anything for you ... Mistress,' Kashika said.

'Anything you want ... Mistress,' Julie added.

The look of anticipation in their eyes kindled a warm tingle deep in Vanessa's loins. She had briefly felt the thrill of mastering another girl with Kashika at home, but she had thought that was a one-off private response just between them. Now Julie was offering herself and making it plain she was not alone.

What was it about her that Shiller girls found so alluring? The white collar? It still marked her as a slave and a submissive, which she knew beyond doubt that she was. The trainers were proving that every night. And yet there was something in her that the girls responded to. Was it because she worked for *GN* and wore her press hat ... or because she had chosen to wear a hat? That decision had marked her out as different. At the time she had thought of it as a small act of defiance and a boost to her self-confidence. But was it symbolic of her willingness to be herself no matter what? Something Shiller had seen in her had convinced her to let Vanessa determine the fate of her girlflesh business. Only a strong personality could do that. Perhaps other girls recognised that power in her. But could one be both slave and master? She looked into the eyes of the two unresisting girls in her grasp and knew she had to find out.

She led them back to the Mall and an empty cell at one end. It was a spartan room with painted breezeblock walls and a concrete floor, fitted out with ceiling hooks, a metal-framed bed, a stack of rubber mats and a basic rack of restraints, sex-toys and punishment devices. She drew the curtains over the inside of the big window and looked round. Julie and Kashika had both gone down on their knees and were waiting with spread thighs, hands folded behind their backs. Their breasts, tipped by hard nipples, trembled as their chests rose and fell in nervous excitement. Their vulvas were already wet with anticipation.

'Did you two plan this?' Vanessa asked.

'No, Mistress,' they said in uncanny harmony.

'What do you see in me?'

Briefly they exchanged glances. Hesitantly Kashika said: 'If you were like us you'd know, Mistress. It's only because you're not that you have to ask. It's that difference we love.'

'You are one of us, Mistress, but also something more,' Julie added.

They were so lovely and inviting, kneeling meekly before her, that she ached to use them. 'So if I was to tell you I wanted to chain you up and give you both a good paddling you'd do it?'

Their eyes sparkled. 'Of course, Mistress.'

'Why?'

'Because you ordered us Mistress,' Julie said. 'It's your right.'

'And we love you and want to please you,' Kashika added.

There was really nothing more to say.

Vanessa took a deep breath: 'Stand up and raise your arms . . .'

* * *

She cuffed their wrists to a ceiling hook and had them stand back to back, their buttocks pressed together.

The contrast between Kashika's dark skin and Julie's creamy complexion was striking and very beautiful. Though both blondes, Kashika's hair was of a deeper, more mellow golden tint, while Julie's had almost a touch of silver. The tension on their arms lifted their breasts, showing off their swollen nipples.

She lashed them with a spanking paddle, taking great care not to cut their precious flesh but delighting in the sharp smacks of rubber on soft skin. She circled them, swiping their thighs, bellies and breasts, making their ripe globes shiver and dance to her tune. They gasped and groaned and twisted and writhed, but they were responding to the blows, not trying to evade them, arching their backs and offering up their breasts for her pleasure and thrusting out their hips and spreading their legs in slavish invitation.

She swiped the paddle up into the fullness of their vulvas, connecting with swollen hot fleshy lips. The paddle blade came away glistening wetly while the mat under them began to be splattered with dark stains.

Vanessa turned them round to face each other and put a belt about their waists, pulling it tight until their breasts bulged against each other and their haunches jutted out. She strapped on a dildo and plundered their hot, tight rectums, ramming hard up all the way, moving round from a coffee bottom to one of peach cream until they gasped and shuddered and came.

How was the pain and humiliation she was inflicting on them different from what Rochester had done to her? Looking into their sweaty but jubilant faces she knew the answer. Because the girls were willing subjects! It was a loving suffering: slave girl foreplay. Now it was her turn to reap its ultimate reward.

She lay on the bed while Kashika and Julie, wrists now cuffed behind them, bent low and used their lips and tongues to kiss and lick and suck at her cleft and breasts. They acted like perfect attendants whose only thought was the satisfaction of their mistress. They were not just company slaves now but her slaves. She had dominated them and they had submitted totally to her will. And it felt wonderful.

The happy memory was still strong two days later when Vanessa knelt on the floor before Zara, who gave her the details of a new assignment for *GN*.

'Have you heard about our outdoor recreational facility in Scotland: Glen Lothy?' Zara asked.

'I think I saw it mentioned in a back issue, Mistress Editor,' Vanessa said. 'A castle and lake in a private valley.'

Zara smiled. 'That's a very minimal description of a wonderful place. You'd better read the article again and anything else we have on file for background.'

'Yes, Mistress Editor.'

'We covered its opening over a year ago, but not from the slave perspective. Cherry and Jade Chains are being sent up to the Glen tomorrow to replace a couple of chains who're due to come home. It'll be Cherry's first time up there so you can go with them and see what they make of it.'

Vanessa frowned. 'So Kashika and I will both be going up there, Mistress Editor?'

'She goes with the rest of her chain, of course. What's the problem? I thought you liked being with her on assignment.'

'Oh, of course I do, Mistress Editor. I just wondered if this was coincidence or if the Director was sending both of us away deliberately.'

'As far as you're concerned, Vanessa, the chains are going because it's their turn on the rota and you're going because I want a story. Any questions?'

'No, Mistress Editor.'

Miss Kyle had charge of her again that night, but this time there was no sex.

A padded board a little larger than a coffin lid was resting against the wall of the room. It had a foot bar to stand on and straps for ankles, knee, waist, neck, and wrists. Vanessa lay back against it as Miss Kyle fastened them in place.

'You won't be allowed to come until tomorrow night,' she told her.

Vanessa was totally restrained but not uncomfortably so. To a slave girl this was luxurious bondage and she could sleep in it quite happily. But she could not touch herself. Like Cherry and Jade Chains, who even now were sleeping in similar restraints in the special rest room block just off the High Street, she was unable to satisfy what she had now come to think of as her natural level of sexual desire. A whole day without an orgasm for a lusty Shiller girl was a terrible deprivation. It would make her desperate to please the next person who made use of her – which of course was the whole idea.

It would be a good ten-hour journey to Glen Lothy, so they were woken for breakfast well before six the next morning. Fortunately Shiller girls normally travelled light and there was no last-minute agonising over what clothes to pack. A collar was all that was needed and toothbrushes were provided at the other end. With her hat, camera, notepad and recorder,

Vanessa looked positively laden down with possessions by comparison – as she had on previous occasions when she accompanied chains being taken to assignments in Shiller lorries.

In fact this time they did have one item of clothing each. These were loose thin T-shirts that were put on before their hands were cuffed: green for Jade, red for Cherry and white for Vanessa. After nearly two weeks of constant nudity the fabric felt strange on her skin and she was grateful that her bottom half at least was 'properly' naked and exposed.

Instead of the normal ball-gags girls wore when being shipped about they had adhesive strips with integral grommet rings taped over their lips. The rings were large enough for a drinking straw to be inserted. From even a few metres away they were almost invisible and yet served as effective gags.

When they were all secure they were marched out of the lift into level B2 in neatly chained columns, with Vanessa being led along by a leash at their heels. They were travelling not in a regular girlflesh lorry but a mini coach, modified to Shiller requirements. It had curtained and tinted windows that virtually hid them from prying eyes while allowing them to see out. All that an outsider might get a faint glimpse of would be their modestly clad top-halves.

They filed in past folding screens around the door that would shield the interior from view while it was open, and took their seats. Vanessa would of course have liked to be put next to Kashika but the chains were all neatly paired up. She was placed on one side of the row of back seats used by the transportation crew, of two men and a woman, who shared the driving and minding the girls.

Naturally they were not allowed to travel without restraints. Seat belts were put on the girls and their wrists cuffed to the armrests. Their legs were spread and ankles cuffed to the seat base frames. Plugs in the seats between their legs were pulled out to reveal flexible hoses ending in plastic funnels that were pressed snugly against their pussies and clipped to their labia, allowing them to pee while still secure in their seats.

There was no practical need to secure them, but there was a psychological one that Vanessa understood. They were all eager to serve in Glen Lothy and there was not the slightest danger of them trying to escape. They could have made the trip unrestrained but it would not have been the same. The process of travelling to an assignment or outlying facility was all part of the experience and preparation. It focused their minds on what was to come. And of course it meant they still could not touch themselves. On top of their night of enforced abstinence they were sure to arrive aroused, excited and ready to please.

They set off, the coach making its way through the sparse early-morning traffic, heading for the M1 and the North. The girls eagerly took in the sights that they so rarely saw while serving. Vanessa felt a perverse thrill knowing they were so publicly yet covertly on display. How many eyes noted the dimly-seen figures behind the tinted glass, never guessing they were looking at two-dozen slave girls naked from the waist down, gagged and chained to their seats?

Once they had settled down on the motorway the crew enjoyed the perks of the job by choosing, after much breast fondling and pussy tickling, from the selection of girlflesh on offer. These were taken to the backseat beside Vanessa, had their gag strips peeled back, and were made to perform oral sex to the accompaniment of music over the speaker system. They were not allowed to cum, themselves, of course. The sucking, snuffling and lapping and the smell of freshly discharged sperm and womanly juices only made Vanessa and the rest more needy.

Between such diversions the girls watched the countryside go by and dozed. At regular intervals they were fed fruit juice and water and peed in their little funnels, all in air-conditioned comfort. It was a novel way to travel, Vanessa thought.

Hours passed. One of the coach crewmen sat beside Vanessa, slid his hand up inside her T-shirt and played with her nipples until they stood out like thimbles under the fabric while his other hand delved between her legs and toyed with her clit until her juices dripped into her plastic funnel. Then he let go of her and wiped his sticky fingers on her shirt, leaving her helplessly simmering with need.

'Don't worry, girl, you'll have plenty of chances to cum when you get to the Lothy castle.'

She desperately hoped he was right.

They arrived at Glen Lothy as the sun was lowering in the sky. For the last half hour they had encountered almost no traffic as they drove along narrower roads deeper into the hills and vales.

Passing between tall iron gates slung between crested pillars and guarded by a gatehouse, the coach followed a long driveway that wound through thick fir woods. Vanessa could feel their excitement mounting as the girls eagerly peered out of the windows. Then a vista opened up before them.

They were descending into a narrow steep-sided glen of heather-mottled moorland merging with belts of woodland that grew thicker as they reached down to a loch dotted with tiny islets. On the near shore stood a granite-grey castle complete with turrets and battlements.

On the landward side a quilt of lawns and walled gardens spread out from the castle. As they passed by them they could see people strolling about enjoying the evening air. Some had naked girls on leashes trotting or shuffling along at their heels. One girl was chasing a thrown stick like a playful dog. A light trap pulled by a pair of girls in pony-head masks appeared on a path that wound out of the woods. It was all entirely open and natural.

Vanessa felt a shiver as she realised that this was a little world on its own; level B3 on a grand scale, isolated from mundane reality, devoted to the use and enjoyment of slaves. Suddenly she was glad to be away from London and worries about Rochester. Here she could simply be herself.

The coach drew up by a side entrance to the castle. The door opened and a big brawny man in shirt-sleeves and a kilt climbed aboard. A lash hung from the belt that supported his sporran. He glanced over the girls with a professional eye.

'We've got an hour to get the lassies ready,' he told the coach crew. 'The laird wants to show them off to the guests at tonight's feast. Let's get them down to the dungeons right away.'

Vanessa sensed the shiver of anticipation pass though the girls even as her own nipples pricked up. They were going down into real castle dungeons!

Six

Stiff-legged from their hours of sitting still, the girls climbed down from the coach, where two more men in highland dress with lashes hanging from their belts chained them once more into coffles. One of the coach crew handed over Vanessa's individual leash and a bag containing her hat and reporting paraphernalia to the big Scotsman. He took it with a nod, looking her quizzically up and down.

'Ah, yes, the famous slave reporter,' he said. 'We must make sure she has plenty to write about. All right, lady and gentlemen, we'll take them from here. There's some tea for you in the kitchen when you're ready . . .'

The girls were led up some steps and through a heavy iron-studded door into a long hallway off which many doors opened, all having the utilitarian look of staff quarters. There came the murmur of voices mingling with the sound of clattering pans. The aroma of cooking wafted past them, and suddenly Vanessa realised how hungry she was. Another studded door at the end of the corridor opened onto the head of a spiral staircase just wide enough for two of them to walk abreast. Down they went into the bowels of the castle.

The stairs ended in a cellar-like space, floored by stone flags over which strips of rubber matting had been laid, which extended away between massive piers bearing the weight of the castle above. It was lit by uplighters similar to those used in level B3. They splashed their light across the heavy white-painted ceiling vaults, making them seem less oppressive.

The girls were led along a passage between waist-high heavy iron grillework cages that were set between the grid of supporting piers. The cages were like jail cells about three metres square but far too low to stand upright within. The cell floors were covered in mattresses and neat piles of bedding. These spartan arrangements were in fact perfectly acceptable to Shiller girls, who preferred sleeping closely packed together. Access was by a low slave door of similar proportions to the ones leading to the dormitory block back in B3. A girl could only enter or leave on her hands and knees.

Beyond the cells was a white-tiled washroom area with communal showers, rows of squat toilets and douche guns hanging from the walls. Opposite were rows of tall metal racks crammed with cuffs, chains, harness, dildos, lashes and other accessories for the restraint, subjugation and punishment of slave girls. Between the two was an open area of rubber matting, set before various charts and maps displayed on the wall. Under these were shelves of books and maga-zines for the use of off-duty girls. Seeing such commonplace luxuries casually displayed adjacent to the racks of restraints reminded Vanessa once again of the unique life of a Shiller slave.

'Kneel,' the big man commanded, and they obeyed, splaying their thighs respectfully. His two assistants went along the rows of girls pulling off their travel gag strips. Vanessa stretched and licked her lips.

The man looked down at them with masterful eyes. 'My name is Kelvin MacDonald, Master of Slaves to the Laird of Glen Lothy. The Laird himself will be coming to inspect you shortly and you will address him as "Laird," should he speak to you. You will address me as 'Slavemaster", and all other staff as "Mister" or "Miss" followed by their name if it has been given, and "Sir" or "Madam" if it has not. Guests are of course to be addressed at all times as "Master" or "Mistress". Do you understand?'

'Yes, Slavemaster,' they chorused.

'Now, Glen Lothy may have only been operating as a slave resort for a year, but it has already gained a reputation for the quality both of its facilities and the girlflesh it has on offer. Even though some of you have only recently taken the collar, I expect you all to perform to the highest Shiller standards, for here the company is Glen Lothy, and any failure on your part will tarnish its name. Remember at all times that the client you are serving is at that moment your lord and master and deserves your absolute devotion. Do you understand?'

'Yes, Slavemaster.'

'While you are with us you may meet with personal slaves some of our guests bring with them. Should you have close contact with them I expect you to treat them with the same courtesy and consideration you do your own chain sisters. They may not be trained to Shiller standards, but they are your sisters in submission. In a manner of speaking they are also our guests, and we want them to leave here with fond memories of the finest slave resort in this country. Do you understand?'

'Yes, Slavemaster.'

'These will be your living quarters when you're not serving in guest rooms,' MacDonald continued. He pointed to a side door. 'Through there are the private dungeon cells the guests use when they want to try their hand at a little torture. You'll become familiar with them soon enough . . .' Vanessa shivered in fear and delight. 'As for the rest you'll learn more tomorrow morning. Glen Lothy is a rare and wonderful place and you should feel privileged to serve here. Now, let's get you washed and ready for the feast . . .'

They were placed on the toilets so they could void their bowels, showered, douched and greased. Finally they were dried and combed. They were given more water but no food. As the Slavemaster explained they would be eating at the feast.

'How well you feed depends on how well you beg like the pretty animals you are,' he said. 'This is how you will behave . . .'

He explained the etiquette involved in their part of the feast. They would also participate in an amusement for the benefit of the guests, which he went on to prepare them for, and which Vanessa thought ingenious and deliciously degrading.

They were all neatly lined up standing with hands clasped behind their necks and feet spread when the Laird strode in.

The Laird was a large powerfully built man in his early fifties, Vanessa guessed. He was clad in full Highland regalia, with dress jacket and kilt, a plaid hanging over his shoulder, a sash belt and a Glengarry on his head. He looked magnificent, but Vanessa suspected it was for the benefit of the guests rather than personal vanity. In his eyes she read something of the same masterful self-assurance that the Director possessed, which did not need to be bolstered by any elaborate costumes. She had to fight the instinct to kneel before him.

He was holding a double chain leash on the other end of which was a pair of redheaded slave girls so similar they might have been sisters. They had neat supple bodies and moved on all-fours like dogs. Their hands and feet were encased in close-fitting mitten-sheaves of black rubber, with pads of the same material stuck to their knees. Instead of plain-coloured collars they had ones in the same tartan pattern as the Laird's plaid. Their bright green eyes flashed as they looked over the new girls with almost predatory interest. Then they lifted their heads and with almost a feral gesture sniffed, their nostrils flaring delicately, as though sampling their scent. Vanessa felt a shiver at the sight of two such magnificent slave girls, yet it was perfectly natural that they should follow along at the heel of such a powerful man.

The Laird inspected Cherry and Jade Chains, squeezing breasts, prodding buttocks and tickling pubic clefts, all the while nodding in approval. When he came to Vanessa he paused.

'So you're Vanessa Nineteen. The Director told me about you. And you're to write about the Glen, I understand?'

'Yes, Laird,' Vanessa said meekly, holding her posture even though the Laird's girl dogs were sniffing at her crotch with uninhibited interest.

'Will you be needing time off from serving duties to do your journalistic work?'

'No, Laird. I'd like to be treated just like any other girl, if it pleases you. I want to write about how they experience working here.'

'That sounds very fine and economical, doing two jobs at once. But mind that the pleasure of the guests always comes first.'

'Yes, Laird.'

The Laird finished his inspection and pulled on the leashes, drawing his pets to heel and putting an end to their pussy sniffing. 'Now, I'll be seeing you all shortly for the feast. Put on a good show and you'll eat well.'

Vanessa thought the banqueting hall of Lothy castle was a magnificent setting for a feast, with its massive timber roof beams and walls hung about with banners and shields. A traditional log fire burnt in the huge hearth even though it was summer, drawing in fresh pine-scented air through the open windows.

The dining tables were arranged in a 'U', with the Laird seated in the middle of the base section, facing inwards like his guests who were arrayed along the outside of the table. There were perhaps thirty-five of them, about two-thirds male with a few obviously couples. Several had brought their own personal pets with them to the table. These knelt beside their chairs with their leashes tied to the chair arms eating food set out on platters on the floor. Some were made to sit up on their haunches and beg for titbits like dogs. The Laird's own pair of bitches ate from golden platters set out on either side of his chair. Every so often he would stroke and pat them, or else hold out morsels from his own plate that they took from his hand.

All the guests were very smartly attired in dinner jackets or evening dress and seemed to be having a fine time as they supped and drank and chatted and admired their surroundings. They had much to admire.

Amongst the genuine shields on the walls were four oversized versions, one on each wall. Against these hung spreadeagled slave girls, bound in place with glittering loops of chain about their ankles, upper thighs, crossed between their breasts and about their elbows and wrists. Metal bridles snuggly encased their heads. Lengths of chain also hung between their

121

thighs issuing from their vaginal mouths. On the ends of the chains dangled a spiked iron ball.

In the centre of each table length was a large silver platter bearing, amid a selection of fruits, a hogtied slave girl. She was both a living table decoration and a display of tender flesh, to be devoured by eye if not with a knife and fork, with her mouth stuffed with an apple and her anus sprouting a large spray of grouse tail feathers. A vertical metal bar bolted to the platter rose up to fasten to the ring in the front of her collar, keeping her head raised.

Moving about the tables, bringing in each course and topping up wine flagons, were the slave girl waitresses. They had plaid sashes slung between their breasts, tam-o'-shanters perched saucily on their heads and their mouths were filled with tartan ball-gags. Hobble chains clinked between their ankle cuffs, forcing them to take dainty steps. The middle of the chains was lifted clear of the floor by another chain that ran up between their legs to a hook protruding from between their buttock cheeks. From chain belts, what looked like miniature silver filigree sporrans hung over their pubes. The inner sides of the sporrans were studded with pins that pricked the girls' vulvas as they swung and bounced against them unless they moved with extreme grace and care.

And finally there were Vanessa and the new chain girls, who were tethered in the space between the tables. They knelt on a circle of rubber matting facing outward with their thighs widely splayed, both out of deference and necessity, so they presented their breasts and pussies to the guests for their appreciation. Their arms were now cuffed behind their backs and individual leashes clipped to their collars ran behind them to a big ring set in the floor.

The guests could not only ogle their pretty naked bodies but also, to their evident amusement, they could feed them.

The girls begged with open mouths and lolling tongues while jerking their hips sensuously to show off their nether mouths. These were bulging with unnatural prominence, for reasons the guests would soon learn. They were also, and quite helplessly, salivating freely and showing their hunger for a different kind of sustenance. If a girl's pleading impressed a guest he might throw her a scrap from his plate, or else something from one of the small bowls that dotted the tables. These contained bone-like shapes pressed out of sweet and savoury biscuit, dried fruit, or candy bar. They were slave girl treats ideal for throwing to them just as one might do for a dog. The girls tried to catch them in their mouths, but if they failed they had to scrabble round for them on the floor and try to nip them up in their teeth, much to the amusement of the guests.

It was of course thoroughly humiliating and Vanessa luxuriated in the sensation. As they scrambled about for dropped treats she exchanged flashing grins of delight with Kashika and the other Cherry Chain girls. The mat under them became wet and smeared with drips from their pouting and swollen vulvas.

The meal drew to a convivial close. The conversation mellowed, wine was being supped lazily and the night was deep and dark beyond the high hall windows. Vanessa saw the Laird raise a hand and a serving girl stepped forward. She had a small copper gong slung between her breasts, stretching her nipples into painfully long cones. In her outstretched hands she held a small radio control handset and a drumstick. The Laird took up the stick and rapped the gong a few times, making the girl wince as her breasts shivered in resonance, and the conversation died away as all eyes turned to him

'Ladies and gentlemen,' he said genially. 'I trust you have had your fill of this humble fare and enjoyed the company of your fellow guests. It is one of life's great pleasures to enjoy good food and sprightly conversation together, feeding as it were both the stomach and the mind. But now it's time for an amusement, the like of which only Glen Lothy can provide. As you can see we have a fresh consignment of girlflesh in the castle, and I think you'll agree what a fine bonnie clutch of pussies they are!'

The guests nodded happily and murmured their agreement, a few applauding the sentiment. The Laird's accent, Vanessa noticed, was markedly stronger than it had been when talking to them in the dungeon earlier.

The Laird continued: 'Now, as is our tradition, we are going to offer up these lovelies for your pleasure tonight. But, we shall have a little fun with the division of the spoils.'

As he spoke the serving girls were going round the tables laying out slender golden keys beside the place settings. The guests examined them with interest. 'You'll see we have twenty-five girls and twenty-five keys. That's one fine slave girl for each of you to take back to your room and enjoy till morning as you please. But who gets which girl? That nobody knows, but we're about to find out. You see these pretty birds come ready stuffed. Each has had a little metal egg inserted in her pussy. Not a comfortable smooth egg but one with wee spikes on its sides. She'd probably like to lay it to make way for something better, but she can't do it without your help.'

He took the remote control unit from the gong-girl's hands, extended its aerial and held it up for the guests to see.

'This sends a signal to the eggs. They start to buzz and the spikes sting like a nest of bees, which is an uncomfortable thing for the lassies to have inside them, as you'll hear from their squeals. But they don't stop and cannot be removed until the right key is inserted in their bases, withdrawing the spikes. But which key is the right one? That's what they've got to find out by presenting themselves to you and begging for you to try your key in their lock.'

The guests were chuckling by now, as they understood the game.

'I think you'll find the girls will be very grateful to whoever has the right key to their lock,' the Laird said with a smile, 'and you can look forward to a fine night as they give thanks in the only way they know how. Now, are we ready?' The guests held up their keys. 'Slavemaster: will you be kind enough to stand by to loose the girls.'

MacDonald stepped up from where he had been watching proceedings from the corner of the hall and took his place by the big tethering ring that secured their leashes to the floor. It was hinged in the middle so it could be unpinned and thrown open, freeing every leash handle simultaneously.

The Laird held up the remote control and pressed the button on its side.

Vanessa and the other chain girls howled and yelped in pain. It was as though a small but angry wasp's nest had erupted inside her vagina. The spikes of the egg crackled with electric sparks while its body buzzed like a vibrator. As the guests laughed, the girls flopped around on the matting, kicking and squirming about as they strained to expel the tormenting objects. But the spikes were angled forward as well as sideways and resisted the natural contraction of their muscles and clenching their sheaves about them only made the shocks more intense. All about her were thrashing bodies, splayed legs and bulging pubic mounds between whose wet lips were exposed vaginal tunnel mouths that alternately clenched and gaped as they tried to spit out the cruel silver eggs that glittered in their depths. They even jerked on their leashes as though they could in some way escape from the pain, but they remained tethered fast. Pain and deep stimulation combined with such urgency that it was impossible to think of anything except that they must get rid of the eggs at any cost.

The Laird struck the gong again and cried: 'Let them loose!' The Slavemaster snapped open the floor ring and their leashes came free.

Vanessa struggled clumsily to her feet, her thigh muscles twitching in time to the electric pulses at their apex so she could hardly stand. Other girls were still crawling forward or flopping about like stranded fish. Juices were dripping from her cleft, stimulated by the buzzing egg and expelled by the helpless contractions of her sheath. She must get rid of the egg, and there was only one way to do it.

In a desperate, bow-legged stumble, gasping and dribbling as she went, she made for the end of the table nearest to her and the plump middle-aged man seated there. Rounding the end of the table she twisted about beside his chair, spread her legs, thrust her dripping, pulsing, buzzing vulva almost into his face and sobbed: 'Please, Master, I beg you, try your key inside me!'

With other girls stumbling past her he thrust his hand between her thighs, grasped a pinch of her pubic hair to steady her and slid the key up into her slot and the keyhole of the egg and tried to twist it. It did not turn.

He smacked her rump, sending her on her way to try somewhere else. Girls were streaming round the outside of the tables now, making for the first guests they could reach and presenting their pussies to them. The hall echoed to their whimpers of pain and desperate pleadings and the guests' laughter at their antics. It was a frantic mêlée of naked flesh as they careened into each other, breasts bouncing and slots dripping, as they desperately sought release from their torment.

There was a cry as the first key fitted and an egg was pulled from the twitching pussy mouth of Jade Chain girl. With a gasp of relief she sank trembling down beside the chair of her saviour, a slender dark-haired woman in a dinner jacket, who picked up the girl's leash and took charge of her prize.

Vanessa found a couple with the man holding the key and she thrust her bottom out at them, begging: 'Please unlock me, Master! I'll be so grateful . . .'

The woman held Vanessa's thighs while the man slid the key up her by-now sopping passage. It did not fit. They pushed her away.

One by one keys were finding their proper homes and eggs were being withdrawn from clutching, tormented pussy mouths with sucking pops and held glistening triumphantly in the air. Through blurred eyes she saw Kashika claimed by a youngish couple who had pulled the egg from her dark sex lips. But where was her saviour? By now there were only a handful of guests left who still had keys held enticingly aloft and the remaining girls were dashing wildly, red-faced and tearful, round the tables between them as the options diminished.

Vanessa almost threw herself at a stocky man with grizzled hair and big hands who was holding out a key and nearly pushed her vibrating, pricking,

127

weeping cunt into his face: 'I beg you to get it out, Master!' she yelped.

His large hands caught hold of her, prising her lips wide, and the key slid inside her. There was a click as it turned. She felt the spikes retract and the buzzing stop. He pulled the egg out of her hot, cloying, feebly twitching passage with a slurp and held it high; dripping for all to see.

With a sigh Vanessa sank trembling to her knees beside him, burbling her gratitude incoherently while he caught up her leash and tied it round the arm of his chair. He was by no stretch of the imagination handsome, but at that moment she thought he was the most wonderful man in the room. He had saved her, and her pussy, though sore, also ached to be used, a fact she had no doubt the stocky man, now her master for the night, would take full advantage of. How easily they manipulated their emotions with a simple perverted game, Vanessa thought dizzily. But then they had also surrendered their rights to those along with their bodies. It was another level of submission and darkly exciting.

The last girl found her key holder, the Laird struck the gong intimately supported by its living hanger and there was a round of applause.

'Well done, all,' the Laird said cheerfully. 'Now you might still find the eggs useful. They won't activate again but if you pop them in their mouths it'll keep their tongues in place. It saves them for more important tasks . . .'

The guests laughed at the notion and followed his advice. Vanessa found her jaws prised open and the egg, still warm and wet with her own juices, was pushed into her mouth. Her master twisted the key and the spikes extended, filling her mouth and pressing her tongue firmly down and leaving the silver base of the egg with its keyhole showing between her lips. It made a fine gag, painfully filling her mouth and totally crushing any desire on her part to attempt to speak or indeed make any sound. She was mute until her new master chose to unlock her.

The Laird pushed back his seat and rose, bowing formally to his left and right. 'And now, as we are replete and ensured warm and willing bedmates, I thank you for your company at my table and bid you, one and all, a very good night.'

The guests rose and bowed back to him in turn. He left the room with his pets at his heels.

Vanessa felt a tug on her collar in turn and scrambled to her feet. Her master joined the other guests as they led their prizes out into the entrance hall and up the broad flight of the main staircase to their bedrooms. At the head of the stairs the company parted. She saw Kashika being led off in the other direction between the couple who had won her. Both of their hands were already fondling the perfect brown contours of her bottom. She hoped they appreciated what a wonderful creature they had so briefly in their possession.

As Vanessa trotted obediently along a thickly carpeted corridor hung with Scottish landscape paintings she realised that, though she was shortly going to serve the man who held her leash in the most intimate manner possible, she might never know his name. As long as she knew the company had vetted him there was no need. For tonight he was her master and she was his slave. There was no chance of mistaking him for anybody else and it made no difference to what was to come.

The perversity of her situation struck her with a thrill of fearful delight. She was about to have sex, of a kind beyond her power to choose or refuse, with a total stranger who had chosen her on the basis of pure chance. He might also punish her first purely for his own amusement, yet she was following after him like a docile animal. Many people would call what she was doing perverted, or think she'd been brainwashed or beaten into submission. A few months ago she would have been one of them. Yet now her nipples only strained a little harder and the familiar warm tingle of anticipation fizzed in her loins.

Perhaps it was this stimulation that caused a fresh insight into the deeper nature of her slavishness to strike her. What a time to get philosophical, she thought, yet on the other hand what better time for a slave?

She wanted to please her master-for-the-night and therefore the Laird and so in turn Shiller because she respected her so much, but her ultimate surrender was always to her own nature. This was because she was not doing this for him or them, but for herself. That had to come first before one could surrender one's body to another with perfect confidence. It meant by submitting she was really doing exactly what she wanted to do. Seen from a certain angle her slavery actually appeared indulgent and rather selfish. Did that make her a naughty girl, she thought wryly? If so she was going to receive her rightful comeuppance. How very moral . . .

Her master-for-the-night's room was a tastefully furnished en-suite, blending old-world architecture with all the modern conveniences. The bed was a contemporary version of a four-poster with a trim canopy, the frame formed of chunky black-stained square timbers. You had to look a second time to see the black metal eyebolts set at strategic points about its posts. In one corner stood a padded trestle set on a wheeled base, while on the wall beside it was a small rack of restraints, lashes and sex-toys. The Laird really did provide his guests with every convenience. She wondered how much they paid for a week's stay? More than she could ever afford, that was for sure. How lucky she was to enjoy all this for free and be herself at the same time.

He stood her on a mat and looked her over, his lumpy features creased in a smile, inspecting her body intimately and noting her reactions. His big hands felt hard and capable, moulding the flesh of her breasts and buttocks as he squeezed them. He's worked a lot with them until recently, she thought. His manner was assured and masterful. She appreciated his taking the time to accustom her to his touch, even if it was entirely for his own satisfaction.

As he examined her he said nothing. There was no need. They each knew their respective roles perfectly. It was nice to be appreciated by a man who understood the value of girlflesh.

He bound her across the padded trestle so that her stomach was doubled over the beam. Her arms and legs were spread and strapped to the splayed legs of the trestle, forcing her bottom up into the air and spreading her groin wide open. He removed the spiked egg from her mouth and replaced it with a thick rubber bit-gag that would give her plenty to bite down on.

Taking a rubber paddle from the rack he dragged the blade over the glistening split-peach of her sex a few times to wet it, and then began to lay it across her buttocks, each firm smack sending shivers through her flesh. It was a methodical punishment and he paused after every few blows to cup her swollen sex pouch, testing its heat and wetness. When her bottom was an even redness he turned his attention to the inviting swell of her vulva, swinging upwards with the paddle. Her puffy inner labia and the erect nub of her clitoris were so prominent they suffered, if that was the right word, with the rest of her pussy, each impact setting mini-firecrackers of pleasure bursting in her brain.

Vanessa groaned and chewed on her bit and felt the lust rising to boiling point inside her. Any moment now she would cum!

Then abruptly he stopped.

She moaned and shook her head, pleading with her hollow eyes, desperate for relief. But he simply hung up the paddle, patted her smarting bottom and went through into the bathroom. After a minute she heard a shower running.

Vanessa squirmed miserably in her bonds, but of course she was utterly helpless and quite unable to relieve her own suffering. Her pussy was throbbing and dripping so much she thought she would faint from need. It was the perfect piece of foreplay by a master, proving his total dominance of her. She was his to use and leave at his whim. Now she was forced to await his pleasure, simmering with unrequited want, by whatever means he cared to exercise it next.

It was a quarter of an hour before he emerged from the bathroom. He had changed into a dressing gown. She raised her pleading face to him and he smiled back, rubbing his hands.

As she watched he took a box out from under the bed and from it removed and laid out an array of broad straps fitted with large hitching rings, two lengths of heavy cords with handles at one end and hooks at the other, a pair of pulley blocks and what looked like a dildo on the end of a rod like a broom handle with a hook on its end. Then he unfastened her from the trestle and, grasping a handful of her hair in one of his strong hands, led her over to the bed and laid her face down. The power in his stocky body was exciting to feel.

After strapping her wrists together behind her back, he passed a broad strap under her belly and threaded the wrist strap through it, holding her arms secure and leaving the ring-ends dangling freely. He crossed her ankles and bent them backwards until her heels nearly touched her scarlet bottom. He threaded a strap through her ankle bonds and the big ring on the end of her belt, but left it slack. Another strap he threaded through the back of her collar, fastening it to her belt ring, also leaving some slack.

Vanessa was now securely hogtied but not tightly. Her master pressed a button on a small control pad hung on the side post of the bedhead. There was a subdued whirr and a large hook on the end of a wire cable descended from out of the bed canopy. The bed had its own built-in power winch.

He slid the hook through the big ring on her belt and sent the hook winding back up. The slack in the belt strap was taken in and she was lifted off the covers. The rising ring pulled on her neck and ankle straps, forcing her body into a taut bow. He stopped the winch and she was left slowly turning in the air a handsbreadth above the bed, her weight spread between her waist, ankles and neck. Vanessa thrilled at her own helplessness, her juices dripping onto the covers. What was he going to do with her?

Her master hung the pair of pulleys on eyebolts set in the frame at the foot of the bed, threaded the cords through them and hooked their ends onto the sides of her belt strap. He hooked one end of the long dildo rod onto the frame between the pulley mounts. Then he pushed the dildo end of the rod into her greased anus and up her rectum. She felt it give as she was impaled on it. The rod was sprung internally, pushing her forward a little.

The man dimmed the room lights and slipped off his robe. He carried a slight paunch but under that he had muscles and his shoulders were broad and powerful. His cock stood out hard and eager.

He lay on the bed and slid under her suspended body, her pendant breasts rubbing and flattening against his barrel of a chest, her hard nipples scratched by wiry greying hair. She felt his erection rub against her stomach and then find her slot that was weeping with frustration. Yes, he was sliding inside her. But she could hardly move to generate the friction and proper penetration she now desperately needed.

Grinning all over his rugged face he kissed her bit-spread lips playfully, took hold of the cord handles that lay by his side and bent his arms, dragging on the cords that ran though the pulleys at the foot of the bed. Vanessa gasped as she was pulled downward in turn by the cord ends hooked to her belt, rubbing across his body, the tension impaling her fully onto his cock even as it drove the dildo hard up her rectum. He relaxed his pull and the resistance of the sprung dildo rod pushed her back up his body again, swinging forward like a pendulum, his cock being pulled half out of her clinging slot. Grinning at the expression on her face he bent his arms again.

She came after half a dozen swings, orgasmic fireworks exploding in her brain as twenty-four hours of pent-up lust was released. Her dangling body convulsed and bounced. But her master was still hard inside her and she realised he had not yet cum. Desperately she squeezed him tightly, feeling the friction rekindling her desire in seconds. God, she was an insatiable slut tonight!

And when she felt his sperm at last pump inside her vagina, her own dam burst for the second time.

For long minutes she hung over him totally satiated, their bodies gummed by sweat where they touched. She could hardly have felt more content.

'Good girl . . .' he said gruffly, ruffling her hair.

Perfect.

Seven

Vanessa would always cherish her next week in the Glen as a special time.

She had a whole valley to explore in which she and the other chain girls could be uniquely themselves. Here their nature was not only tolerated but encouraged and celebrated. It was the same sisterly warmth that existed in the Shiller building and level B3, but on such a scale that she could easily imagine the world had changed to accept the presence of slave girls as a normal part of everyday life. She was surrounded by them being used as they desired by people free to do so without any pretence or sign of guilt. In the midst of constant domination, forced labour and bondage she could be free.

It was a natural consequence to her recent insight about the possible selfish nature of her submissive side that she began to wonder if slave girls might even be said to lead a pampered existence. In the castle dungeons they were firmly but good-naturedly cared for by the staff who treated them according to proper Shiller discipline. They did not have to worry about food or shelter, their health was closely monitored and they even had people to flush out and grease their bottoms for them, and they were all doing what they most wanted to do. Didn't that seem like pampering?

In the normal world a pampered environment usually produced spoilt people, and yet the chain girls were the nicest bunch you could hope to meet: supportive, lively and apparently quite unselfish.

The fact that it didn't spoil the girls or, she hoped, herself, had to be down to the practical consequence of their chosen lives. Regular punishment, no consideration for privacy, zero freedom of movement for long periods and forced sex for the pleasure of others soon taught you that your wishes counted for very little. Of course living like that would normally lead to spiritless, terrified creatures too fearful to take any initiative, which equally bore no relationship to the apparently well-balanced girls she knew.

Did that mean Shiller girls existed in some magical state of equilibrium between the two conflicting forces? Were they simply content because they were fulfilled and guilt-free? Was it down to Shiller's guiding principles and their unique chain training? Or had she got it all completely wrong? She made a mental note about another possible column to start in *GN*: the psychology and philosophy of slavery.

The day following their arrival the new chains were allowed to sleep in to recover from their exertions of the previous evening and given a late breakfast, during which they recounted their bedroom activities and sore pussies and smacked bottoms were displayed and sympathised over. Kashika looked tired but pleased with herself after satisfying the demanding couple who had won her in the egg race. Jade Chain, who had served in the Glen before, they were then taken off for other duties, while Cherry Chain and Vanessa knelt on the big square of matting in the middle of their dungeon dormitory so that Slavemaster MacDonald could gave them an orientation lecture.

Yes, an orientation lecture for slaves, Vanessa thought. It was marked down on an office planner hung up on the wall: CHERRY CHAIN – 8.00AM TO 12AM: REST AND ORIENTATION. The planner showed with appropriately tinted blocks and bars what each chain's duties would be for the coming days. Next to it hung a helpful plan of the castle and glen, which showed the location of the tennis courts, stable yards and boathouse, amongst other facilities. She and the other Cherry girls had huddled excitedly round the chart earlier, speculating about the meaning of some of their forthcoming duties, which included PRIVATE DUNGEON DUTY, PONY TRAPPING, HOUSE SERVICE, GAME HUNT, GALLEY CREW, DOG WALKS. Coming up in ten days and intriguingly marked in red was: HIGHLAND GAMES.

Surely only Shiller slaves, Vanessa thought with pride and delight, would have their activities so neatly colour-coded.

They listened attentively while the Slavemaster expanded on his brief lecture of the previous evening, making it clear what was expected of them during their time in the glen. Using the map he then indicated key locations around the castle and glen. Sometimes they would be participating in planned events or entertainments and at others they would be made freely available to the guests for their own use, either in the castle or grounds. There was a rota for serving on day or night shifts.

'Outside of your quarters and unless serving a guest, when your degree of restraint will be at their discretion, you will be properly confined, corralled or chained down. Whenever you need to be moved within the castle or grounds it will be in a standard chain coffle.' He glanced at Vanessa. 'When necessary

I or one of my men will take charge of your leash, girl.'

Vanessa would have liked to be linked to the Cherry Chain, but rules were rules. She wanted to share everything with them and not feel her white collar meant she was being treated specially. Of course it might simply be inconvenient to accommodate her as they were used to handling girls in batches of twelve. The restraints were designed for that number ... or perhaps having thirteen girls on a chain was considered unlucky.

'This'll be a good time to show you the private dungeons through there,' he continued. 'The guests don't usually require them this early in the morning ...'

Chained in a coffle with the Slavemaster holding Vanessa's leash, they were led through the access door into a set of corridors lined with heavy studded dark oak doors. The walls were unpainted and there was no rubber matting on the floor, so the stone slabs were cold under their bare feet. The dungeon was lit by what at first appeared to be medieval flaming torches mounted on scrolled wall brackets, but on closer inspection they proved to be large flame-effect moulded electric bulbs with flickering multiple elements inside them. They cast a dim yellow light and sinister deep dancing shadows. Instant medieval mood without having your lungs filled with smoke and soot, Vanessa thought.

The Slavemaster showed them the inside of a few cells. They were filled with hanging rings and chains and numerous ingenious devices of iron plate and heavy pegged and bolted timbers. There were chairs, frames, racks and posts, spikes, screw threads and unyielding rods. The girls goggled at them nervously, both awed and impressed. The Slavemaster noted their reactions and grinned.

139

'Pretty things, aren't they? A guest can keep a girl in one of these for up to twelve hours. I never think you're a true Shiller girl until you've served your time in a Castle Lothy torture cell.'

Vanessa knew it was only another part of the castle cellars dressed up to look sinister, but the atmosphere was quite different to their own section. These felt like classic dungeons where unlucky maidens might be imprisoned to face unspeakable torment and degradation. It was clichéd, frightening and yet also tempting. How well would she survive twelve hours in one of those? It was almost like a challenge to prove her credentials as a true submissive.

They were allowed a brief interval for a light lunch. Then they were formed up again into a coffle. This time Mister Stewart, one of MacDonald's assistants, strapped rubber bits between their teeth. Vanessa had noted on the planner that Cherry Chain's duties for the afternoon were: 1.00PM TO 5.00PM: GALLEY DRILL. She hoped it did not mean a maritime cookery course.

'Like all good castles,' the Slavemaster said, taking up the leash of Amber 1, who was the first girl in the coffle, and leading them to a dark corner of the dungeon, 'we have a secret passage.'

He unbolted a small door that opened onto a narrow tunnel mouth little higher than their heads. He threw a switch and a string of electric bulbs lit up, curving away into the distance.

'This leads along the loch shore to the boathouse from where a branch turns inland to the stables,' the Slavemaster continued, enjoying the look of wonder on their faces. 'It was dug a few hundred years ago in less settled times when the owners of the original Tower of Lothy, before it was extended to form the manor you see today, still feared being laid siege to by their warlike cousins and thought a clandestine means of egress might be a good idea. We find it serves as a convenient means of moving chains from the dungeons to the stables and galleys without having to take them up through the house. Follow me . . .'

They padded after him, a string of flesh charms on chains. Mister Stewart brought up the rear leading Vanessa by her single leash.

The tunnel sides were of natural rock interspersed with sections filled by dressed stones. What the original builders would have thought about its new use Vanessa could not imagine. She hoped they would at least be intrigued by the image of thirteen naked girls chained in a tight coffle passing down the tunnel they had so laboriously hacked through earth and rock. After perhaps three hundred metres they passed a junction where the tunnel branched left. Then ahead of them was a flight of steps closed at the top by a wooden trapdoor. The Slavemaster climbed the steps, threw open the trap and led them on up after him.

Vanessa had seen the boathouse on the map of the glen. It was constructed partly over a natural inlet where the woods came down to the shore. But she had not realised how large it was. It had three berths formed by the landing stages that ran about the inside and projected out into the waters of the loch that lapped and slapped lazily about the hulls of the craft moored within.

She hardly noticed the rowing boats and pedalos in the first berth. Her eyes were transfixed by the craft next to them. They were two miniature oar-driven galleys, one about twice the length of the other.

The Slavemaster led them along the wooden decking. 'Most other duties in the glen will be familiar enough to you, but the galleys are something you won't have come across before. They're one of our unique attractions. The guests take them out onto the loch to admire the scenery or to carry them across to the islets that can be reserved for special parties. So we train new chains on them from their first day so you'll be ready to serve properly when called.'

The two craft were of similar general design. Vanessa was sure they were not in any way accurate historical reproductions, even allowing for their reduced dimensions, but they looked right. They were long and low with an ornate carved sternpost that curved up and over the rear deck and eyes painted either side of the inward-curving bow stem. Rows of benches ran down each side with shipped oars by each one. A planking catwalk ran between the benches connecting small decks at the fore and aft of each vessel. The smaller galley had six benches on each side and the larger twelve. On the smaller galley, in contrast to the utilitarian backless benches, a pair of comfortable reclining garden loungers had been mounted on the rear deck under the overhanging sternpost. Behind them was a waist-high rod hinged to a pair of steering paddles that pivoted through rowlocks and hung over the stern.

'They take one or two chains to crew with options for personal slaves as decoration,' the Slavemaster explained.

As they got closer the modifications for slave-girl use became apparent. The benches were fitted with upright pivoting dildos, chains and ankle cuffs. The oars had matching wrist cuffs and both bow stem and sternpost were fitted with chains and cuffs. There was an electronic control box of some sort resting on one of the loungers, each of which had lashes in holsters hung from their sides. The rod linking the steering paddles also had a dildo rising midway along its length and chains and a belt hanging from it.

Vanessa had already fallen in love with the sheer perverse purpose of the vessels. This was classic exploitative slavery, combining forced labour and humiliation. Forget a hundred sweaty men in rags hauling on the oars *Ben-Hur*-style, what about twelve or even twenty-four shapely naked girls chained in their place?

'Before you board them there's the matter of safety,' the Slavemaster said. 'The galleys have integral buoyancy chambers, so they won't sink if holed, but in case they should somehow capsize or you get thrown into the water, you'll be wearing these at all times . . .'

Hanging on rows of hooks were what looked like heavy leather slave torso harnesses. The Slavemaster took one down and showed it to the girls.

'These function as self-inflating lifejackets. In addition all the cuffs onboard are secured with soluble hinge pins. If they get wet they'll come loose in seconds.'

Vanessa mentally kicked herself. She had not even thought of the safety aspect. She just wanted to get on board the galley. Of course girls wearing metal collars and chains were not the most buoyant of objects. Fortunately she and the other girls were under the control of people who did think about such things.

The harnesses were buckled onto them, with straps going over their shoulders, crossing their sternums and then about their chests above and below their breasts, squeezing their flesh and making them bulge slightly further. Looking at the other girls Vanessa thought the additions emphasised their bondage.

They made their way onto the smaller of the two galleys.

While Vanessa was taken to the back of the vessel, the Cherry girls were arranged according to size, girls of equal strength on opposite sides. They were positioned over the benches, which were covered in black vinyl-wrapped padding, with the hinged dildos projecting through slots in the cushions. Vanessa now saw the dildos were banded in metal down their black rubber shafts and there were cables running out from under each bench.

'Sit!' the Slavemaster commanded, and a dozen anus rings bulged and gave way as they were breached and a dozen hot rectums were filled as bottoms squirmed and settled on the wooden benches.

Ankle cuffs were clicked into place, holding their feet against bracing rails and forcing the girls to sit with their thighs splayed. The dangling cuffs on the oars were clipped about the girls' wrists. The galley was untied and pushed clear of the landing stage, allowing the oars to be slid out though the rowlocks and into the water. The oars were not long and light enough for even inexperienced rowers to use.

Now it was Vanessa's turn to become an intimate part of the vessel. Her hands were cuffed before her and then attached to a slack chain hanging from the arching sternpost that hung over the stern deck like a tail. There were chains and cuffs bolted to the deck and these were clipped about her ankles, again leaving some slack in the chains. The linking rod that connected the two steering paddles was behind her with its dildo nuzzling her bottom. The Slavemaster lifted her up onto her toes and impaled her upon it, filling her rectum with a hard rubber plug. He buckled the belt hanging from the rod about her waist. Two chains ran off either side of it to rings in the steering rod. She could not lift herself off the dildo and could only shuffle to the left and right as far as her restraints allowed, moving the steering paddles with her. Now she noticed an electric cable with a crocodile clip end was coiled about the linking rod on each side of her. The Slavemaster unwound them and clipped one to each of her nipples. Vanessa could guess how they would work. She'd become a living remote-controlled rudder.

Kashika, chained to a bench three rows back, flashed her a quick smile of sympathy round her bit.

The Slavemaster seated himself on one of the loungers and picked up the control box. From her position behind him Vanessa could see the box simply held a couple of buttons and a joystick. Meanwhile Mister Stewart took up one of the holstered lashes and strode along the catwalk between the girls on the benches.

'Now we'll just activate the system,' the Slavemaster said, pressing a button on the box.

Electric needles stabbed through Vanessa's nipples, making her flinch, while the other girls jerked and whimpered, instinctively clenching their knees together.

'Did you all feel that?' the Slavemaster asked.

They all nodded, a few blinking back tears.

'Good. Now the guest only needs to use the joystick to select direction and speed and this box turns it into signals controlling you. Vanessa Nineteen will steer and you will provide the propulsion. She'll feel steady pulses in her teats to hold a course and uneven pulses to tell her to move left or right until they become balanced again. You'll feel a regular sequence of pulses in your arse dildos, from weak to strong and then down again. That's the stroke rate. Starting position is bent forward with oars in the water ready to pull. You pull as the pulse gets stronger, lift your oars and return to starting position as it diminishes. Pull, lift, return and dip. The faster the pulses, the faster you row. The box can control each row of you separately so the galley can be turned. The command to back water, that is to push with your paddles, will be signalled by two rapid sharp even pulses, with another two to resume normal action. Three rapid pulses means raise your oars clear of the water. We'll practise until you know the responses by heart. You don't want to be seen thinking when guests are onboard, just obeying . . .'

He pulled the joystick backwards. The girls whimpered as the command shocks jolted through them and fumbled clumsily with their oars, backing water. Vanessa felt pinpricks begin to pulse through her nipples. The left side was slightly stronger. Clenching her anus about the dildo inside her she shuffled sideways, feeling the resistance of the water against her steering paddles, until the pulses evened out. Slowly they backed out of the boathouse onto the open water. The Slavemaster shifted the joystick sideways. The left row of girls continued to back water while the right fumbled to change direction. Mister Stewart's lash swished across their bare backs, encouraging them to concentrate. What was required now was simple mindless instant obedience to their electric commands, Vanessa thought. They must become part of the vessel.

The joystick went forward and they set off parallel with the shoreline. Gradually, encouraged by Mister Stewart's lash, the girls found their rhythm, rocking to and fro about the pivoting dildos inside them, their breasts swaying in time. The joystick went forward and they picked up their stroke rate. Their knees spread as they made the return stroke and came together as they pulled, flashing their pouting clefts.

After a few minutes the girls began to drip sweat onto benches and deck planks that bore the stains left by their sisters who had gone before them. She saw the shining beads standing out in sharp contrast on Kashika's skin and the even darker flesh of Olivia 8. The girls' pussies, stimulated by the dildos churning with their bodies and intense excitement at their usage, also began to drip. The breeze of the galley's motion carried the girls' scent back to Vanessa. She gazed at the double row of straining glossy naked chained bodies with their hard-nippled breasts and gaping pink glistening clefts. She doubted they would ever win any prizes for speed, but was equally certain no guest would care with a view like that.

What a wonderful sense of power it would bestow to sit in one of those easy chairs and hold in one hand a box that linked to the intimate parts of thirteen girls. To make them obey simply by pushing a joystick. Being borne across the waves by their sweat and exertion. And if they faltered then a little lashing would soon put them right. And when they were allowed to rest how grateful they would be to their captain. No need to unchain them, just pull out a gag bit and they would gladly provide oral pleasure. He, or she, would have the pick of a dozen oar girls, the steering girl and maybe a girl pet chained to the prow like a figurehead, showing her off as a prize for all to see.

For a moment Vanessa imagined herself in the lounger resting her feet on Kashika's chained body. Julie 5 Canary would take her place with the other girls, and then ... she gasped and clamped hard on her bit as a mini orgasm rippled through her loins and she dribbled onto the deck. What a wonderful place this was ...

* * *

That evening they staggered back to their quarters stiff, sore and utterly exhausted. Their anuses, used for hours as pieces of living machinery, were bruised and numb. Vanessa felt tired enough from steering and she knew the oar girls had worked even harder. But they had learned to propel and steer the tiny galley to the Slavemaster's satisfaction, and that knowledge filled them with a sense of pride and achievement. They were now real modern-day galley slaves.

The stimulation without relief they had been subjected to all afternoon had left them all aroused and horny, but they were so tired they barely had the strength to wash and eat. Then they collapsed in a warm huddle in their cell and slept straight through to morning.

The Glen Lothy stables nestled in a clearing in the woods at the focus of many picturesque pathways stretching right round the glen that guests could explore in their ponygirl carts. Besides the stable stalls where serving ponygirls were housed and the harness and traps stored, there was an outdoor corral and an indoor sand-floored training yard. This had stand seats along two sides so that it could serve as a display space and arena.

Cherry Chain was sent to the stables after mastering the rudiments of galley-slave service to learn the techniques of being good ponygirls. Cherry Chain had received basic ponygirl training in B3, but further instruction was judged necessary before they were fit to pull carriages about the glen. Vanessa was grateful to Mister Winston for having helped her overcome her irrational dislike of pony masks and enjoy the experience to the full.

Apart from the flesh-tinted head masks they wore bridles and harness that included binder sleeves to keep their arms folded across behind their backs. It not only restrained them but also helped conceal their hands to reinforce the transition to true ponygirls. They had tails fitted that matched the colour of their own hair that flowed out of the slots in the backs of the masks like horses' manes. The tails jutted out from the small of their backs to hang in graceful plumes clear of their bottoms. They were not fastened to their harness but glued to their skin with triangular pads of transparent pliant plastic. The lower points of the triangles ran down into their buttock clefts and had springy carbon fibre strips sandwiched within them. These strips connected with the base of the tail plume and helped give the tails lift and bounce, making them bob and swish as they moved about.

To protect their feet they wore bracing ankle boots with moulded horseshoe-like pads under the balls of their feet. Curving carbon blade tongues projected backwards from under these horseshoes. These gave a spring to their steps and kept them up on their toes as though wearing invisible high heels. This, added to the projecting ears of their masks, made them seem taller and more elegantly equine.

The first time Vanessa saw them all fully attired in their pony guises she was astounded. They were erotic female chimeras; half centaurs, harnessed and bridled and ready to be broken in for use.

As it happened there was no spare girl available for Vanessa to train with and the chain pairs had to take priority in learning to work together, so she was relegated to watching them pull their lightweight pony traps around the stable block and then set out along the tracks through the woods for training runs. As compensation she did receive some dressage practice in the training yard so she would have some direct personal experience to write about for her article.

With a long rein attached to her bridal ring she was made to circle round a trainer, urged on by flicks of a carriage whip. With her arms bound behind her the sway of her hips and breasts was exaggerated and she felt her intimately attached tail swishing, its bracing rod transmitting the movement down to the sensitive skin of her buttock cleft. Then she was made to start lifting her knees higher and higher, almost prancing. Her breasts began bouncing in sympathy. A course was marked out on the arena that she had to follow with precise steps, trotting and cantering when told, stepping sideways, nodding her head and tossing her mane. The trainer's long whip flicked across her breasts and haunches when she made a mistake, motivating her to try harder.

She luxuriated in the thrill of losing herself, becoming a true ponygirl-being, responding automatically and instinctively to commands. Perhaps the mask hiding her features made it easier to dissociate her thoughts. It was strangely satisfying and deeply arousing.

Vanessa was put in the corral to wait for the rest of Cherry Chain to finish their training. A pair of girls were pressed up against a fence with their masked heads resting on each other's shoulders, rubbing their supple bodies together groin to groin and breast to breast. While watching them Vanessa almost unconsciously moved over to the sawdust pit on one corner, spread her legs, bent forward and peed freely. A passing middle-aged guest couple saw her and commented admiringly. From their accent they sounded American. She trotted over to the fence when they called and offered her a slice of apple. By tossing her head back she managed to pass it through her fake snout and catch and chew it with her real teeth, despite the internal bit, and swallow it down.

They petted and handled her intimately, reaching through the fence rails and commenting on her build and the strength of her thighs and firmness of her breasts. They behaved as though she really was a mute friendly animal and she did nothing to dispel that illusion, rubbing up against their hands. It should have felt degrading but it did not. It was another part of the adventure she was on. She knew what she was and nothing they did or did not do would change that. But what they were doing was not wrong. They were making a fuss over her, treating her as something special. And so she was.

The woman's fingers slid up her vagina and toyed with her erect clitoris. The moment was perfect. Vanessa shuddered, jerked her hips and came with as close to a whinny of pleasure as she could utter,

'Why, this pretty thing has spent herself right in my hand!' the woman exclaimed.

Vanessa was aching to try the dungeons, wanting to test her new-found confidence in herself, but according to the planner they were due to participate in a hunt first.

A storm blew over the Glen the day and night before, driving most staff and guests under cover. However, there was no lack of indoor activities when you had dozens of willing slave girls to hand. The morning of the hunt dawned bright and clear.

By nine o'clock a string of hunters was moving across the valley side, reaching from the loch shore to the ridge where a security fence guarded the boundary of the estate. Ahead of them three chains of girls had been let loose. These were their prey.

Panting for breath and lathered with sweat, Vanessa stumbled onwards. Behind her she could hear the shouts of the hunters and the flat *phut* of their rifles as they shot at one of her sisters. An occasional cheer went up when a girl was downed. Today she was literally going to be hunted down like a wild animal and shot.

She was costumed appropriately. Small dark-tinted goggles protected her eyes, making them look larger, appealing and more animal-like. Rising from a plastic pad glued to her forehead along the hairline, like her ponytail had been fastened to her back, was a spread of realistically moulded lightweight foam-rubber antlers. Her hands were confined in dark brown rubber mittens with sock-like versions for her feet with thicker soles. A small white deer tail hung over her bottom. A female deer with stag-like antlers was nonsense of course, but it would make sense later. And hunting a creature that truly enjoyed the experience was so much better than killing an innocent animal.

The hunt was taking place across the more open and less wooded stretch of the Glen on the other side of the loch from the castle. There were a few stands of pine, but mostly it was scattered boulders, scrubby grass and clumps of heather, with hollows and gullies providing the best cover. If she could keep going she might work her way round the glen and reach the thicker woods where she had a better chance of losing her pursuers, but she doubted if she would get that far. In fact she hoped not. It was a very slavish paradox. She wanted to be captured yet natural fear of the guns and the desire to please drove her on.

Occasionally she saw other antler-headed girls in the distance, breaking cover to make a dash for a new hiding place as the hunters advanced. The chains had been encouraged to scatter when they had been released earlier and she had no idea where Kashika was. She was on her own, feeling a wild joy in running naked over the hillside.

Suddenly she heard men's voices and gunshots ahead of her. A line of hunters crested the rise a couple of hundred metres away, working their way up the hillside. They had gone along the shore road to get ahead of them. They were cutting her off!

She turned uphill, making for the crest. She might still be able to get past them.

A cry went up. She'd been spotted. There was the *phut* of a gas-powered gun, something whizzed past her and hit a boulder where it stuck, crackling with electricity. It was a dart-like projectile with a bulbous adhesive rubber tip through which metal studs bristled, no doubt the product of some Shiller technical division. And if one hit her it would hurt!

Gasping for breath, she struggled on up the hill, her crown of antlers bobbing on her head. If she could just make the next rise . . .

There was a smack like a punch on her left buttock and then a crackling numbing electric fire that coursed through her body. She went sprawling face down, her limbs twitching convulsively, stunned by the shocking pounding pain.

Then the capacitor in the dart drained and the terrible pain was gone, leaving cold/hot pins and needles in its wake. She lay where she had fallen, trembling helplessly, too dazed to think or move.

Dimly she realised there was a man holding a rifle standing over her. She felt her skin pulled as he tore the sticky dart from her rump. Then he rolled her over onto her back. She had an impression of a face contorted by elation and desperate lust. He kicked her unresisting legs wide, unzipped his flies to free his erection and fell upon her.

153

His weight flattened her breasts and drove the air from her lungs as his cock rammed into her vagina. At that moment he cared only about his own pleasures. She was just an animal he had brought down: symbolically, and for all practical purposes at that moment, dead meat under him.

The successful hunter was claiming his prize.

When he'd satisfied his need the man pulled out of her ravaged passage and zipped up. He took a tag from his pocket and clipped it to her collar. He bound her wrists and ankles with plastic ties, picked up his rifle, grinned at her once more and then walked away.

Vanessa lay limply where she had fallen, too weak and drained to try to move even if she'd been free to, feeling his sperm oozing out of her. Her bottom stung where she had been struck, and not just from the electric shock: she'd have a bruise there tomorrow. There was a twitchy tremble in her limbs similar to that she had felt after Rochester's machine had zapped her. And yet it was all completely different in one vital respect. She'd chosen to do this, and beneath her pain and exhaustion was a sense of elation. She'd been a good sporty prey. And now she was going to be shown off for all to see, as a prize should.

A pair of castle staff men came up to her. They pushed a gag into her mouth, slipped a long pole between her bound limbs, hoisted her onto their shoulders and carried her down the hill. Slung beneath the pole like a carcass she hung limp but satisfied. More pampering. They were carrying her down the hill in style.

A Land Rover with a trailer hitched behind it was waiting on the shore road. Half a dozen other girls, bound as she was, were already stacked in the back like carcasses of meat. She saw Kashika and Rachel 9 of Cherry Chain amongst the others as she was slid off the pole into the trailer, and managed to squirm between them. They were bedraggled and smelled of earth and sweat and wild grass, but their eyes shone with a triumphal light she recognised. The three of them huddled together, perfectly content.

After they had recovered another four girls off the hillside, the men drove their trailer full of freshly bagged girlflesh round the loch to the castle. As they passed by the estate offices, a group of outbuildings tucked away amongst the woods not far from the stables, they braked to a sudden halt. Another vehicle had pulled up sharply in front of theirs with a squeal of brakes and in a spray of gravel.

Vanessa heard doors opening and angry raised voices. She raised her head far enough to see over the side of the trailer.

Four security men were manhandling a youngish man and woman, both dressed in shorts and hiking boots, out of a castle Land Rover and shoving them towards the estate office.

'. . . fascist sex-trafficking pigs!' the woman was shrieking. 'I saw what you were doing to them! When I tell the police about this evil fucking place you're all finished . . . do you hear, finished!'

Cold fear clutched at Vanessa's heart. The special time was over.

Eight

The angry couple disappeared through the estate office door that was hastily closed behind them, leaving one of the escorting guards outside mopping his forehead and scowling. Vanessa heard their driver wind down the window and call out to him: 'Where did they come from?'

'We found them down by the shore. We think they've been in the grounds for a few hours.'

'How'd they get in?'

'I don't know. But they've seen too much for us to risk letting them go.'

'Bloody hell! What do we do with them?'

'That's up to the Laird. Just don't let the guests know anything's wrong. Get that lot sorted and then come back here. We'll probably have to do a sweep of the grounds to check there are no more.'

'Right . . .'

The Land Rover pulled away again, jerking Vanessa back down onto the huddle of bound girlflesh. She looked into the now troubled faces of the girls around her and shook her head helplessly.

At the side door of the castle their ankle binders were cut and they were handed over to Mister Stewart to be taken down to their dungeon quarters for cleaning up. In a few words their driver told him the news. While they were being washed and toileted they overheard Stewart conversing with Jamison, another attendant, and both became very grave and quiet. Nothing more needed to be said. They all, girls included, understood the implications. Glen Lothy could only operate if absolute security and discretion were maintained. If the guests feared their privacy was compromised then they would leave and it was all finished. Vanessa saw grim, fearful faces all around her. Kashika looked at her as though appealing for some hopeful sign, but all she could do was smile hopefully back and shrug.

It was a cleaner but unnaturally subdued string of girls, still wearing their antlers, mittens and ball-gags, who were taken up to the entrance hall a while later for mounting. The walls above ground-floor level on either side of the hall, between the main door and the great staircase, had traditionally been used to display the stuffed heads of animals hunted down across three continents by previous owners of the castle in times gone by when such trophies had been popular. The heads remained, a dozen on each side, arranged in regular double staggered rows, though the boards on which they had been mounted had been unobtrusively modified.

Two narrow galleries leading off the first-floor corridor had been constructed behind the trophy walls against which were a dozen narrow curtained alcoves. At the end of each gallery stood a slave girl on a long leash chain holding a douche gun. Within the alcoves a circle of wall behind the trophies had been removed, leaving the mounting boards covering them like lids. On the gallery side of these apertures were polished wooden mounting blocks set within frames fastened to short rails, so they could be slid into the holes like plugs. The blocks were divided into two halves that could be closed together leaving an oval hole in the middle edged with thick black rubber.

Stewart and Jamison arranged the girls in the alcoves, alternately kneeling on all fours and standing bent at the waist. Vanessa was one of those standing. The men fed the girls' heads, shoulders and breasts through the halves of the mounting blocks and closed and locked them, the foam rubber making a tight seal, pressing their arms to their sides. A hook on the upper half of each board fastened to the backs of their collars, keeping their heads up. The original trophy heads were slid to one side of the apertures on concealed runners and the girls were shuffled forwards until their upper torsos took their places.

They had become living trophies amongst the stuffed specimens. Their heads, shoulders and stiff-nippled breasts jutting out proudly from the mounting frames, they looked out over the hall. From the gallery side they presented an equally appealing sight, forming a row of alternately kneeling and standing posteriors begging to be mounted, with greased anal puckers and pouting clefts at the ready, all neatly framed within their alcoves. Stewart and Jamison clipped on ankle cuffs set in the side of each alcove to ensure they kept their legs spread, then left them to be enjoyed.

The guests were of course free to admire them from the front and make use of them from the rear. Trying to take her mind off the problem of the intruders, Vanessa thought how economical it was that while one half of her was being decorative the other could be providing more intimate pleasure.

A little later another string of girls was led in and mounted on the opposite wall.

Now Vanessa could see them as the guests did, and for a while she was able to lose herself in the erotic tableau they presented. With their antlers on and heads braced firmly facing outward, at first glance they very nearly merged with the trophies they had displaced. They were simply more exotic animals that had been hunted down by the masters of the house. Their red ball-gags showing between their teeth were a unifying splash of colour. Only when their eyes moved or the tremble of their breasts showed was it apparent they were still living creatures.

Guests passing through the hall or using the stairs paused to admire them. Later the hunters would return and no doubt boast about the ones they had caught. That night their prizes would be delivered to their rooms. Would that be the last time hunters celebrated their success in the castle?

Vanessa suddenly felt frustrated and angry. Being on display gave her too much time to dwell on her new fears. What if the Laird could not reason with the couple? They could not simply keep them in detention indefinitely.

The face of one of the girls opposite changed. Her eyes screwed up and she clenched her teeth about her gag. Vanessa knew somebody had entered her alcove and was now using her. Lucky thing. She became aware of people moving along her own gallery. Please pick me, she thought, wiggling her hips invitingly. She wanted to get screwed. It would help distract her from worry. But instead she saw along the wall to one side of her the antlered head of one of the other girls begin to bob rhythmically to the muffled sound of energetic grunting. After they were done, the girl with the douche gun would clean them up ready for the next guest.

Perhaps two hours passed this way, and then Vanessa felt somebody was touching her, but not as a prelude to intercourse.

She was pulled back through the aperture, the block was unclamped from about her torso and her ankle cuffs were released. It was Slavemaster MacDonald. He clipped a leash to her collar and then peeled the fake antlers off her head and tossed them aside.

'The Laird has said you're to be taken to his office,' he said gravely. 'Director Shiller wants to talk to you.'

The Laird's private office overlooked the gardens at the back of the castle. Through the window Vanessa could see a guest walking between the flowerbeds with a leashed slave girl trotting along at his heels. On the walls hung paintings of the castle and glen. The Laird himself sat behind a massive, ancient and well-worn desk on which rested the inevitable modern incongruity of a computer terminal. The screen was currently angled so it was visible to those seated on both sides of the desk. On it was an image of Director Shiller.

Vanessa felt instinctively that she should be kneeling, but the Laird pointed to one of the high-backed leather-seated chairs in front of the desk. 'Sit there, girl. The Director wants to speak to you.'

Nervously Vanessa sat, the leather cool on her bare bottom. MacDonald took the other chair. It felt strange to sit amongst these powerful people like an equal. She felt the weight of expectation descending upon her. It was so much easier being a slave.

Shiller looked out at her from the screen and a brief smile crooked her tight lips. 'Sorry to disturb your stay, Vanessa, but a situation has arisen that I think you might be able to help us with. Perhaps you already know something about it?'

'I saw two trespassers being brought in, Director. I heard the woman shouting about what she was going to do. I understand the implications if they can't be kept quiet about what they've seen.'

'Yes, perhaps you more than any of us,' Shiller agreed. 'A few months ago that angry woman might have been you. Independent, outspoken and strong-minded . . .'

'She's an unreconstructed feminist!' the Laird muttered. 'You should have heard the names she called me!'

Shiller again smiled thinly. 'Be that as it may, from what has been reported to me of her words especially, you sound like kindred spirits, Vanessa.'

Vanessa blushed and hung her head. 'Director, I didn't know the truth then, I didn't accept what I was . . .'

The Director raised a reassuring hand. 'Vanessa, your loyalty to the company is unquestioned. I asked for you to be brought here because you might be able to provide insight from your recent personal experience into how this couple might be thinking as outsiders suddenly confronted with slave life on such a scale, so we can determine the best way of handling them. The Laird has of course tried to explain, but –'

'They flatly won't listen to reason!' the Laird cut in angrily.

'You did your best, Malcolm,' Shiller said gently.

'But it was not good enough! They can't believe our girls can all be here of their own free will. Before we found them they'd seen some ponygirls being driven through the woods. Their driver was using the whip on them. Just a few licks to put a bit more spring in their steps, but they didn't see it that way.'

'That sounds familiar, doesn't it, Vanessa?' Shiller said. 'You were not convinced by my assurances the girls in B3 were there voluntarily either.'

Vanessa forced a wry smile of her own. 'No, Director. It was all such a shock.'

'Yes, that is the state these people are in right now. In one respect only is the situation different from yours. They appear to be innocent trespassers.'

'Are you sure, Director?' Vanessa asked, feeling the hair rising on the back of her neck. 'After what Rochester tried with Kashika and me he might do anything. We know he's after incriminating evidence to use against the company. Glen Lothy must be the biggest company facility outside London. It would make a good target if he knows about it.'

'That we're looking into, girl,' the Laird said. 'We have their names and home addresses and checks are being made to be sure they are who they say they are. Mike Kendal and Jennifer Morton, both from London. He works in the city and she's a freelance writer. So far they seem genuine enough. They had the usual camping gear with them. We're taken that, their mobile phones and cameras, and made a superficial search of their persons for any hidden devices such as Rochester wanted you to use. They're objecting to anything more intimate and we're not forcing them to comply just yet.'

'As innocent people might, Laird,' Vanessa said.

The Laird scowled. 'Yes, and until we know better we must continue to treat them as innocent. But if we want to win their confidence we have to begin by showing them we're not the monsters they think we are. Some of my less reputable ancestors would simply have locked them in the dungeons and thrown away the keys . . .' He sighed. 'But these are more enlightened times and we can't keep them prisoners indefinitely. They seem to be on a walking holiday which might give us a few days, but eventually somebody will raise the alarm if they don't contact them.'

'Which is where you come in, Vanessa,' the Director said. 'In your case I had to act more forcefully. I also had a suspicion you might be a potential convert to our ways. But this time we have nothing like that to work with. Perhaps if this couple were able to talk to a slave girl face to face they might at least begin to admit the possibility that this is not a haven of sex-traffickers and exploiters.'

'We don't expect miracles from you, girl,' the Laird said, 'but it might make them a little more amenable and it would be something to do while we wait for background checks.'

Vanessa thought furiously, aware of their eyes upon her. The reporter in her wanted to know more facts. 'May I ask how they got into the grounds, Laird?'

'Kendal told us that. It was up on the hill there where the woods run against the boundary fence. Yesterday's storm must have brought down a tree. It fell outwards over the fence making a bridge of sorts without triggering the alarms. Late last night they climbed in over that. My men have checked it out and the tree's there right enough.'

'Did they know this was private land and they were trespassing?'

'He said they missed the notices in the dark and thought it was forestry land. They just wanted a bit of shelter to pitch their tent if the weather turned worse.'

'Did you believe him, Laird?'

'It sounds reasonable enough. At least he was a bit more forthcoming than his girlfriend. All she does is curse me and promise disgrace and damnation for us all.'

Vanessa took a deep breath. 'I'll do what I can, Laird. Director, if I make any progress, do you or the

Laird want to take over and try to make some sort of deal with them?'

'You must use your own judgement, Vanessa,' Shiller said. 'In business negotiations you do not jeopardise any personal trust established between the different parties by changing negotiators halfway through the process. I will fully support any agreement you make.'

Vanessa felt pride swell within her even as the weight of daunting responsibility seemed to settle on her shoulders. 'Thank you, Director, I promise I'll do my best. Slavemaster, can I fetch my reporting gear from the slave quarters, please? And something from the magazine rack . . .'

MacDonald led Vanessa to where Kendal and Morton were being kept in the detention room of the security office. A castle security man stood in the corridor outside. As he unlocked the door the Slavemaster unclipped Vanessa's leash and said: 'Good luck, girl . . .'

Vanessa took a deep breath and strode boldly in.

The intruders were seated at a plain table in the middle of an otherwise empty room with bars on the window. Vanessa had only caught a glimpse of them earlier. Now she saw they were both in their mid-twenties. Mike Kendal was a bristle-cut blond, well groomed and lean with grey eyes, at the moment looking nervous and uncertain. Jennifer Morton had a nice figure, dark brown hair and dark eyes under full straight brows and a determined set to her lips.

They looked up as she entered and their jaws dropped.

'Hallo,' Vanessa said brightly, 'I'm Vanessa the Slave Reporter for the *Girlflesh News*.' She pulled up a spare chair and sat down opposite them, putting her camera, recorder and a folded magazine on the table. 'Sorry about all this trouble you've been having, but you understand this is private land and you were trespassing. Still, I'm sure it'll all be sorted out. Meanwhile I thought as you were here you might be ready to do an interview? I'm sure my readers would be interested in your story.'

She had achieved the effect she intended. They were thrown off balance, both goggling at her incredulously. Whatever else they might have been expecting she was sure it wasn't the offer of an interview by a naked slave-collared reporter in a white fedora.

Vanessa took the hat off and fanned herself with it. 'Hasn't it been a lovely sunny day? I hear you were caught out in that storm yesterday. We were all indoors. You must have got wet. I don't blame you for wanting to pitch your tent in the woods; they're lovely. Are you on holiday for long?'

Mike was dividing his attention between her face and her breasts while Jennifer was struggling to find her tongue. At last she managed to say: 'Who ... who the hell are you meant to be?'

Vanessa smiled sweetly. 'I said, I'm Vanessa the Slave Reporter for the *Girlflesh News*. Do you want to see a copy?' She unfolded the magazine in front of them.

It was last month's issue with a picture of a dozen girls in orange collars and chains kneeling in a semi-circle and smiling brightly at the camera as they showed off their newly depilated pink pussy lips. The heading read: 'A CLOSE SHAVE FOR PEACH CHAIN', with the tagline: '*Why did clients request the trim? See page 4*'.

Vanessa was not risking any further security breach. Nothing in *GN* ever mentioned Shiller or her company by name. She was always: 'The Director'.

Nor did it give away anything that would reveal the location of its headquarters or the identities of its clients. What it did feature in great detail were incidents and achievements in the lives of working slave girls reported in a matter-of-fact manner as though they were of personal interest and everyday familiarity to its readers, which they were.

The pair already thought the worst, Vanessa decided, so any attempt at a cover-up would only seem to confirm their suspicions. Therefore she might as well push them all the way until they were forced to re-examine their prejudices about the alternate lifestyle into which they had stumbled.

'The next issue will have my article about the Glen,' Vanessa continued brightly. 'That's why I was up here. I think it'll make a great read because this is such a wonderful place. Anyway, I'd like to do a little piece on you as well. Maybe I'll call it: UNEXPECTED GUESTS, what do you think?'

Still looking dazed, Mike had started to flip though the pages of *GN*, perhaps looking for page 4. Jennifer suddenly snatched it out of his hand and waved it under Vanessa's nose.

'Is this pornography some sort of joke?' she demanded.

'Of course not,' Vanessa said.

'You expect us to believe this is a magazine about slave keeping . . . and you write for it?'

Vanessa took the copy from her hand and opened it at the page featuring her last article with her own by-line and picture, of which she was very proud. 'Yes I do. Unless you think I've just thrown this together in the few hours since you turned up.'

Mike finally found his voice. 'So . . . this is for people who want to read about slave girls?'

'No, it's primarily aimed at slave girls to read

166

about things of interest to them,' Vanessa explained, 'though of course other interested people see it as well.'

Jennifer's lips pinched. 'That's . . . sheer nonsense!'

Vanessa recalled the words Zara had used when she had first expressed her incredulity that such a publication could exist. 'Why do you find it so hard to believe? Sportsmen read sports magazines and engineers read technical journals so naturally slave girls read about slavery.'

It was such a self-evident statement it was hard to counter. Jennifer fell back on her argument of faith. 'I don't care about this filth. This is evil and I'm going straight to the police as soon as I get out of here.'

'And what exactly do you think is going on here? I understand the Laird told you earlier it was all voluntary.'

Jennifer looked contemptuous. 'He was lying of course. I know what I saw! Those girls chained to the carts being whipped like animals!'

'And that boat on the lake,' Mike added helpfully. 'It looked like a slave galley. There was this girl tied over the prow and there was this man who looked like he was –'

'He was raping her!' Jennifer said.

Vanessa wished they hadn't seen a galley but it was probably preferable to witnessing the hunt. That would really take some explaining. Aloud she said: 'But did you ask any of the girls if they were enjoying themselves?'

'Don't be absurd!'

'But would you if you had the chance?'

'I know women would never want to behave like this of their own free will!' Jennifer declared with absolute conviction.

'Why?' Vanessa asked simply.

She looked at Vanessa with disbelief. 'You have to ask?'

'I was just wondering what your reasons were for making such a universal statement about what a relative handful of women amongst a few billion on this planet enjoy doing.'

'Because it degrades and dehumanises them, that's why! It makes them objects of exploitation. Nobody can want that!'

Vanessa arranged her recorder on the table. 'If we're going to debate the morals and philosophy of slavery can I record this? My readers will be interested. I'll show you a transcript first, of course, so you can check it's accurate.'

Mike sat back, frowning at the device. Suddenly he took in a rasping breath, pulled an asthma inhaler from his shirt pocket, shook it and sucked from its spout a couple of times.

Jennifer turned aside to look at him in concern. 'Are you all right, Mike?'

He took a deep breath, nodded and tucked the device away again, looking slightly embarrassed. 'Sorry . . . it catches me like that sometimes. All this . . . is a hell of a shock.'

Jennifer looked back at Vanessa, her anger returning. 'Are you seriously telling me you'd print what we say in that disgusting paper?'

'As I said, slave girls are interested in anything concerning their lifestyle. Especially coming from people who want to destroy it. After they read this at least they'll understand you meant well, even if you were misguided.'

She had them confused again and that was good. This was where being who and what she was gave her an advantage over the Laird. She started the recorder.

'Now, you were saying nobody could want to be a slave.' Vanessa pointed to her neck. 'See the collar? Note the absence of clothes. I'm here of my own free choice and I'm a happy slave. Do I look dehumanised and degraded?'

Jennifer was shaking her head. 'You must be part of it. Or they've got some hold over you . . . or you've been brainwashed.'

Vanessa laughed. 'Make up your mind which one it is! Or better still, admit the faint possibility that I'm telling the truth and every girl here is happy with what she is. Don't condemn them or the people in charge just because they don't conform to your narrow view of what's right and wrong.'

'My views aren't narrow!'

'But you didn't know about this place until today, did you? How does this fit in to your preconceptions, or are you too frightened to try to expand them?'

'I'm not frightened of anything,' Jennifer said angrily. 'I'm talking about fundamental human rights!'

'All right, we'll talk about them. Do you believe women should have the right to freedom of choice in all things?'

'Of course.'

'Even the freedom to choose when not to be free?'

'What? That's nonsense.'

'Why not? It's a valid option. Unless you only believe in those freedoms that conform to your rigid idea of the way the world should work and people should behave. That's how dictatorships and religious fundamentalism gets started. What does it matter if some women honestly and freely choose to be slaves as long as it doesn't hurt anybody else? I take it you've heard of natural submissives and masochists. You accept they exist.'

'A few maybe. They're sad women who need help.'

'Oh, like lesbians and gay men used to be thought to "need help" to conform?'

'That's quite different,' Jennifer said dismissively.

'But how?' Vanessa asked. 'And why shouldn't submissives be allowed the same freedom to be who they are?'

'What a few do in private perhaps,' Jennifer conceded grudgingly. 'But that's not what's going on here. We saw the girls pulling carts and that slave ship. Then there was a woman being led around on a leash like a dog. There must be dozens of them here.'

'Over a hundred,' Vanessa said.

They both blinked. Jennifer said: 'And you say they are all here voluntarily? I don't believe it!'

'So you might believe in one submissive but not a hundred? Use your imagination. They've simply come here from all over the country to live as they choose.'

'To be chained up and whipped, to be treated like animals, like men's playthings!'

'So they're letting the side of free, strong, non-slave women down by inconveniently enjoying being dominated by men? And a few women as well, just for the record. Nobody's forcing you to do the same, it doesn't reduce your personal freedom by one iota, so why should you worry?'

'It's the principle!'

'What principle exactly? And what's the alternative? Have them live an unhappy lie for your peace of mind? Re-educate them? Lock them up for being abnormal? Except they're into bondage and might like that.' She saw Jennifer was getting confused and pressed on. 'Not long ago I thought the same as you. Then I was forced to confront the same things you've seen today. I didn't think women could want

170

to like this. But they do. And gradually I found I did too.'

Mike had been watching this verbal interchange with an expression of bemused fascination. It suited Vanessa that he kept out of it for the moment. She'd handle him later. Jennifer seemed to be the stronger more outspoken one, and for now she focused on her.

Jennifer said: 'But how can you want to be a . . . a slave?'

'Because I am uniquely me and I get pleasure out of doing so,' Vanessa said proudly. 'It's the way I am. Some people like music I hate or get obsessed with sports I think are dumb. That's the way we are. Can't you accept that?'

Jennifer shook her head. 'No. It's simply not right. It's exploitation!' Her brow furrowed for a moment. 'This place is big. It must cost money to run. Where does that come from? Do people make money out of these women?'

Vanessa was expecting this. 'Yes.'

Jennifer looked triumphant. 'Then it is exploitation!'

'Only of the willing. And we get well cared for and earn our living.'

'You're paid slaves?'

'We get a proportion of the money we earn the company. Why not?'

'That sounds like prostitution.'

'No, it's a lifestyle choice. The girls here have certain natural talents that can be employed to the mutual advantage both of our clients and us. They get pleasure dominating and we get pleasure being dominated. Isn't it far better for a submissive to be managed on a sound commercial basis by people who care about her than get trapped by people who don't? Yes, we are commodities in a way, but then so is

171

anybody with a special ability, a look or a skill that others value and want to make use of. The idea of enforced slavery or prostitution disgusts me as much as you. That really is evil! But this is exactly the opposite and it works.'

'You're saying this is . . . ethical slavery?'

'Exactly. I know it's a startling concept. I couldn't believe it when I first heard it. But it's true, and just because it doesn't fit with your preconceptions of right and wrong doesn't make it less so. What's more important: your principles or the happiness and well-being of the girls here? The chosen lives of real people versus a set of theoretical ideals? But you won't believe any of this unless you take the time to ask them for yourselves. Will you open your minds and give us the chance to prove it?'

As Jennifer hesitated Mike suddenly spoke up: 'I suppose it wouldn't hurt, Jen.'

She turned to him in surprise. 'What?'

'To find out the truth. I mean if these girls really are here voluntarily that's a big difference to what we first thought.'

Vanessa suddenly found herself taking a liking to Mike.

'They can't be,' Jennifer protested.

'Then we're got nothing to lose, have we?' Mike pointed out. 'You're the one always going on about equality and choice. What if they have chosen to be slaves?'

Vanessa jumped in. 'Just give us a week to prove it. You'll be our guests and you can talk to as many of the girls as you like. Hear their stories. See for yourself how happy they are. If you accept it's all consensual then everything you've seen remains confidential.'

'That sounds fair enough,' Mike said. 'We've got more than a week of our holiday left.'

Jennifer was still looking suspicious. 'You think a bit of hospitality will buy us off?' she asked Vanessa.

'No, I'm doing you the courtesy of believing you meant it when you talked about rights and principles. If I thought you were the kind of people who could be bought off then I'd tell the owners to close down the Glen right now rather than pay bribes. You don't have the monopoly in principles, you know.' She felt the emotion building inside her again and thought of Shiller's speech in B3 before all the girls and added huskily: 'To us honesty is everything.'

Jennifer was peering at her curiously for the first time. 'All right, I'll do it, but not for a week. It won't take me that long to know for sure. Three days.'

Vanessa took a deep breath. 'Three days – starting from tomorrow.'

'Agreed.'

'And you promise not to try to leave during that time.'

'Fair enough,' Mike said.

'Also, you can talk to as many girls as you like but you don't trouble the guests,' Vanessa said. 'They didn't come here to debate the morality of slavery. They know they're not doing anything wrong enjoying our girls.'

'I wouldn't trust what they said anyway,' Jennifer said with contempt.

'And . . . you've both got to be strip-searched.'

Jennifer looked startled. 'What? No way!'

'Listen to me,' Vanessa said patiently. 'We have to be careful of spies. There are far nastier people around than you can imagine who'd love to destroy us. You might be working for them trying to smuggle a camera in here. Your baggage has been checked and now it's your clothes and you.'

'Nobody's laying a finger on me!' Jennifer insisted.

Vanessa allowed a trace of scorn to enter her voice. 'So you say you care about the dignity of the girls here but you're not prepared to sacrifice a little of your own on their behalf?'

'Come on, Jen,' Mike said. 'It's no worse than if you get unlucky at an airport. We're in this thing now, so let's just get it over with, eh?' He flashed a sudden easy smile. 'Anyway, I'm hungry. Any chance of getting something to eat around here?'

'They've got a fantastic chef in the castle,' Vanessa promised.

Jennifer took a deep breath. 'All right. But none of those security guards are touching me.'

'I'll see to you, okay?' Vanessa said.

'Then let's get this over with . . .'

Mike was taken out so Jennifer could strip. Vanessa handed her boots, clothes and pocket items out the door for the guards to check.

Jennifer had a nice body. Pale, neatly shaped high breasts with well-proportioned nipples, a trim waist, strong thighs and nicely rounded buttocks. Her pubes were a thick dark delta of fluffy curls.

Once she was naked Vanessa ran a bug scanner one of the security men had shown her how to use over her body. Jennifer's lips tightened to a pinched line but she said nothing. When Vanessa put on a rubber glove and applied KY jelly, she scowled but turned round and bent over the table.

As she probed Jennifer's vagina and anus, which were very nicely formed and invited thoughts that Vanessa had to suppress, Vanessa was alert for some subtle response to this intimacy. But all she felt was the other woman's tension, resentment and desire for the search to end. Jennifer's clothes and possessions were handed back into the room by a guard who shook his head. Jennifer dressed and they left the room for Mike to be searched.

As they waited outside they saw Mike's clothes and possessions being handed out and minutely dismantled and examined. His boots, watch, inhaler and wallet were scanned for electronic devices and then put through a portable x-ray machine.

'Just how paranoid are you?' Jennifer demanded as she watched the guards at work.

'Very, I'm afraid,' Vanessa said. 'You might understand one day.'

Ten minutes later Mike had been checked and cleared and was dressed once again. He grinned broadly, looking Vanessa up and down with approval. 'Well, that wasn't so bad. Now, what about some food? We're your guests now, you've got to keep us well fed or else we'll tell on you.'

'Mike, this is serious!' Jennifer snapped.

'Sorry.'

While Mike and Jennifer were found a room in the castle and provided with a meal, the Slavemaster took Vanessa back to the Laird's Office to report her progress. She felt utterly drained after her verbal confrontation and wished she could have done better.

'I made the best deal I could, Director,' Vanessa explained to Shiller's image on the screen. 'They're very suspicious of us, Jennifer especially. I think Mike's beginning to realise what a good time he could have here, which might be helpful, but she has her principles. I was hoping she might show some sign that slavery had a secret appeal to her, like I did even though I tried to deny it. But I don't think she's a potential submissive.'

'That would be too much to expect to happen twice,' Shiller said.

'And we have three days to convince them to keep our secret,' said the Laird grimly.

'Three days is better than none,' said Shiller. 'For the moment, Vanessa, as you have established a degree of understanding, I think you should continue to represent us. Your presence will serve as a constant reminder that our girls are all volunteers. From now until this problem is resolved you are excused all other duties and are free to act at your own discretion. Is there anything you need?'

Vanessa had been giving this some thought. 'First, can I have Cherry Chain to act as escorts and sample slave girls, please, Laird? I know how they'll respond to questioning. And the use of whatever facilities I need when I show them round? Also, can the security presence please be as unobtrusive as possible?'

'You can have all that, girl, if it gets the result,' the Laird said. 'Meanwhile I'll tell the hunter that downed you that you're ill and offer him another prize girl.'

'No, Laird, if you please I would like to go back on display and serve normally. The guests should not suspect anything is wrong. Mike and Jennifer will keep to their room tonight. It'll give them time to calm down a little and perhaps take in what I said. Tomorrow we can all start fresh.'

The Laird looked at her with renewed respect and observed dryly: 'I like this girl, Director.'

'I knew you would,' said Shiller.

As she was put back on display Vanessa tried to put all thoughts of the task ahead of her out of her mind and surrendered to the simple rewards of slavish life. With the ball-gag in her mouth and fake antlers once more glued to her head she knew who she was and what was expected of her. The knowledge that the guests looking up at her got enjoyment from seeing her mounted amongst her sister slaves pleased and excited her. If they cared for more her lower body projecting out into its tiny alcove on the gallery side could provide it.

Over the next few hours, two men made use of her. The feel of good hard cocks filling her vagina was a great comfort. That she never saw their owners' faces did not matter in the least. Afterwards the chain girl with the douche gun cleaned her up and gave her a little pat and tickle when she was done. It was so nice to belong. This must not be allowed to end!

That evening she was taken to the room of the man who had bagged her in the hunt. Afterwards she did not recall much of his face, but again that did not matter.

He put a big rubber bit in her mouth and chained her standing with feet spread wide to the foot of his bed, facing towards its head. He ran down a large rubber hook from amongst the devices hidden away in the bed canopy and slid it up into her vagina. Winding it tight lifted her onto her toes and pulled her hips forward and up, tensioning her body so there was no slack in her posture. Then, very slowly and carefully, pausing between each stroke to feel the warmth of her flesh, he gave her a thorough paddling until her bottom was an even scarlet.

Only when the saliva trickling from between her clenched teeth was dripping onto her breasts and the juices from her hooked vagina were making a stain on the floor and she was moaning desperately for relief, did he ram his shaft up her backside and sodomise her again and again.

* * *

In the small hours Vanessa woke up with a start as though from a bad dream.

She was chained on her back spreadeagled under the softly snoring body of her master. Fortunately she had not disturbed him.

Her contentment had melted away with the cooling of her backside and now the enormity of her task had hit her. It had taken a month to convince her that Shiller's slave business was ethical and she'd been a convert-in-waiting all the time. Now she had committed herself to accomplishing the same task with two people, one of whom was implacably opposed to everything related to the girlflesh business, in just three days. And the pair of them might yet turn out to be Rochester's spies.

She felt like the defender of the castle under siege with the battlements about to be stormed by the enemy. And it was not only Glen Lothy that was under attack but the whole company and what it stood for: the castle of girlflesh. And if she failed it would all come tumbling down.

Nine

Having served all night the Cherry Chain girls were allowed a lie-in. However Vanessa had to cut their rest period short to brief them. While the other chains left to serve about the Glen, they sat in a tight huddle in the cell round Vanessa while she explained her plans.

Amber, Charlotte, Fiona, Hollie, Kashika, Lisa, Madelyn, Olivia, Rachel, Tina, Victoria and Yvonne. She'd seen them accepted into the Shiller slave-training programme and she'd seen them graduate. Now, as she looked into their anxious faces, Vanessa desperately hoped she would not see them depart from the life they loved, because it would mean she had failed.

'For the next three days your only duty is to be ready when I need you,' Vanessa said. 'That might mean talking to Mike and Jennifer about what you feel about being slaves, giving demonstrations or serving them or me in some way. I don't know for sure because mostly I'll have to play it by ear. Basically be honest and be yourselves.

'Now I think Mike's going to be easier to win over. Like any bloke his age this place is a dream come true. So anything you can do to keep him happy is fine, but don't be too obvious so it offends his girlfriend.

'Jennifer is the real challenge. She simply can't believe we like being dominated, especially when that means being mastered mostly by men. I'm going to suggest she interviews any of you she wishes individually and in private. She's going to be trying to prove her suspicions that you're all really being pressured or brainwashed into this. This is where all your individual stories will help. I want her to get to know you as individuals who've come together here out of choice, not coercion. But no mention of Shiller by name or how big the company's operation actually is. I threw a little of that at them yesterday to get their attention, but I don't want this to get sidetracked. For now we'll just work at getting her to accept Glen Lothy as the home of happy, consensual slaves. Any questions?'

Kashika said solemnly: 'You know we're ready to do whatever's necessary. Just ask us.' The others nodded. Vanessa felt the warmth of their companionship and loyalty wash over her and had to swallow hard. If Jennifer could just feel as she did now all her doubts would be blown away.

'Should we make it all seem like more of a game?' Charlotte wondered. 'If she's worried about us suffering then we could say the whips and stuff are softer than they look and we're just playing along when we cry and howl.'

'No, no pretence of any sort,' Vanessa said firmly. 'That'll make this seem more like elaborate prostitution. I said this was a lifestyle choice and I think she might respect that if she's absolutely convinced it's true. If she thinks we're putting on any sort of act then it's finished!'

Before she began her day with Mike and Jennifer, Vanessa had an early conference with the Laird and Shiller.

180

'We've had some results from our enquiries into the backgrounds of our uninvited guests,' Shiller said. 'Miss Morton is a freelance writer and illustrator with a modest but growing reputation in her field. Some of her work had been published by Dominion Press, which Rochester owns, and she attended at least one literary gathering where he was present – along with a few hundred other people.

'Mr Kendal has not been strictly truthful with us. He said he worked in the city. In fact he lost his job with Kingston Reed a few months ago and has since then been looking for fresh employment while offering his services as a financial advisor, so far with limited success.'

'Any link with Rochester, Director?' Vanessa asked.

'Rochester was a client of Kingston Reed, but then so were many others. Kendal was in a very junior position and would have had little opportunity for direct contact with him. We're still running checks.'

'In other words we have slight grounds for suspicion against both of them but no proof,' said the Laird. 'If we found one or both of them were working for Rochester then we can simply toss them back to him empty-handed, since it's incriminating photographs he wants to use as a lever. If this pair are innocent and genuinely concerned about the welfare of our girls then we have to let them go eventually. And then, even without hard evidence, they might induce the authorities, or even worse the press, to investigate the Glen. We have friends in high places but there are limits to their influence.'

'Couldn't you close everything down until the danger was past, Laird?'

'We have a plan for that. In an emergency, inside an hour we can conceal everything connected with our girlflesh business and turn the Glen into the model of an innocent private resort. But it would be the end of our guests' trust in us.'

Vanessa took a deep breath. 'I'll do my best to see that doesn't happen.'

Vanessa decided Mike and Jennifer's inspection tour should start in their dungeon dormitory. It would give her a chance to introduce them to Cherry Chain while inspecting the facilities so they could see the girls were well cared for.

Mike attempted not to stare openly at the display of bare flesh around him but failed dismally, while Jennifer averted her eyes in disgust and largely succeeded.

Vanessa had hoped their night in a luxury apartment with excellent food might have mellowed her, but if it had she gave no outward sign.

With Slavemaster MacDonald looking on with barely concealed indignation at the intrusion and Cherry Chain kneeling patiently on the mats, Vanessa showed the couple round. She kept her press hat on, hoping the juxtaposition between it and her naked body would serve as a continual reminder that things were different here . . .

'There are twelve girls to what we call a "chain", who train, work and live together,' Vanessa explained. 'They're called Cherry Chain. I thought you might like to talk to them later. You can pick another chain if you want but they're available right now. These are the cages they live in . . .'

Apart from Cherry Chain most of the chains were out in the castle and grounds so the cages were almost all empty, except for a couple with heavy curtains drawn round them. 'They were up late serving guests,' Vanessa explained in a whisper.

'You mean being forced to have sex with them,' Jennifer said distastefully.

'If that's what they wanted,' Vanessa admitted. 'We're here to give pleasure.'

'Why are these cages so low and the doors so small?' Jennifer asked.

'It makes us stay on our hands and knees,' Vanessa said.

'Forcing you to act more like animals?'

'It makes us look up at our masters. That feels right for a slave girl.'

'Or a collared animal,' Jennifer persisted.

'If you like.'

She showed them the recreation space, showers and toilets. All were immaculately clean, but Jennifer still looked displeased.

'Don't the women have any privacy?' she asked.

'Almost none,' Vanessa admitted cheerfully. 'We don't expect any.'

'So you're caged like animals and also have to pee and shit like animals!'

'Captive animals have no choice about their captivity, we do,' Vanessa countered.

'That's what I'm here to decide!' Jennifer retorted.

Hell, she's taking this seriously, Vanessa thought.

'What are those?' Mike asked, examining the douche guns hanging by the toilet pans.

Vanessa explained their purpose as part of their daily routine. Mike looked surprised while Jennifer grimaced. 'These things are specially made for cleaning and greasing women for anal sex?'

'That's right,' Vanessa said. 'They're hygienic, effective and quick to use.'

'Just so a man can shove his cock up your behind more easily,' Jennifer said with contempt.

183

'Well, would you rather we did it dry and dirty?' Vanessa replied.

Mike said slowly: 'So right now all of you have . . . er . . . grease up your . . .'

'We're prepared for intercourse through every orifice at all times,' Vanessa said helpfully.

They moved on to the racks of restraints and punishment devices. She took them so much for granted by now that it was only as she saw Jennifer's expression harden still further that Vanessa realised what a shock such objects might seem to the uninitiated.

'How can you live next to such things?' Jennifer asked, gingerly picking up a spanking paddle.

'They're just part of everyday life for us, like your computer or paints and paintbrushes. The things we need to enjoy being ourselves.'

Jennifer smacked the paddle experimentally into her palm and winced. 'But they're designed to hurt you!'

'Yes, pain is part of our life.'

'But if you have to get a fix of pain can't you do it to yourselves privately?'

'It's not the same,' Vanessa said. She sought for the right words. 'We don't just like pain, or else we'd spend all our time sticking pins under our fingernails . . . and that would be stupid and it would simply hurt. It's pain with sex, exposure and stimulation. It's restraint, helplessness and anticipation. It's the thrill of surrendering to another person's will. It's . . . it's being a slave!'

Jennifer simply shook her head. *What a chasm we've got to bridge*, Vanessa thought hopelessly.

They returned to where the Cherry girls were still patiently waiting. They were kneeling in a line with hands cuffed behind their backs, thighs splayed and mouths filled with cherry-red ball-gags. They were individually leashed so they could be separated but the leash handles had been clipped to the collar of the next girl in line to form a coffle. They were spotlessly clean, brushed and combed and their eyes sparkled with anticipation. Vanessa thought they looked adorable. How could anybody not see they were happy exactly as they were and aching to please?

'Why are they gagged?' Jennifer asked suspiciously.

'That's how girls are normally presented ready for being taken about the estate,' Vanessa explained

'Part of what you call being a slave, I suppose?' she said with contempt.

'Exactly. It all helps focus the mind on serving our masters . . . and mistresses.'

'Can't you take their gags out?' Jennifer asked.

'If that would please you,' Vanessa said.

'Not for me, for them.'

'Well, why not ask them if that's what they want?'

Hesitantly Jennifer stepped forward in front of the girls. 'Do you want to be ungagged?' she asked, speaking slowly and clearly.

The girls shook their heads.

Jennifer glowed at the watching MacDonald and the lash hanging from his belt. 'I don't suppose they had any choice.'

'They had a choice in becoming slaves,' Vanessa said. 'That's the only one that mattered.'

'They look happy enough to me,' Mike ventured.

'Mike, can't you see they've been maltreated?' Jennifer snapped. 'Look at the marks on them!'

A few of the girls bore some light strap marks on their behinds. Vanessa had hardly noticed them. Was her backside still red? She hadn't checked.

'Well, even so, you've got to admit they look healthy and well fed,' Mike said.

185

'So, they keep their animals healthy,' Jennifer said scornfully. 'That way they can earn more money for their masters. It doesn't mean it's right!'

Mike's attempts at being reasonable were welcome but at the moment they weren't helping. Vanessa cut in: 'Look, you can talk to the girls down here, but it's a lovely day so I thought we could take them out into the grounds. Then you can choose any of them you like and talk in private where you can be sure you won't be overheard and they'll have no reason not to tell you the truth. We could even have a picnic lunch sent out. How about it?'

They gathered in the shade of a big cedar tree that rose from the rolling lawns to one side of the main drive. At their backs was the green curtain of the woods while before them were the dark waters of the loch, across which a galley was cutting a shimmering wake, and then the purple and tan swell of the far hillside. The lawns and gardens about them were dotted with guests and their slaves at play. To Vanessa it seemed a perfect idyll, but glancing at Jennifer's face she could tell the feeling was not mutual.

Vanessa hoped none of the other guests would intrude on their little group. Fortunately it was not considered good manners in the Glen to impose oneself on others unless there was a clear invitation.

Separating the girls' leashes Vanessa handed Amber's to Jennifer. 'There, this is Amber One Cherry. You can take her away and ask her what you like. You can work your way through them in order if you like.'

Jennifer wrinkled her lip as she saw Amber's collar. 'You all have numbers.'

'We all have numbers in real life,' Vanessa countered. 'Just because we wear them on our collars it doesn't mean we're not people.'

Looking uncomfortable and self-conscious, Jennifer led Amber away. Vanessa turned to Mike.

'Do you want to question any of them?'

Mike grinned sheepishly. 'I think she'll do a good enough job for both of us.' He glanced about cautiously to ensure Jennifer was well out of earshot and lowered his voice. 'Look, don't tell her but it's bloody obvious to me you lot want to be here, once I thought about it. It would only need one of you to slip her leash, or whatever, and get away and tell the police and that would be it. And I could tell the fences were designed for keeping people out, not in. So if you're happy and your guests are happy, that's fine by me. Live and let live, right? But Jen has these principles. I mean I admire her for them, but sometimes . . . well, they can be hard to live with.'

That gave Vanessa an opening. 'Talking of principles, we've been doing a bit of checking up and it turns out you haven't been entirely honest with us. You don't work in the city any more, do you?'

Mike looked pained. 'Ah . . . you found out. Look, don't tell Jen about this either. It's embarrassing. She still thinks I work for Kingston Reed.'

'Why don't you?'

In answer Mike pulled his inhaler from his top pocket and held it up for her to see. 'Because of this. I thought only kids or old people got asthma. Then I had a few attacks and that got me frightened. I'd been the proverbial rising star, earning good money, working hard and playing harder and suddenly this came along and made me feel . . . well, mortal, I guess. I got cautious and you can't be too cautious in my job . . . my old job, I mean. You have to take risks and I didn't want to any more. Suddenly I wasn't performing like I had been and hating it. So I got out. Tried to get other work but my heart wasn't in it. I got tired of London, and that's something I never believed I'd ever do. That's why, when I got together with Jen again, I suggested coming up here.'

'You had a break in your relationship?'

'I first met her a few years ago. There was a physical thing between us, but emotionally . . . maybe it was my fault. I was probably being a bit of a dick! Anyway it cooled. But I caught up with her again a couple of months ago and things were better. Being a Green she went for this holiday. I like the fresh air but I'm not very good at the countryside bit. Fucked up the map reading and the weather forecast, which is why we ended up here.' He looked Vanessa up and down with an approving grin. 'Not that I'm complaining . . .' his eyes suddenly shied away '. . . uhh, sorry.'

'That's all right,' Vanessa assured him. 'Look at me all you like. I'm here to be enjoyed.'

Mike laughed. 'If anybody had told me a week ago I'd be having a conversation with a naked girl in a collar in a place like this I'd have said . . . well you can guess.' He paused and frowned. 'Actually, about that. I don't know what the usual procedure is, but do you think there's any chance of me getting a job here? I'd do anything. For Christ's sake don't tell Jen I asked, but seriously . . . is there?'

Vanessa was surprised at the request. 'That's not up to me. You'd have to ask the Laird, I suppose. I wouldn't think the money would be what you were used to.'

'It's not something I ever thought I'd be saying either, but the money really doesn't matter. The air's clean and the scenery . . .' he looked around at the Cherry girls and grinned happily '. . . is perfect!'

By lunchtime Jennifer had interviewed all the girls, each one taking less time, Vanessa noticed. Vanessa knew what the girls would have told her because not so long ago she had asked the same sceptical questions. Every one would have said with absolute honesty that she was a happy, consensual, well cared-for slave. But this did not seem to have satisfied Jennifer. To be fair, Vanessa conceded, it hadn't satisfied her either.

'They all say they enjoy being slaves and have not been coerced,' Jennifer announced.

'Well, that's good, isn't it?' Vanessa said. 'You've found out they're not being held against their will.'

'Assuming for a moment that it was true and not a result of indoctrination and that all the other women here believed the same, that doesn't mean I'm satisfied,' she said.

'It sounds pretty good to me,' Mike said.

'People are making money out of these women's unusual . . . desires, obsessions, whatever you call them. Probably a lot of money. Is that right, legally or morally?' Jennifer looked deeply troubled.

Vanessa sent Amber and Charlotte off to the kitchens and they returned carrying a large picnic basket between them. The Cherry girls laid out the cloth, plates and cutlery and served the food. While Vanessa, Mike and Jennifer ate they knelt close by and Vanessa threw them titbits. Mike copied her only to stop when Jennifer glared at him.

'They're not animals!'

Desperately Vanessa tried to get some positive reaction out of Jennifer.

'Look at us here,' she said lightly, sitting back in

the grass. 'Manet would have approved. A modern *Déjeuner sur l'herbe.*'

The allusion was to the famously controversial Impressionist panting mingling nude women and clothed men in a wood, but Jennifer merely said: 'As far as I know none of his subjects were slaves.'

'I hear you're an artist,' Vanessa persisted. 'Wouldn't you like to draw any of the girls? You can't pretend they're not pretty enough.'

For a moment she saw a flicker of interest in Jennifer's eyes, then it was replaced by suspicion. 'Are you trying to trick me into something?'

Vanessa barely controlled her annoyance. The woman was bristling with distrust. Why had she taken this task so much to heart? Was there no way of getting through to her?

'No, I was just suggesting you might take advantage of being in a figure-painter's paradise, that's all. I was then going to add, humorously, that you'd have no problem with your model getting fidgety, since you could always tie her down so she couldn't move, but I suppose you'd think that was some sort of double-meaning trap as well! You know what, the girls and I could do with some fun. Let's find out if there's a court free. They've got a version of tennis here that you've got to see . . .'

Quadruples slave-girl tennis would probably never feature at Wimbledon, Vanessa conceded, though the viewing figures would have gone through the roof if it did.

It was a show game for a chain of girls to play, eight on the court and four serving as ball girls. Just watching them crouched down by the net with their bottoms up ready to retrieve a ball and the bounce of their breasts when they darted forward was a delight in itself, but that was nothing compared to the antics of the players.

They had their arms cuffed behind them. Two of the girls on each side had an oversized wire-cored foam rubber racquet with a curved handle plugged into their vaginas and two had them plugged into their rectums. Elastic cords from their collars held the racquets at an angle of about forty-five degrees. The ball, a lightweight inflatable beachball, was thrown in from the sidelines to the team whose serve it was and they tried to swat it over the net for the other team to try to return.

Cherry Chain threw themselves heart and soul into the game. Frantic shouts went up of: 'Mine!' or 'Leave it!' or 'No, mine!' and it was a joy to watch the girls dashing off after the lazily bouncing ball, their bound arms accentuating the swing of their hips and their absurd racquets wagging in front or behind them. When they did get into striking distance and braced themselves the frantic hula-swing of their hips as they batted it back sent their breasts gyrating and buttocks shivering.

Sweat soon beaded their bodies. The stimulation caused by the intimately clenched racquets also meant that the rubber-sheathed racquet handles soon became wet and the insides of the girls' thighs shiny with exudation. This did not help either their technique or racquet control, and the bizarre devices were soon flapping about even more wildly than before as the game became a cheerful shambles. There were many collisions and tumbles, but nobody on or off the court seemed to care. The watching guests cheered and applauded every frantic dash, swing and bouncing breast.

Everyone was enjoying the show . . . except Jennifer.

'Come on, Jen, you can see they're having fun,' Mike protested.

'They're being degraded and humiliated!' Jennifer said simply and turned and walked away.

Hell, this is all going wrong, Vanessa thought as she followed her. Jennifer seemed to be retreating into a shell. It was mid-afternoon and she felt she had made no progress with her. Mike looked like he was going to be no trouble, especially if the Laird offered him a job, but Vanessa could hardly take credit for that. And it would count for nothing if Jennifer blew the whistle.

She caught up with Jennifer near the car park.

'What's the matter?' she asked. 'You can see the girls are having fun?'

'Perhaps it's the audience,' Jennifer said. She pointed at the row of expensive cars lined up under sheltering awnings. 'They're just rich men's playthings. You can't pretend that's right.'

'It's human nature for some people to enjoy having power over others,' Vanessa agreed. 'But surely it's better that they do it with willing subjects than unwilling ones. Luckily the flipside is that there are people who like being dominated. Bring them together and everybody is happy. And here it's done openly and honestly and safely.'

'Even if I really believed all that, I still don't know if it's right ... not deep down! Wanting to master another person, to humiliate them and to force them to obey you and please you. Even if she was willing, what does it say about the dominator? How can anybody live with such sick desires inside them? They should fight it. But this place is like a sweet shop; it makes it too easy to give in to temptation. I think it's obscene!'

Vanessa did not know what to say. Even after talking to all the girls Jennifer was barely conceding they were here voluntarily. She must get her to accept that at least, but it would need a dramatic demonstration. So be it, then.

Leaving the girls in the charge of MacDonald, with Mike still enjoying the match and Jennifer sitting on a bench wrapped up in her bitter thoughts, she went to see the Laird.

The girls were cleaned up after the game while Mike and Jennifer had tea. When Vanessa greeted them once more she was carrying a large holdall. She gathered up the Cherry girl coffle, ball-gagged and with hands cuffed behind them, together with their uninvited guests and led them all round to the side of the castle where the Land Rover and trailer used to carry them back from the hunt the day before was waiting. MacDonald himself was at the wheel.

The Cherry girls clambered into the trailer while Mike and Jennifer sat in the back and Vanessa took the passenger seat. As they headed off along the trail through the woods and up the hillside, Vanessa turned round to Mike and Jennifer and addressed them resolutely.

'We're going up here to prove something to you, so there's no shadow of a doubt left in your mind,' she said. 'I shouldn't have to do this, not after what you've seen and heard today, but you don't leave me any choice.'

Mike looked anxious while Jennifer asked: 'What are you going to do?'

'You'll see,' Vanessa said.

As they reached the hilltop they turned onto the narrow track that ran along the inside of the summit boundary fence that enclosed the entire Glen. It was a tall structure of heavy-duty chain link capped by angled brackets facing outwards holding five strands of barbed wire. Beside the track was a carefully cultivated screen of shrubs and trees that shielded the interior of the Glen from prying eyes.

Where an arm of the woods came up to the fence they passed the tall splintered stub of a pine tree broken some height above the ground. A little way along the track lay the rest of the trunk, now sawn in half, where it had been dragged clear of the fence.

As they left it behind them Mike said with a sudden chuckle: 'That's where we came in. They've moved our bridge. Did we climb that in the dark? I must have been mad! Sorry about that but the weather was crap and this place looked so tempting. Still, it'll make a great pile of firewood for the winter.'

Vanessa smiled slightly at his good humour but Jennifer made no response.

Mike pointed: 'We camped just down there. Never imagined what we'd find in the morning, eh Jen?'

'I never wanted to climb that tree,' Jennifer said coldly.

'But you wanted to find some shelter the same as me.'

'Yes, and look where it got us,' Jennifer snapped back. 'We should have got out once we'd seen those girls being whipped as they pulled that cart.'

'Come on, who wouldn't be curious to see more?'

'But then they wouldn't have caught us,' Jennifer continued bitterly. 'We could have told the police and this whole stinking place would have been shut down by now!'

Macdonald could not contain himself any further. 'This is private land, Miss Morton. You were the trespassers. What we do on it with our girls is our business.'

'Not when it tempts people to do such evil things!' Jennifer said shrilly.

She's beginning to sound dangerously self-righteous,
Vanessa thought. *Is she religious or lapsed and stuffed
full of suppressed guilt? Maybe this is bringing it back?
Oh God I hope this works . . .*

The Land Rover pulled up in a little scrubby
hollow in the hill where the line of the fence was
broken by a heavily padlocked service gate. They all
climbed out, Vanessa carrying the holdall with her.
MacDonald unloaded the girls, then climbed back
into the cab and drove off.

For a moment Vanessa had an image of the odd
group they made. A dressed man and woman, herself
naked but for her fedora and the dozen Cherry girls
naked, cuffed and gagged, while below them lay the
castle in its wonderful valley.

'Right,' she said firmly, 'as you can see we're alone
and nobody's going to disturb us.' She focused on
Jennifer. 'You've said you still can't believe the girls
are here voluntarily. Well, now's your chance to put
that to the test.' She fished a key out of the holdall
and held it up for them to see. 'I'm going to open that
gate in a moment and I trust you'll keep to our
agreement and not try to leave yourselves. Instead
you're going to choose which of these girls goes out
there.'

She had their undivided attention once more. Even
the Cherry girls stirred uneasily. They knew nothing
about this. Vanessa hoped their honest surprise
would register with Jennifer.

'Now, if they're being held here against their will
they should be ready to take any opportunity to
escape, right?'

'You expect one of them to walk out of here
naked?'

'No.' Vanessa pulled out a parka, T-shirts, jeans
and a pair of walking boots from the bag and laid

them on the ground. 'If she follows the path along the outside of the fence she'll come to the main road soon enough, or she can cut across the hills ...' She brought out an OS map and put it on the clothes. 'She can take her choice and with a head start there's not much chance she could be caught, agreed?'

'I suppose so,' Jennifer said.

Next Vanessa held up a clear plastic wallet packed with banknotes for Jennifer to see. 'A thousand pounds in cash ... want to count it? Enough to hire a car or pay somebody to drive them to a railway station or get a room for a night and certainly enough for them to get away from here. And once she was safe she could inform the police and get this place raided and save her sister slaves, agreed?'

'All right, agreed,' Jennifer snapped. 'Get on with it!'

Vanessa laid the money on top of the other items. She went over to the gate, unlocked the heavy padlock, and swung it to and fro a few times to show it was really open. She came back to Jennifer. 'Now, you've talked to all these girls. Pick the one you think most wants to escape.'

'But they all said they liked it here,' Jennifer protested.

'Obviously that's just because they were too frightened to tell the truth,' Vanessa said, reversing their roles with relish. 'But now they're just ten steps from freedom, surely they'll make a break for it. Come on, pick one of them.'

Jennifer was looking confused and angry. 'All right ... her!' she said, pointing at Olivia Eight.

Olivia had her mane of dark frizzy hair tied back in a ponytail, matching the tight curls of her pubic triangle. Her lips were full and sensuous, her skin the colour of rich coffee, her buttocks chubby and rotund and her heavy conical breasts capped by thick dark-chocolate nipples.

'A safe, politically correct bet,' Vanessa said dryly. 'Of course, how could a black girl possibly want to be a slave?'

She freed Olivia from the coffle, uncuffed her hands and removed her gag. 'You're free to go, Olivia,' she said. 'There are clothes and money and there's the gate.'

Olivia did not move. 'I don't want to go, Mistress,' she said.

'But Miss Morton thinks you do.'

'Then she's wrong. Like I told her this morning, I like it here. I'm happy. Why should I want to spoil it?'

'Go, please, for God's sake get out of this terrible place!' Jennifer suddenly cried out, making Mike flinch.

Olivia looked at her with large liquid brown eyes but still she did not move. 'I don't want to, Mistress.'

'Maybe she needs some encouragement,' Vanessa said. She took a lash from the holdall and swished it through the air in front of Olivia. 'If you don't walk out that gate I'll use this on your rear, understand?'

'As you wish, Mistress,' Olivia said, getting down on her hands and knees and raising her bottom into the air submissively. Her glossy smooth cheeks made a perfect target, cleft by the dark valley of her bum cleavage which opened out round the pitchy ring of her anus and melted into the ripe swell of her full-lipped vulva.

The wonderful offering made Vanessa shiver with pleasure while liquid warmth began to fill her loins, but she forced her voice to remain level. 'Easy choice, pain versus freedom. Should be a no-brainer. Maybe she thinks I'm kidding . . .' She drew back her arm.

'You can't do this!' Jennifer said.

'If she wants to stay here she gets treated like a slave,' Vanessa said and swung the lash across Olivia's upraised bottom. Its many tongues hissed through the air and curled round the contours of Olivia's buttocks with a crack. Olivia jerked and gave a little grunt but held her position. Darker stripes burned on her soft skin. The heady sense of power Vanessa had last felt while dominating Julie and Kashika in the B3 cell infused her and she swung the lash again. Crack went the leather tongues again as they licked round the dusky orbs, making Olivia's bottom flesh shiver. The slave girl whimpered and her eyes sparkled with tears but still she did not move.

'Stop it, stop it!' Jennifer shouted.

'All right, what about a different girl?' Vanessa demanded. 'Pick another!'

'I can't!' Jennifer said wretchedly.

'Then we'll try all of them. Get over here! Kneel down!'

The rest of Cherry Chain hurried forward and knelt in number order beside Olivia. A dozen lovely raised bottoms all in a row; different hues and degrees of rotundity and fleshiness, each with its own distinctive sex pouch peeking from beneath it, and at that moment all utterly subservient to her will.

Vanessa walked along the line trailing her lash across the range of fleshy hillocks. 'I'll lash each one of you in turn and keep on until one of you gets up and goes to the gate. You'll save yourself pain and your sisters as well, understood?'

They nodded. Vanessa positioned herself behind Amber's pale body and swung upwards with the lash, catching the fullness of her buttocks and causing the leather thongs to cut up into her cleft. Amber yelped behind her gag but did not move. Vanessa took a step forward to Charlotte and repeated the motion.

Swish and crack, down the line she went. Even Kashika's darling bottom received its due punishment. She could not stop now. It had to be done. She hoped . . . no, she knew, they understood. This was for all of them.

And then there were a dozen rosy bottoms and a dozen smarting, glistening quims. But not a single girl had attempted to rise. They had reacted as true Shiller slaves and she was so proud of them.

Vanessa wiped her brow and turned to Jennifer, who was looking on in mute incredulity. 'Do you want to have a go? Maybe you think I'm holding back my arm. Can you beat some sense into them?' She held out the lash handle-first towards her.

Jennifer snapped out of her trance and shrank back in horror and disgust. 'All right, you've made you point! I believe you. They want to be here. But it's still evil! Just stop hurting them . . . and leave me alone!'

And she turned and ran off along the track back towards the castle.

Mike looked between Jennifer's retreating back and Vanessa and the girls, and then shrugged helplessly and ran after her, calling out: 'Jen love, it's all right . . .'

Vanessa frowned at Jennifer's dwindling figure and then looked down at the Cherry girls. 'You were all fantastic,' she assured them. 'But I might have screwed up. There's something going on in that woman's mind I don't understand . . .'

Ten

The mystery about Jennifer troubled Vanessa all that night in her cell, despite the warm company of the Cherry girls huddled close about her and Kashika sleeping in her arms.

She had kissed the lash marks she had put on their bottoms and they had kissed her in return, assured her they would do whatever she asked of them, and given her pleasure as only slave girls knew how, but still she was restless. She had forced Jennifer into accepting the girls truly wanted to be slaves. That should have left her with the problem of deciding if it was right to make money from their activities. Jennifer might fret over this but surely it was an order of magnitude less challenging than believing she was witnessing forced slavery and could be viewed with much greater emotional detachment. Instead she was becoming steadily more anxious and distressed. Why?

Jennifer was clearly an intelligent and caring woman with a strong will and social sense. Discovering what she at first thought was a nest of slave traffickers had obviously shocked her, but that must begin to pass now it had been demonstrated beyond doubt that it was consensual. She didn't have to approve of the girls' chosen lifestyle to accept it. That might give rise to displeasure but not the intense level of feeling she had displayed.

Vanessa turned the problem over in her mind long into the night. If Jennifer was trying to deny a secret craving for slavery then she might understand the turmoil in her mind and the attempt to deny what was going on around her and wish it destroyed so as to remove the temptation. She herself had gone through something like that. Yet Jennifer was not a submissive, that Vanessa was sure of. She knew the signs from her own responses.

Could Jennifer be Rochester's spy after all? Might she now be torn between unexpected sympathy for slave life in the Glen and her mission to bring it down? Had she been misled in the same way Vanessa had been? She and Mike might be working together, or had she been lying to Mike and was now fearful of telling him the truth?

Then sometime before dawn the solution came to her. Of course, that explained it all! Really, it was so obvious. And now she knew what she must do to defend the girlflesh castle.

The next morning she carefully briefed the Cherry girls, then MacDonald, Shiller and the Laird. They agreed with her reasoning but thought her plan was risky. However they had no better alternatives to suggest. The matter of their unwelcome guests had to be resolved soon.

As the Laird said: 'We've got the Highland Games due in two days. Apart from our regular guests we've got several visitors dropping in just for the event. I don't want that being raided by the police! Let's get this couple sorted out.'

When Jennifer and Mike were escorted down to the dungeon they both looked tired and from the stiff looks they exchanged Vanessa suspected they had been arguing. Well, she was sorry she might have contributed to their falling out but for the moment it suited her plans. With Cherry Chain kneeling attentively to one side she addressed the unhappy pair.

'Now, I think its true to say that you're fairly relaxed with what we're doing here, Mike, yes?'

Mike frowned and glanced at Jennifer. 'Well ... yeah, I suppose you can say that.'

Vanessa laughed lightly. 'Oh, I think we've got past supposing. I mean you wouldn't exactly turn your nose up at a job here, would you?'

For a fraction of a second Mike looked dismayed, then forced a quick chuckle. 'No ... I can't say I would.' Jennifer glared at him and he added hastily: 'But only as I'm sure the girls are volunteers and as long as no lasting harm's done to them. A bit of S and M's all right in its place, but I couldn't agree to real suffering.'

'Which is a perfectly reasonable attitude and I respect you for it,' Vanessa said sincerely. She turned to Jennifer. 'But you've still got some reservations about what goes on here, right?'

Jennifer chewed her lip, scowling at Mike as she did so. 'Yes, you could say that.'

'And you two have been arguing about these reservations?'

'I like to think we've been trying to discuss them rationally,' Mike admitted. 'When she's not running off and hiding in the woods like she did last night.'

'I just wanted to be on my own for a bit and think,' Jennifer said simply.

'I spent half an hour looking for you!' Mike retorted.

'Why not spend the morning apart so you can both sort things out in your own minds?' Vanessa suggested, soothingly. 'What about it? Mike, you can take half the Cherry girls for a walk. Talk to them yourself so that you're absolutely sure they're happy. Try out some of the facilities.' She chuckled again. 'See if you'd fit in here.'

'That sounds good,' he said quickly.

Vanessa motioned and girls Amber One through to Lisa Six stood up and came forward. They'd been linked together in a half coffle. Vanessa handed Mike their lead leash, then glanced at Jennifer's set face.

'Don't you trust him with them?' Vanessa asked. 'Of course it's understandable. The Glen's a tempting place for anybody with normal desires and urges. But we try to be honest about them. It's a place where people can be themselves. I hope you'll remember that.'

Jennifer looked at her oddly, but before she could reply, Mike said lightly: 'It's okay, Jen. One girl you might worry about but six would be too much excitement!' He tapped the inhaler protruding from his chest pocket meaningfully.

They watched him leave and then Vanessa said: 'There's something I haven't shown you yet. I thought it might be too hard to take. But now you believe the girls are here voluntarily I think you should see it. It might help you understand what it's really like between master and slave . . .'

Taking up the leash of the remaining Cherry girls, she led the way through the small heavy door and into the corridor of private dungeons. Jennifer shivered at the changed atmosphere, peering about in the flickering light of the electric torches.

'Fantastic place, isn't it?' Vanessa said cheerfully. 'This is where the clients can take their time with us one to one. There are different sizes of cells. The one at the end is a king-size deluxe for regular group orgies. You've got to see it . . .' She led the way to the last door, opened it up and turned on the lights. 'There . . .'

It was a large room with piers and buttresses dividing the walls up into shallow alcoves. Straw was scattered about the stone-flagged floor. Fresh warm air whispered through wall grilles; it was an air-conditioned dungeon. In the flickering electric torch-light loomed massive and ominous devices.

'Go on, have a good look round,' Vanessa said, giving Jennifer a gentle shove forward. In a daze the woman wandered between the implements of re-straint and torment.

The walls were hung with tethering rings and chains and racks of canes, lashes, paddles, ropes, gags and strap-on dildos. But these were just adjuncts and accessories to the mechanisms that dominated the chamber.

There was a high-back torture chair built of heavy baulks of blackened timber, fitted with numerous hinged metal cuffs. Its seat was hollow and under it were the thrusting spikes of impaling mounts. A backbreaker rack with its bow of ribbed bars and heavy cuffs and chains rose like the arch of a bridge. Assorted chains and straps dangled from ceiling hooks above it. Resting against a wall was a big flogging frame with a heavy rope net strung across it. The frame had a footboard fitted with double pairs of cuffs and a second double set hung from the top bar of the frame, so two girls could be accommodated side by side. A big timber box, hung about with ropes and rings, had a massive square timber post rising from one side. From the front of the post hung a heavy spreader bar on a winch chain. There was a 'Y' frame festooned with straps along its arms, mounted on a waist-high tilting stand. On a slightly higher stand was a short riding horse beam, its serrated ridge jutting upwards like the pitched roof of a house and stained with the juices of the girls who had ridden it. Chains and cuffs hung from the roof above. Then there was a massive table stretcher rack, with solid upright securing panels at its head and foot, pierced with holes for wrists and ankles. The panels slid along grooves in the tabletop driven by gear rods controlled by hand wheels projecting from each end of the table. A set of stocks was braced on a baseboard that also supported a set of leg spreaders. Finally in one corner stood a huge mummy case complete with a gold leaf decorated death mask. Its glittering eyes seemed to survey the room with satisfaction.

'What do you think?' Vanessa asked.

Jennifer gulped. Her eyes were flicking round the room nervously and she appeared to be sweating. 'What do you expect me to say? This place is used for inflicting pain and humiliation on helpless girls.'

'No,' Vanessa corrected her gently, 'it's used for fun and entertainment which comes from pain and humiliation being applied to willingly helpless girls in the way they like it. For instance, the Cherry girls have been missing out on dungeon practice in the last few days so I thought I'd give them a few hours in here to make up for it. No pain, just restraint. Do you want to give me a hand?'

Jennifer went pale. 'To help you strap them down . . . fit cuffs on them?'

'That's right,' Vanessa said easily. 'Unless you have a problem handling women's bodies? Are you exclusively hetero?'

'No, I've had female lovers. I think women's bodies are lovely.' She spoke those words with perfect confidence and openness, then the look of fear returned and she seemed to retreat into herself again:

'But this is . . . something else. Don't ask me to abuse them!'

'I'm not asking you to abuse them or use them sexually, just to help me restrain them,' Vanessa said patiently. 'I'm going to do it anyway so you might as well help. Besides, you haven't had much hands-on experience with the girls yet. Leading them on a leash hardly counts. You can't pass judgement on Glen Lothy if you haven't felt what it's like to handle a girl properly and fit her into restraints. OK, so it's not your thing but it would help you get an idea how the guests feel when they use them. It doesn't mean you agree with it, just that you're trying it out, you see?'

'But I don't even know what half these things do –'

'You can guess . . . unless of course it'll upset you again.'

Jennifer looked alarmed. 'Upset?'

'Like you were last night. That was one reason I wanted to talk to you alone. I've seen how seriously you're taking this decision you've got to make. You're trying so hard to be fair it's upsetting you. That is why you ran off last night, right? The responsibility of making the right choice was getting a bit too much. It's a compliment to us, really.'

Jennifer appeared to clutch gratefully at the flimsy suggestion. 'Uh, yes . . . that's right. It was stupid to get so emotional. This place is such a shock. I just want to do the right thing . . . to be fair.'

'Well, I wanted to say how much I appreciate that,' Vanessa said sincerely. 'Not many people in your situation would do the same.'

Jennifer smiled for the first time that morning. 'Thank you.'

'So in the spirit of that fairness and understanding you can help me now.'

Jennifer gaped at the patient coffle of Cherry girls with their eyes shining and nipples hard with anticipation and seemed to shrink away.

'Mike's not around to see and we won't be disturbed,' Vanessa persisted before Jennifer could say anything. 'Look, I'll bolt the door . . . there, now it's just us girls having a bit of fun.' She grinned. 'So, just for fun, and I accept you don't do this sort of thing normally, who do you think should go where? I know what their favourites are but can you guess? Look at them carefully. Which girl will most enjoy what device?'

Had her verbal manoeuvring been too obvious, Vanessa thought anxiously as she forced her expression to remain guileless and open. She had pushed the idea of it all being innocent as much as she dared, trying to make it seem as painless and casual as possible. Now she watched as Jennifer looked along the line of bound female flesh and licked her lips. *Come on, girl, let go a little . . .*

'Well,' Jennifer said slowly, pointing. 'Perhaps she could go on that table . . .'

'Call her by name: Rachel Nine goes on the stretching table. Good choice . . .'

Rachel was a tall slender brunette. Vanessa unhitched her from the coffle and led her over to the table, then sat her up on it and swung her round.

'Can you lift up the top halves of the foot stocks?' she asked Jennifer. The girl obeyed and Vanessa had to smother a grin of elation.

Rachel's wrists were uncuffed, and her arms were drawn above her head to be laid in the upper stocks, which were closed about them. Her ankles were similarly confined. Both sets of holes were lined with dense foam rubber to prevent marking the skin and also to ensure a firm grip. Now Rachel was stretched out flat along the length of the narrow table, her feet and hands protruding through the holes in the stock boards. Vanessa turned the control wheels, winding the upper set of stocks along the table and dragging Rachel's arms with them. She stopped only when Rachel moaned and her slim body was drawn out to a trembling tautness. Her ribs were showing under the tight skin of her chest and her breasts had been elongated into lozenges capped by hard pink nipples.

Vanessa reached under the table and brought out a sprung rod with a dildo on it. Jennifer goggled. 'What are you going to do with that?'

'Match her discomfort and helplessness with a bit of pleasure, of course. It's what slave girls like . . .'

She pushed the base of the rod against the foot-stock board and slid the dildo end into Rachel's tight pale slit, which swallowed it eagerly. Rachel clamped her teeth about her ball-gag and closed her eyes, wiggling her hips as far as her tensioned body allowed.

'There,' Vanessa said with satisfaction. 'Doesn't she look happy?'

'I suppose so . . .'

'And she can suck on that for hours. Perfect choice. Right, who's next?'

Jennifer looked round her. 'Well, what about, uh . . . Tina Ten on that post and box thing . . .'

Tina was small and neat with straight black hair, olive skin and almond eyes.

'The spreader post,' Vanessa said. Yes, it suits her . . .'

They uncuffed Tina and laid her on the box with her head pressed up against the side of the post. Her arms were pulled out and tied to rings at the back of the post.

208

'Tie a rope over her middle, will you?' Vanessa asked.

Hesitantly Jennifer drew a dangling rope across Tina's slim stomach and threaded it through one of the rings on the box side.

'Tie it tight,' Vanessa said. 'Don't be afraid to be firm. That's what they like. Loose cuffs and ropes look silly and they're an insult to a true slave. They want to feel properly secured.'

Jennifer gritted her teeth and pulled the rope until it dug into Tina's flesh and tied it off.

Vanessa raised Tina's legs and doubled them over until she could tie her ankles to the spreader bar hanging from the post above her. The rope across her middle resisted the upward pull on her body. This forced her small rounded pubic mound with its neat pink slit to bulge from between her smooth stretched thighs and showed off the puckered mouth of her anus.

'Now let's give her something to play with,' Vanessa said. She brought a rope up from the front side of the box, ran it through Tina's cleft and between her small apple-round breasts and tied it to her collar ring. Tina moaned and squirmed, the rope sliding though her wet slot.

'A little pain and a little pleasure, see?'

Jennifer nodded, her eyes lingering on Tina's contorted body.

'Who next?'

Jennifer chose to put Olivia on the torture chair. She sat with her thighs spread wide and her bottom and pubes hanging over the seat hole while they closed the cuffs about her ankles, wrists and neck. There was a set of broad straps that crossed over her chest, dividing her breasts and squeezing them outwards.

'Big-titted girls know their boobs are going to get extra treatment, don't they?' Vanessa said to Olivia with a smile. The helpless girl nodded mutely, wide-eyed with anticipation. There were light sprung chains and clips hanging down the sides of the chair back. Vanessa ran a couple of these over the top of the chair and clipped them to Olivia's plump nipples, stretching them upwards.

'And I suppose you're going to put one of those things up her as well?' Jennifer asked, looking at the bristling rods under the chair.

'Two of them,' Vanessa said. 'Slave girls are used to having both holes plugged at the same time . . .'

She fitted a pair of dildos from the tray under the chair to the rods and screwed them upwards until they penetrated Olivia's plump cleft and her dark anal pit. Olivia grunted as they slid inside her, clenched her buttocks and began to work her hips up and down.

Vanessa stepped back to admire her handiwork, wiping her brow. 'Phew, isn't it warm in here? And we've still got three to go.' She looked Jennifer up and down. 'You're dripping with sweat. Why don't you strip off and get comfortable.'

Jennifer looked aghast. 'What? Be naked like them? No, I couldn't.'

'No, you're definitely not one of them,' Vanessa assured her, 'not with your personality. And you haven't got a collar on. That makes all the difference. We're totally private in here and you can do what you like. You'd be a mistress who chose to work on her slaves naked for comfort. Go on, you've got a lovely body . . . enjoy the freedom of not having it wrapped up in sticky clothes. You can bet that's what almost everybody else does down here.'

'I don't know . . .'

'Keep your shoes on. The heels give you a little extra height and make you look superior, but get rid of the rest. You don't have to be shy around slaves. And I'm one as well, remember . . .'

With a deep breath and a sudden slightly naughty smile Jennifer began to strip off her clothes. In a few seconds she was naked but for her shoes. Vanessa looked at her with approval. 'There, that's better. Now, who next?'

Dark-haired, pale-skinned and Celtic, intense Madelyn Seven went on the riding horse beam, its serrated ridge polished smooth by so many thighs and vulvas before her, dividing her pubic lips and digging up into her cleft to grind against her clitoris. Her ankles were cuffed behind her to the base frame of the horse and its height was adjusted so that she had to stand on tiptoe to take any weight off her crotch. A ceiling chain hooked to the back of her collar kept her upright. Even as they stepped back Madelyn began to work her hips back and forth, happily rubbing her pubes along the wooden teeth.

Out of the corner of her eye Vanessa noted a flicker of a satisfied smile playing about Jennifer's mouth. Yes, it was working.

Strawberry blonde Victoria was strapped on her back to the 'Y' frame, with her arms above her head and her legs splayed almost painfully wide, showing off her fiery pubic bush. Jennifer got quite involved in checking the tightness of the many straps that bound her immovably in place.

'What are you going to give her for pleasure?' she asked.

Vanessa pulled out Victoria's gag and replaced it with a rubber plug from which a chain ran between Victoria's pale breasts, cutting through her red pussy, and dangled between her spread legs. On the other end hung a lead weight. Every time Victoria turned her head a few links ground across her clit.

Finally blonde and busty Yvonne was bent over the backbreaker. Cuffs held her arms over her head and ankles wide. The bow of the rungs pushed her hips and stomach up high, while her large breasts flowed up her chest to hang almost inverted, their brown nipples hard. They were not allowed to stay that way. Cuff straps linked to ceiling chains were bound about them and pulled tight, lifting the heavy globes into the air until they bulged like fleshy mushrooms. A big rubber hook with a bulbous tip was also deployed to dig deep into her vagina. Squirming and wriggling her hips rubbed its shaft against her clitoris.

Vanessa looked sideways at Jennifer as she surveyed the girls writhing in their happy bondage. She seemed to have forgotten her own nakedness as she stood with her hands on her hips. It was a good pose, Vanessa thought. There was definitely an expression of satisfaction on her face.

'Can you smell it?' Vanessa asked.

'What?'

'The scent of girl juice. Look at it dripping out of them. There are half a dozen pussies in here pumping it out. They know they've been mastered. Isn't it an incredible perfume?'

Suddenly Jennifer frowned and became self-conscious. Her eyes turned away from the girls. 'Well, this has been ... weird but interesting. I agree the girls seem to like it. But it does make them so open to abuse by the guests. Can they ever be safe? I'm not sure. I need to think ...'

She's making up excuses for herself again, Vanessa thought. Right, phase two goes ahead as planned. Sorry, Jennifer ...

Aloud she said: 'Before you go you have to look at this ...' She led Jennifer over to the magnificent mummy case. 'Now ...' she raised her arms dramatically 'Open Sesame!'

And the lid of the mummy case swung open.

Slavemaster MacDonald stepped out of the case and grabbed Jennifer by the arms even as Vanessa reached round and rammed the ball-gag she had surreptitiously picked up into Jennifer's gaping mouth. Then together they pushed Jennifer face forward against the inside of the lid, ignoring her frantic gurgling cries of fear and rage. The lid was fitted with an array of projecting foam-covered blocks, snap cuffs and quick-fastening straps designed to hold a standing figure clear of its curving shell. They secured her neck, arms and waist and then forced her feet up onto the broad inner lip of the lid, spread and cuffed them in place.

They stood back. Jennifer was straining at her bonds and wailing and grunting furiously, but she was securely fastened within the lid frame, with her nose about twenty centimetres from a small flatscreen display that was mounted on the inside of the bulge of the lid's face.

'Good luck, girl,' MacDonald said to Vanessa gruffly.

'Thank you, Slavemaster,' Vanessa replied.

He strode to the door, unbolted it and left. Vanessa went over to a rack, took down a strap-on dildo and buckled it about her hips. The rubber phallus shaft was already greased.

The girls strapped to their frames had all twisted their heads about to watch Jennifer's capture and confinement. Now they nodded and smiled at Vanessa round their gags and then lay back again. She smiled back at them. They knew what to do.

213

The mummy case was deep enough for Vanessa to climb in behind Jennifer. It was also fitted with restraining straps. Interesting combinations of slaves and masters could be played out in here, but today the principal activity was going to be outside.

Vanessa pulled the heavy lid shut and they were enclosed in darkness. The tip of Vanessa's strap-on dildo brushed across Jennifer's bottom. Jennifer wailed. Vanessa turned on a dim red glow tube above their heads.

'Sorry about this but you wouldn't jump so you had to be pushed,' she said, putting her arms about Jennifer in a friendly hug so the dildo bent upwards and slid along her buttock cleft. She laid her chin on Jennifer's shoulder and said in her ear: 'Don't waste your time struggling or trying to scream because this thing's soundproofed. We won't suffocate because it also has its own air supply. An air-conditioned mummy, eh? Only in a Glen Lothy dungeon!'

Jennifer snuffled and jerked at her straps, not appreciating the finer points of her strange prison.

'Now you are going to respond properly whether you want to or not,' Vanessa told her, cupping and squeezing Jennifer's breasts. 'You've got lovely firm tits, do you know that? Anyway, we won't get bored because we've got our own closed-circuit TV channel. Shall we see what's on?'

She switched on the screen and an image of the chamber appeared as seen through the mummy's camera eyes. They could see the girls lying in perfect repose in their straps and chains.

'Aren't they lovely? We've got sound as well and we can even pan and zoom in on them,' Vanessa said, working a tiny joystick mounted below the screen to demonstrate. An image of Madelyn's pussy lips spreading on either side of the wooden horse beam

214

filled the screen. 'See, we won't miss a single detail. Now, I reckon things will start to happen very soon, so I'm going to get you in the right mood. You've got a lovely body and I'm going to have some fun with it . . .'

She grasped Jennifer's hips and nuzzled the phallus tip against her anus. Jennifer shivered and wailed but Vanessa kept pushing. The sphincter gave under the unequal pressure and bulged as the bulbous rubber head forced it wide. The rest of the shaft slid smoothly in after it, filling Jennifer's rectum. The helpless girl groaned and screwed her tear-filled eyes up in shame.

Vanessa caressed her, sliding her hands down to cup and toy with Jennifer's pubes. They were staring to unwillingly weep a little. She could have such fun with her victim but she had to stay focused.

'Did that hurt? Now you know why we grease ourselves. You'd better get used to it and watch the screen. In about five minutes you'll see something interesting. Not nice, maybe, but interesting . . .'

In the close space and despite the air-conditioning their mingled pussy scents began to perfume the air. Vanessa continued to caress and kiss Jennifer's neck and cheeks, ignoring the angry twists and jerks of her head. Gently she pumped the phallus up and down inside her rectum. She had to keep her aroused, albeit unwillingly, but not risk bringing her off. Jennifer must be frustrated as well as angry, ready for the moment when . . .

The dungeon door opened and Mike walked in leading Kashika on a single leash. There was no sign of the other Cherry girls. Jennifer ceased to struggle and stared at the screen.

Mike peered round the room, his gaze trailing across the bound bodies of Cherry girls Seven to

Twelve. A huge grin split his face and he patted Kashika on the head as though praising a dog. 'Good girl! You said she'd be leaving them down here . . .'

He closed and bolted the door behind him, then strode around the room, leading Kashika after him. He stroked wet vulvas, tweaked hard nipples and hot bottoms. The girls watched him with mute expectant eyes, squirming happily at his touch and straining against their bonds to push their flesh into his hands.

'So you're here for a couple of hours and you've got all these toys and there's no one to play with you,' Mike said, shaking his head in wonder, 'and I can have any one of you any way I like.' His smile faded for a moment and he turned to Kashika, grasping a handful of her hair and turning her face up to his. 'You girls are like priests in confession, you never tell, right?' Kashika nodded. Mike looked round at the others. 'That goes for all of you? Jennifer never knows I was here.' They nodded. He smiled again. 'God, I like this place!'

He walked around the room again, with Kashika trailing behind him, examining the canes and lashes on the wall racks. 'You really enjoy having your arses whipped? You're genuine pain sluts?' They nodded. 'And afterwards that makes the sex better?' They nodded again.

He took down a paddle with a long semi-rigid rubber blade and flexed it experimentally. 'Now, which one of you do I have? I'd like to screw the lot of you but I don't have the time! Shit, you are all so fantastic! All right . . . you!'

Hooking Kashika's leash handle over a wall hook he went over to Victoria spread out on the 'Y' frame. He examined her body, running his hands over the twin mounts of her pale breasts with their glossy red conical summits. Then he stroked the soft insides of

216

her thighs and the taut tendons that stood out either side of her pubic mound. Lifting the chain that was cutting into her cleft he ran his fingers up her flushed slot. 'Hell, you're wet already!' He slid stiff fingers deep into her vagina. She grunted and closed her eyes. 'You are really hot!' he exclaimed, pulling his wet fingers out. 'But I want you hotter. I want you gagging for my cock!' He pulled the rubber plug and its dangling chain out of Victoria's mouth and tossed it aside. 'I want to hear you beg to be fucked!'

'Yes, Master,' Victoria said.

Mike stood back and swung the paddle. It struck the undersides of Victoria's breasts with a crack, making them leap and bounce like wild things. A red blaze blossomed across the soft pillowy curves.

Victoria yelped, her cry echoing back from the walls. 'Ahhh . . . Master . . . I want you inside me!'

Inside the mummy case Jennifer flinched as the blow fell. Through the phallus embedded in her Vanessa felt Jennifer's anus clench about the shaft that transfixed it. Vanessa began to pump into Jennifer a little harder. A moan of what might have been despair came from behind her gag, but she did not look away from the screen.

Mike laid the next stroke over Victoria's stomach, leaving a band of scarlet flesh right across her navel. 'Uhhh . . . Please screw me, Master!'

Crack! The next two blows went across her spread inner thighs. Victoria howled and sobbed and begged to be filled, her eyes now streaming with tears. The next landed on the red curls of her pubic bush, turning the soft flesh lips between them as red as the hair. 'Screw me, Master . . . ahhh . . . I want your cock up me . . . I beg you! Fuck me now!'

Mike threw the strap aside, ripped open his flies to free a straining erection, took hold of Victoria's thighs and rammed into her hard enough to make the frame shake and send a shiver through her scarlet breasts. Victoria gave a sobbing wail of relief. 'Ohhh . . . thank you Master . . . yes . . . more . . . please . . .'

Wildly Mike's hips jerked back and forth and inside the mummy Vanessa matched him thrust for thrust, feeling herself caught up in the raw spectacle of his animal need. A shaft of rubber sliding in and out of a clenching anal passage moved in synchrony with a shaft of living flesh sliding in and out of a clenching vaginal passage. Sweat formed a slippery film between Vanessa's breasts, where they were flattened against Jennifer's smooth back, and her hips and Jennifer's bottom. Continuing to stab with her hips she reached round Jennifer's pinioned body and rubbed her helplessly hard and pulsing clitoris. Juices of arousal brimmed over and ran down their thighs and dripped to the floor and their scent filled the close space. Jennifer gasped and whimpered as Vanessa ravaged her rectum, her hands clenched into fists, her strong thighs bulging as they strained at her straps, the muscles hard under the soft curves of her buttocks, her head waving, blinking the tears from her eyes but quite unable to resist or expel the shaft that was sodomising her or to look away from the tiny screen.

And then with a grunt Mike ejaculated. On the brink herself, Vanessa frigged the wet cleft in her hand one last time as she herself came, wrenching a moaning, choking, unwilling orgasm from Jennifer's body. Then she sagged against her victim, weak-kneed and gasping for breath.

When she could focus on the screen again both Mike and Kashika were gone.

She wanted to rest but there was no time. With an effort Vanessa pulled her dildo from Jennifer's anus with a slurping suck and threw open the mummy case. As the bound Cherry girls looked on intently she loosed the straps and cuffs and released her victim.

Red-faced from anger and orgasm, blinking the sweat from her wild eyes, Jennifer staggered backwards out of the lid and nearly fell. With a trembling hand she tore the ball-gag from her mouth and turned to face Vanessa, her face contorted with bafflement and incredulity. She fought for words.

'You . . . bitch! You set all this up! Why?'

Vanessa shrugged and said with contempt: 'Why not? We're sex sluts. It's what we do. You're too weak to control your boyfriend and too wrapped up in your own self-obsession to notice. I bet you two haven't had sex since you got here. Now you're surprised he took advantage of us? What did you think he was going to do in a castle full of sex slaves?'

'But why trap me, why do this . . .' She clutched at her backside. 'It hurt . . .' She wiped her fingers though her cleft, still glistening with her discharge 'and you forced me to . . . Oh shit I feel so . . . dirty!'

'Oh, stop whingeing!' Vanessa said. She slapped the phallus still sticking out from between her hips. 'I've just stuffed this up your arse and made you cum and you enjoyed it! Why? Because you're soft and you deserved it! We like dominants around us. You talk tough but you act like a wimp! If you don't like what I did then do something about it!' She gave Jennifer a shove. 'Or are you really a submissive slut underneath just like all of us?'

Jennifer slapped her on the cheek so hard her teeth rattled.

At last! Vanessa thought dizzily as she fell to the ground.

Eleven

Before Vanessa could pick herself up Jennifer had taken hold of a handful of her hair and began dragging her across the straw-covered stone flags, so she had to scramble along awkwardly on her hands and knees.

'You think I'm weak, do you!' Jennifer snarled. 'Think you can use me like a slave and humiliate me and stick that thing up my backside? I'll show you . . .'

She rammed Vanessa head-first against the ropes of the flogging rack and tore the phallus belt off her. As Vanessa tried to pull her face away from the lattice of rough hemp that was rasping against her cheek Jennifer gave her a stinging slap on the rear that left a print of her hand in her flesh, then caught hold of Vanessa's right arm, doubled it up painfully behind her back, grasped her hair again and heaved her onto her feet. Slamming her into the net again so that her breasts were squeezed though the voids between the ropes, Jennifer held her in place with the weight of her own body as she snapped a spring cuff about Vanessa's left wrist. Dragging Vanessa's twisted right arm out sideways she secured that as well. Then she pulled Vanessa's feet wide across the footboard and cuffed her ankles.

Jennifer stood back breathing heavily, looking Vanessa's spreadeagled figure up and down with eyes filled with a burning desire for revenge.

'A wimp, am I?' Jennifer said. 'You humiliated me, you slut! And I was actually worried how your paying guests treated you! Well, we'll see how you like it . . . '

Her heels clicking on the flagstones, she strode over to the equipment rack and examined the array with sadistic calculation. A long-handled paddle with an open lattice blade caught her attention. She took it down and swung it though the air where it made a loud and satisfying hiss.

'That'll do nicely. I want you to hear it coming . . .' She took up position behind Vanessa. 'You're going to say how sorry you are for what you've done. You're going to say what a treacherous slut you are and beg to lick my boots!'

'You haven't got the nerve to use that on me!' Vanessa goaded.

'Oh, haven't I?' Jennifer drew back her arm and swung with all her strength.

The blade hissed though the air and connected with Vanessa's left buttock with a sharp crack that imprinted its pattern on her skin. A ripple spread out from the point of impact through the soft flesh and the net heaved as Vanessa recoiled against it. Her breasts, poking though the net lattice, jiggled. A shrill yelp of pain burst from her lips as fire burnt her bottom and tears sprang to her eyes. For a moment she sagged against the ropes, then she twisted her head round. 'Is that the best you can do?' she taunted.

'What about this! And this! And that!'

Jennifer rained blows down on Vanessa's rear. The hiss of the blade singing through the air and the smack of abused flesh filled the chamber. Vanessa squirmed and twisted in her bonds, her bottom weaving about in a futile effort to evade the paddle. But her cheeks turned from pink to rosy scarlet as they were mercilessly belaboured and her taunts were lost in ever more feeble sobs of pain.

Suddenly Jennifer dropped the paddle. Through her mist of tears Vanessa saw Jennifer was looking at her hollow-eyed with a new need that had to be satiated. She took a fresh strap-on dildo from the rack and feverishly put it on, pressing the rubber prongs on the inside of the mounting pad against her cleft with wonder and fierce delight. Stepping up onto the footboard between Vanessa's spread legs she took hold of the ropes and rammed the rubber shaft hard into Vanessa's anus and all the way up her rectum until her lower stomach slapped against Vanessa's bottom. Now their positions on the mummy case were reversed. Reaching through the rope mesh she grasped Vanessa's bulging breasts and pinched them cruelly.

'I want to hear you beg!' she said.

She reamed out Vanessa's rectum with hard deep bruising stabs of the phallus, driving a grunt and a sob from Vanessa with each one. And all the time she was kneading and twisting Vanessa's breasts and pinching and stretching her nipples. Jennifer's tight springy breasts flattened against her shoulder blades. Vanessa felt the liquid heat filling her. The pumping phallus up her rear was building up the pressure. She was dripping on the floor. She was going to cum . . . and she was going to go . . .

'Please . . . no more . . . I'm sorry . . . I beg you . . . uhhhhh.' Vanessa gasped as a jet of pee, punctuated into fitful spurts by the thrusts of the dildo, and a spray of orgasmic discharge left her engorged vulva together.

'How dare you enjoy this,' Jennifer cried angrily, and then came herself.

For a minute Jennifer lay pressed against Vanessa's own limp strung-out body. Sweat glued their bodies together. The Cherry girls gazed at them in mute wonder. Dazedly Vanessa wondered if she had had her fill. Then Jennifer grasped her hair and twisted her head round. Jennifer's eyes were shining with an unnatural light and her pupils were dilated. She was high on the elation of her first taste of domination and her triumphal orgasm.

'Now you're going to kiss my boots.'

She pulled the dildo out of Vanessa's tender distended anal mouth. It was quite clean and glistened with grease. Leaving it strapped on Jennifer took cuffs, a riding crop and a leash from the rack, freed Vanessa's arms only to re-cuff them behind her back, clipped a leash to her collar and then freed her legs.

Jennifer swiped the crop sharply across the back of Vanessa's knees and Vanessa dropped to the ground. Jennifer pointed at her shoes. Vanessa bent down.

'I'm a treacherous slut and deserve everything I get and I beg to kiss your boots, Mistress,' she said, and did so.

Jennifer jerked her leash, lifting her head. 'Were they all in on this?' she demanded, pointing at the Cherry girls with her crop.

'Yes, Mistress.'

She looked round at them, her lips curling in a cold smile. 'You say you like pain and sex and humiliation. Well, you're going to prove just how much.' She swished the crop through the air. 'I'm going to beat you one by one until I see you cum, and then . . . and then you're going to thank me for it!'

Dragging Vanessa after her on her knees and with the dripping black dildo bobbing in front of her,

Jennifer went over to where Olivia sat impaled on the torture chair. She unclipped the chains and clips that had been suspending Olivia's nipples and fondled her heavy breasts as they ballooned from between her chests straps.

'So big-titted girls expect to get special treatment do they?' she said. 'Well I'm not going to disappoint you . . .'

She used the crop methodically, covering Olivia's globes in horizontal stripes. When she hit the dark rubbery nipples they folded inwards and then sprang back for more. As her face screwed up in pain, Olivia's hips began to work on the dildos plugged into her. They were already wet with her juices and, driven by pain, it did not take long for her to pump out a spray of juice past the rubber shaft filling her vagina.

Jennifer stayed her hand. 'You really are a proper pain slut,' she said with contempt as she pulled Olivia's gag out.

'Thank you for punishing me, Mistress,' she gasped.

Jennifer moved on to Rachel on the stretching table. Her taut body was laid out for punishment. She was already sucking at the dildo lodged inside her that was braced against the base panel closed round her ankles. Jennifer cupped Rachel's small conical upstanding breasts. 'Are these tits as sensitive as big ones?' she asked rhetorically. She sliced the crop across them, fascinated by the way they sprang back upright, even as their pink nipples changed to dark red. She was working her way across Rachel's smooth flat stomach when the girl groaned and discharged onto the dark stained tabletop. When her gag was pulled out she also thanked Jennifer even as her eyes brimmed with tears.

Madelyn riding the horse beam was almost ready to cum by the time Jennifer got to her, working her cleft back and forth along the wooden ridge, her breasts heaving and bobbing. A few swipes across her haunches were all that it took to have her rolling her eyes up and grunting through her gag while her juices dribbled down the sides of the beam.

'You really are shameless,' Jennifer observed as she pulled the girl's gag out.

'Yes, Mistress. Thank you, Mistress,' Madelyn said.

Jennifer paused as she came to Victoria spread out wide on the 'Y' frame. The chain that had cut through her cleft and teased her clitoris had not been replaced after Mike had used her so she had no means of working herself off. Mike's sperm still oozed from her gaping vaginal mouth. Vanessa wondered if Jennifer would resent her for providing her boyfriend with such intimate relief?

Curiously Jennifer felt the still hot skin of Victoria's breasts where their natural paleness was mottled red while Victoria gazed up at her fearfully. She stroked her thighs and tickled her erect clitoris until it was straining painfully, making Victoria roll her eyes and moan. Suddenly Jennifer grasped Victoria's hips and rammed the dildo brutally hard into her lovemouth. Victoria gasped and clenched at the shaft with slavish instinct. Just half a dozen thrusts were all that it took for her to climax.

'Thank you, Mistress,' she said with feeling when her gag was removed.

Tina, doubled over on the box and post with her legs in the air and her neat little pubic peach bulging was just begging for a beating or sex or both, Vanessa thought as she was dragged to her side. With every little wiggle and jerk of her hips the rope sliding though her slot grew steadily more stained and her eyes grew rounder and fuller with lust. Jennifer undid the rope and delivered three quick slashes with her crop that made the rubbery lips shiver, and then impaled her with her phallus, still shiny with Victoria's juices, making Tina's stomach bulge. So close was she to orgasm that just three lunges was all that it took for her to cum, her slim body seeming to vibrate in her bonds.

'Thank you, Mistress,' she said meekly.

And then there was just Yvonne left.

By now the air in the chamber was reeking with the scent of sex as eight highly active pussies dripped with lust. Jennifer was looking haggard and desperately aroused, dizzy with power and once again consumed by renewed need. Licking her lips, she staggered over to Yvonne's bowed body, pulled the hook from her vagina, slashed the crop across her stomach a couple of times and then threw it aside and climbed on top of her, sliding her head and shoulders through the chains that stretched Yvonne's cuffed breasts to the ceiling. Without prelude she mounted her, ramming her dildo into Yvonne's ready and very willing cleft.

With desperate urgency she rode the living arch of sweet sweaty flesh, thrusting and grinding hard and fast without any thought for the slave girl beneath her. At this moment she was supreme mistress of the chamber and only her will counted and her desire that must be satisfied at any cost. It was more than the friction of the rubber prongs on the inside of the dildo stimulating her clitoris, more than the lovely body across which her own slid with primal need. It was having that proxy synthetic presence inside Yvonne, it was having the right to use her helpless body as she chose. As she came with a little cry and a look of wonder and triumph in her eyes, Vanessa saw for the first time that Jennifer truly understood what it meant to master a slave.

Her eyes closed and Jennifer collapsed across Yvonne's body, utterly exhausted by emotional shock and the exertion of three closely spaced orgasms. Except for the slow rise and fall of her chest she was quite still.

Minutes passed. The other Cherry girls looked on in anxious silence. Vanessa was beginning to wonder if Jennifer had actually fallen asleep when she stirred.

Slowly she lifted her head, brushed aside a straggling lock of hair and looked round with disbelief at the bound girls with their paddle-marked breasts and dripping clefts, and then at Yvonne's body under her. Her face suddenly crumpled as shame filled her eyes. Clumsily she pulled herself off Yvonne and sank to the floor in a huddle, sobbing. 'Oh, God ... what have I done ...?'

Vanessa shuffled over to her and kissed her trembling shoulder and nuzzled reassuringly against her. 'It's all right. No need for tears. You've nothing to be ashamed of. This is exactly what I was hoping you'd do.'

Slowly Jennifer looked up, wiping her eyes. 'What?'

Vanessa smiled. 'I realised what you were early this morning. It took me that long to work out why you nearly freaked when I offered you the lash last night. Then all your actions made sense, especially the way you kept talking about "evil" and "temptation". All the time you were struggling with your own secret desires, not as a submissive but as a natural strong *dominant*. The trouble is, being in denial about that meant you might have forced the Glen out of business, not because it was wrong but to remove the temptation you personally felt. I couldn't let you do that. I'd do anything to defend this place.'

Jennifer blinked. 'This was all a set-up to bring me out of the closet?'

Vanessa smiled. 'That's one way of putting it. But I also had a deadline so there was no time for subtleties. You had to be pushed. Sorry for being so brutal but you needed a kick up the backside to let go. I had to tease you out, get you used to handling the girls, breaking down your inhibitions so that when we manoeuvred Mike down here you'd get angry enough to want to take a proper revenge. Don't be too hard on him. He can be led by the genitals like most men, especially with half a dozen slave girl pussies dangled before him.'

Slowly Jennifer said: 'Mike is Mike. But how do I live with what I am?'

'The same way we live with what we are: joyfully! There are unhappy submissives in this world and unhappy dominants who can't accept their needs and are too decent to force them onto anybody, but haven't met a willing partner and are too inhibited to join the BDSM scene and seek them out. That was you, I think. Am I about right?'

Jennifer pinched her lips and nodded. 'Something like that. I couldn't believe these urges I had were right. I tried to bury them.'

Vanessa kissed her cheek. 'You were a prisoner of guilt. Well, you've no need to hide any more and certainly not from us. We need people like you to appreciate what we have to offer. Be strong so we can go weak at the knees serving you.'

'But I hurt you.' She looked round 'All of you. I'm sorry.'

'Don't be. I planned it. You don't have to apologise any more.'

'You knew I'd take my revenge like this. You knew you'd suffer.'

'It was in a good cause: to bring in a new Mistress and to save the Glen. Anyway, it only really hurts if it isn't done with respect for what we are. This is no place for brutes. But you're not one of them because you do care. Glen Lothy is where submissives and dominants can be themselves safely and happily. Welcome home . . . Mistress.'

It was an hour later in the Laird's study.

Jennifer sat before the Laird's desk. Shiller's face showed on the screen turned towards her. Vanessa, relieved to be free of her extra-slavish responsibilities once more, knelt by her chair, a position she felt was much more natural.

There was still a post-orgasmic flush lingering on Jennifer's cheeks and she looked acutely self-conscious, but her words were firm and clear. 'I won't reveal anything about the Glen,' she said. 'I can't be such a hypocrite as to condemn people for indulging in activities that I've just found out I enjoy as well.'

'I'm very glad to hear that, Ms Morton,' Shiller said. 'And of course you must consider yourself our guest for the rest of your holiday.'

'Aye, you and Mr Kendal will be welcome,' the Laird confirmed. 'You must attend the games at least.'

Jennifer smiled. 'Thank you, I accept, but I can't answer for Mike. I think we may be going our separate ways.'

'I'm sorry,' Shiller said. 'I hope we have not been responsible for any antagonism between you.'

Jennifer shrugged. 'It probably would have happened anyway. I've changed . . . but I think deep down he hasn't.'

'Well, you'll certainly be seeing more of him for the next few days,' the Laird said. 'He asked if he can work here. I've said he can make himself useful helping prepare for the games while I consider his request.'

Jennifer gave a rueful chuckle. 'Now why doesn't that surprise me? Oh, well I hope he's happy. And once again, I'm sorry for the trouble I caused you.'

Shiller's eyes briefly flicked down to Vanessa. 'I think our security needs these occasional tests to remain alert. And it also does our principles good if they are held up to the light for close examination once in a while.'

Vanessa smiled.

'I accept that you're trying to be ethical and have certain standards and that the girls are here of their own free will,' Jennifer said, 'but I do worry that they are vulnerable to real abuse by your guests. I couldn't have that on my conscience.'

Shiller looked thoughtful. 'Then perhaps we can also offer you a job, Ms Morton. You could become an independent inspector of our facilities to ensure our girls are being well treated.'

Jennifer blinked. 'Are you serious?'

'Perfectly. Don't make any decision now. I'll be attending the games and we can talk more then.'

'Well then, I'll think about your offer. And thank you.'

'My pleasure.' Shiller looked at Vanessa. 'And once again well done, Vanessa. You resolved our problem with a whole day to spare.'

Kneeling on the bed, hands bound behind their backs, Vanessa kissed Kashika passionately, their breasts mashing together.

Ropes ran over pulleys hanging from the bed canopy, connecting the backs of their collars to large anal hooks embedded in their rectums, so that as their heads lowered their bottoms had to rise. They pulled and twisted on these like unruly puppets as they kissed, their mouths working down each other's bodies, finding hard nipples and hungrily sucking and nipping at them. Motors whirred and they were dragged back up the bed to lie across Jennifer as she sprawled naked on her back. Their mouths immediately fastened onto Jennifer's nipples, one to each teat. She shuddered and closed her eyes as they worked on her.

Kashika moved downwards across Jennifer's belly to the hot moist well of her sex, half-suspended from her pulley, dipping her head and lifting her bottom. Meanwhile Vanessa had moved to one side and taken over both Jennifer's breasts and was sucking and nibbling her nipples with greater vigour. Kashika twisted about, straddling Jennifer and presenting her mistress with an intimate view of her own dark-lipped sex pouch and her hook-pierced bottom, as she buried her head between her thighs. Jennifer gasped as Vanessa nipped harder on her breasts even as Kashika's tongue probed Jennifer's slot and curled about her straining clitoris.

Jennifer pressed a button on the control box she held. Current flowed down wires threaded through the ropes leading to their anal hooks. They yelped and their buttocks clenched tight as they were shocked, driving them on to greater efforts. In a minute Jennifer gasped and bucked her hips, wetting Kashika's face with her discharge and then collapsed, leaving her two slaves dangling over her.

After a minute Jennifer let some slack into the ropes and pulled both girls round to lie on either side of her in her arms and looked at their flushed faces.

'Well . . . you two really are fantastic together. I didn't think I could cum again today, but . . . wow!'

'Thank you, Mistress,' they both said.

'If anybody had told me this morning I'd be doing this right now I wouldn't have believed them,' Jennifer said, then smiled wanly. 'How Mike would love to watch!'

The three of them were alone in the room. At Jennifer's request Mike had moved to another bedroom. She had not told him what she had seen from the mummy case, just that she wanted to be alone and that she didn't mind if he made use of the castle girls. He'd been hurt at being rejected but clearly appreciated the compensation.

'I feel responsible for your break-up with Master Mike, Mistress,' Vanessa said sorrowfully.

'And I'm sorry I led him to the dungeon, Mistress,' Kashika added.

'Only because I ordered her to, Mistress,' Vanessa said quickly.

Jennifer thumbed the button on the handset and they yelped as the anal hooks delivered warning jolts.

'Stop it, both of you! There's nothing to apologise for. You've made me accept what I am and I'm more grateful than you can imagine. As for Mike it would have happened soon enough. I think I was outgrowing him. When he got back in touch with me I thought he had changed for the better. He had a bit, but not enough.' She chuckled softly and hugged them both. 'Though I suppose I'll always be grateful for him getting me in here. In fact, at first he handled this better than I did.'

'You had your own problems, Mistress,' Vanessa reminded her.

'I know. And I suppose they weren't helped by you people treating us like spies. Who are these enemies you have that you're so frightened of anyway? You never said.'

'I must leave that to the Director to explain if she thinks it best, Mistress,' Vanessa said. 'Let's say it's somebody rich and powerful who runs a rival slave business not as caring as this one. They'd love to get their hands on incriminating photos of our guests, or better yet our Director, together with slave girls, to use as blackmail and take over the Glen. They've tried once before to smuggle micro-cameras into one of our buildings.'

'So that was why those searches were so bloody intimate?'

'Yes, Mistress. I'm afraid it was making us paranoid. I'm glad you and Master Mike turned out not to be spies.'

Jennifer looked thoughtful. 'Still, we could always pretend you and Kashika were spies.'

'Mistress?'

'Tomorrow shall we play "Interrogations" down in the dungeons?'

'That sounds like a great game, Mistress,' said Vanessa happily.

Twelve

The day of Glen Lothy's unique Highland Games dawned bright and clear.

Vanessa had been up early. While Cherry Chain were putting in some last-minute practice, Vanessa, with her reporter's hat on and camera in hand, was recording the background preparations before the guests started to arrive and she would have to put her camera away. With the shots she'd got yesterday of the girls in practice and formal pictures of the winners she could take after the event, she'd have enough images for her article.

The Games were held in a large clearing amongst the trees on a shelf of land a little way up the hillside above the castle. Pavilion tents had been erected around the perimeter the day before and track and field event lanes and markers had been laid out on the grass. Now chairs were being set out and catering arrangements made. Carts laden with the necessities were being hauled up from the castle by teams of slave girls.

Vanessa saw Mike hurrying between the castle and the field, fetching and carrying with enthusiasm. He was now dressed in his shirt with a borrowed kilt and long Highland socks and was clearly trying hard to impress the Laird. He and Jennifer appeared to have come to a cordial understanding over the parting of the ways. At the moment she was enjoying a ride on a ponygirl trap, but she would be back in good time for the Games.

Vanessa liked roaming about naked in such a beautiful setting taking pictures. The staff all knew her by now, were flattered to answer her questions and pose for photographs while they worked, but otherwise generally left her to go where she pleased while she had her hat on and was in full journalistic mode. It was a freedom few other people would ever know and an undeniable perk of being a slave reporter.

She wandered down through the trees to the service yard at the back of the state offices. A Land Rover came down the hill track and turned into the service yard towing on the end of a chain behind it half of the tree that had blown down over the fence. It parked by an open shed where a couple of sawhorses had been set up. Mister Stewart climbed out of the passenger door.

Vanessa took a few snaps and then asked: 'Please, Mister Stewart, what are you doing?'

'The old log for the hauling contest has split, girl, so we thought we'd put this to good use.'

Vanessa snapped the tree. She should have taken a picture of it earlier for her UNEXPECTED GUESTS article, but she'd had other more pressing concerns at the time. This would have to do.

Then she paused and looked closer at the trunk.

'Stand clear, girl,' said Stewart, 'we want to trim it down.'

'Please, Master, wait a minute. What's that?'

Stewart peered closer, reached between the branches and rubbed at the trunk. 'That's just a scrape in the bark with some earth in.'

'But how did it get there? It didn't come from the chain you used. That's nowhere near it.'

'Must be a gash from the fence then.'

'It looks too broad . . . Please, Mister Stewart, have you got some water? It's important.'

Looking at her very oddly he took a water bottle out of the car and handed it to her. She poured some on the truck and rubbed. A pale gash appeared running halfway round the trunk.

'This is quite a smooth mark, very even and fresh,' Vanessa said. 'Something scraped across it. But why was it covered with earth?'

'It must have come off the ground when it came down,' said Stewart.

'But with the branches in the way how could that part of the trunk touch the ground?' She took a close-up photograph. 'Somebody must have rubbed earth into it to disguise the gash.'

'Don't be silly, girl, who'd want to do that? It's probably a splash. It was wet at the time.'

'So why wasn't it washed away . . .' Suddenly she shivered. 'Oh . . . of course!' It felt like pieces of a puzzle falling into place in her brain. It was so obvious! But she had to be absolutely sure. 'Please, Mister Stewart, can you get the key to the gate nearest to where the tree fell and drive me up there? This is very important.'

'I've got plenty to do down here, girl, instead of worrying about a bit of mud.'

Vanessa took a deep breath and touched her white collar. 'If you don't help me now, Mister Stewart, I'll tell the Laird and the Director. If I'm wrong you can beat me for it but please do this for me!'

Grumbling, Stewart went into the office and fetched the key while his companion unhitched the tree, and then, with Vanessa in the passenger seat, they roared off up the hill.

He opened the gate and drove them through and out along the outside of the fence until they got close to the place where the tree had come down. She saw the broken stump with its splintered top through the fence and said: 'Stop here, please, Mister Stewart.'

Vanessa sprang out and began searching the ground while Stewart looked on with a disgruntled frown. She didn't even consider that she was naked but for her hat and beyond the Glen's protective fence, or that there was a chance a walker might come along. Even if it had she would not have cared. This was too important.

She found the tracks and a scattering of sawdust where the Glen vehicle had gone out to salvage the tree three days earlier and then moved further away from the fence across the tussock grass. There had to be some sign. She kicked at a raised sod of turf. It came loose. She looked around. Yes, there was the other one. A thrill coursed through her as she took a picture of her find. She'd been right.

'Come and look at this, please, Mister Stewart,' she called out.

She showed him what she'd found and explained her reasoning and his scepticism vanished.

'I'll inform the Laird,' he said grimly.

'And find Jennifer Morton,' Vanessa said. 'I have to ask her a question.'

An hour later Mike Kendal knocked on the door of the Laird's study and entered when he was bidden. 'You wanted to see me, Laird . . . oh.'

Besides the Laird the study contained MacDonald, Stewart, Jennifer, who was looking confused, and Vanessa.

'If you're busy, I can come back . . .'

'No, Mister Kendal,' the Laird said gravely. 'This won't take long. I just want you to hand over your camera.'

Mike blinked and looked confused. 'But I haven't got my camera. Your security people kept it and our phones. They said we could have them back when we left.'

'I don't mean that camera, I mean the one concealed in your so-called asthma inhaler,' said the Laird, pointing to where, as usual, the mouthpiece of the inhaler protruded from the breast pocket of Mike's shirt.

Jennifer cut in. 'Look, I don't understand this. Your security people examined Mike's inhaler. They took it to pieces. I saw them. It was perfectly ordinary.'

'It was,' Vanessa said, 'but that's not the one he's carrying now. That one has a micro-camera concealed inside it that he was going to use to take photographs of our guests together with slave girls, so they could be used for blackmail!'

Mike scowled. 'This is getting ridiculous! I cooperated before, I put up with a very humiliating body search and they found nothing. If this is what working here means then I don't want the job . . .'

He made to leave but MacDonald and Stewart blocked his way. Mike turned back to the Laird, his fists clenched. 'You can't keep me here like this!'

'We'll keep you here until Vanessa has finished her explanation,' the Laird said coldly. 'Or you surrender that inhaler.'

'It's just an inhaler and I'm not handing it over to anybody. I need it. It's the only one I've got!'

'Then you'd better listen, Mister Kendal. Continue, Vanessa.'

'Yes, you were very cooperative,' Vanessa said to Mike. 'Unusually so. But I was working so hard trying to win Jennifer round I didn't think about it. She was the obvious threat to the Glen and such a good diversion. Strong-willed, outspoken, socially aware . . . is that why you picked her?' Jennifer drew in her breath sharply. Vanessa continued: 'You knew what her reaction would be when you got caught. Oh yes, you planned to get caught all along. You had to get up close to the guests to use your hidden camera and what better way than to have it accepted as an obvious but innocent object? You agreed so quickly to that search. And you were so happy when you got it over with.'

'That's only natural,' Mike snapped. 'And remember all my gear was searched as well. This is the only inhaler I've got and its been checked!'

'I asked Jennifer a question a little while ago,' Vanessa said. 'On the night you climbed over the tree into the top wood and pitched camp, did you afterwards leave the tent for any time? She said you were gone for some time, despite the weather.'

Mike gave a mocking laugh. 'Well, what do you think I was doing? I was having a crap, of course!'

'I think you were arranging a good safe hiding place for that inhaler. One you could find again easily when you needed to swap it over for the genuine one after that had been passed by the security team! All the time you were practically pushing that inhaler in our faces until we'd all got used to seeing it hanging out of your pocket, which is a great place to carry a camera. Then you swapped them over the second night you were here when we were up by the hill gate and you went off after Jennifer.'

Mike looked disbelieving. 'You mean I carry round a micro camera on the off-chance of being able to get inside secret estates full of millionaires playing with slave girls so I can practise a little blackmail! That's mad!'

'No, because none of this was chance! This was all planned months ago. You were just waiting for the right weather. That tree didn't blow down by itself. It was pulled down just before you got there by people in an off-road vehicle with a winch, who work for the same man you do. I found their disguised tracks up on the hillside. They must have used a pole to reach over the fence and get a sling round the tree. But they scraped the trunk when they pulled it down. After you'd gone over, dragging Jennifer with you to play her part as a decoy, they rubbed some earth into the mark to conceal it because the tree had to stay there it make it all look natural. It took a lot of work and planning but then we are dealing with a ruthless man playing for big stakes. This was ready to go if another scheme went pear-shaped . . .' she grimaced, 'which I happen to know it did. By the way, how much is Harvey Rochester paying you?'

Mike snarled and lunged at her, but MacDonald and Stewart caught his arms and twisted them up behind his back. Vanessa snatched the inhaler out of his pocket, put it down on the Laird's desk, picked up a carved granite paperweight and smashed it down on the device.

Shards of plastic and lens glass and a tiny spool of photographic film spilled out across the desk.

The Laird poked at the debris. 'A plastic microfilm camera that wouldn't register on a normal detector. You were taking no chances, Mister Kendal, but you've still lost. And don't think of attempting some petty act of sabotage. Rochester wants the Glen intact, not ruined by scandal. It's all or nothing, and you have nothing. Now throw him back to his master!'

But before MacDonald and Stewart could hustle Mike to the door, Jennifer, now pale-faced, said in numbed voice: 'You're working for Sir Harvey Rochester?' She looked at Vanessa. 'He's your rival?'

Vanessa nodded.

'I went to him after I'd lost my job,' Mike grated. 'I'd couriered some stuff over to him once before and I bluffed my way in. I told him I'd do anything for him, anything! And he said he did have a special job in mind –'

'For somebody bright, enthusiastic and go-getting, I suppose,' Vanessa interjected contemptuously.

'No!' Mike said scathingly. 'For somebody who had the courage to do what was necessary and see a job through!'

Jennifer was shaking her head in disbelief. 'How could you use me like this!'

'But I did it for us!' Mike said with passion. 'We can still make it work, Jen. They can't hold us against our will. People know we're here. Even without the photos we can both be witnesses to what we've seen. That might be enough to give Rochester a lever! He'll pay a packet to get his hands on this operation!'

Jennifer took a deep breath. 'You think I'd do that? At least these people are honest about what they do! They don't cheat and blackmail for money or to extort a business takeover! I don't know if you love me now or ever really loved me. I don't care any more! If you make any accusations anywhere about this place I'll deny them!' She suddenly seemed to slump in her chair and closed her eyes. 'Now please just take him away . . .'

MacDonald and Stewart dragged Mike out and the door closed behind them.

Vanessa knelt by Jennifer's chair and took her hand. 'I'm so sorry, Mistress.'

'So am I, Ms Morton,' said the Laird. 'But in this life we must look forward, not back. This afternoon we have a gathering planned. Would you do me the honour of allowing me to escort you to the Glen Lothy Highland Games?'

Jennifer took a deep breath and wiped her eyes. 'I would be delighted,' she said.

'Do you have a girlpet to take with you? It is traditional.'

'No.'

The Laird smiled down at Vanessa. 'Then one will be provided . . .'

Shiller arrived before just before lunch and had a conference with the Laird, who brought her up to date with the latest developments regarding their uninvited guests. In her turn Vanessa was brought into the office and knelt before her.

'Well done, Vanessa,' Shiller said. 'You have done both Glen Lothy and the company a great service.'

Vanessa swelled with pride. 'Thank you, Director, but it was just luck. It turned out I hadn't solved our problem in two days after all. It was too good to be true. I should have known better.'

'Well, you solved half the problem, and you were quick enough to see the truth when luck came along and that's what mattered,' Shiller said with a smile. 'And you didn't even have to reveal that we had video recordings of Ms Morton and Mr Kendal dominating the Cherry Chain girls and yourself in the dungeon, which could have been used to encourage them to remain silent if necessary.'

'No, Director. I know it was my back-up plan, but I'm not proud of it and I'd rather Mistress Jennifer didn't find out. I told her I would do anything to protect the Glen, but she's been hurt by one person's blackmail scheme and I don't want her to think badly of me.'

'There should be no need for that. You won her over by fairer means.'

'Do you think Rochester will try again, Director?'

'I'm afraid so. But that's a problem for another day. Let us enjoy the Games.'

Guests ringed the event field by the time the Laird appeared, attired once more in full Highland regalia and with his striking pair of red-haired slave-bitches straining eagerly at their leashes ahead of him. On one side of him walked Shiller with, Vanessa had been delighted to discover, Sandra as her pet.

They had exchanged brief welcoming nuzzles and kisses earlier. Sandra had said: 'You save us from Rochester again! I knew you were something special the first day I met you!'

Vanessa had been too moved to reply.

On the other side of the Laird was Jennifer, smiling nervously and holding Vanessa on a leash: her pet for the afternoon and, if she wished, the night.

Vanessa shuffled along on all fours like the other girls, with black rubber socks, mittens and kneepads. She glanced up adoringly at Jennifer, who looked very attractive in a borrowed kilt and tartan sash. The lines of her Mistress's kilt were even more appealing because Vanessa knew there was nothing underneath it. Like a good inquisitive dog she had checked earlier, which had earned her an affectionate smack on the rear.

They assembled in front of their seats set on a low podium and the Laird stepped forward, taking up a microphone. 'I welcome one and all to the second Glen Lothy all-girl Highland Games,' he said. 'I know we shall have a fine afternoon of sport to entertain you. Four chains are competing today: Jade, Cherry, Violet and Azure. I hope you will give them all your support. There will be both team and individual events, all points won to count towards the final team score. Now let us welcome the competitors!'

Vanessa crouched by Jennifer's chair and laid her head against her knee where she could be stroked and petted. For now she should forget being a reporter or an amateur detective and enjoy herself like any other slave girl. That was the most important thing. That was what being a Shiller girl was all about.

The four competing chains were marched onto the field and paraded round the track to the applause and cheers of the onlookers.

They were cuffed and chained in their customary three-by-four grid. Their chain numbers had been painted in their collar colours on their backs, chests and thighs, with matching coloured ribbons in their hair. As they jogged round the track beaming with excitement their breasts jiggled prettily. Vanessa caught sight of Kashika and felt a thrill of pride and happiness.

The first event was the slave girl version of 'Putting the Stone'. The stone in question was a sphere of granite the size of a lawn bowling ball. It hung on the end of a short length of chain with a perfectly smooth polished wooden dildo on the other end. In fact it was not so much putting as carrying, and since their arms were cuffed behind them their options were limited.

The Azure team were lined up by the edge of the track first, with their number one girl standing on the starting line with her legs spread. MacDonald slid the dildo up into her vagina as far as it would go, leaving the stone dangling between her legs at about ankle height. She gripped the wooden rod tightly with her internal muscles and set off along the track, with the rest of her team following her on the inside.

Of course there was no way she could support the weight of the stone by gripping such a smooth object inside her for very long, and the dildo immediately began to slide out of her. Despite clenched thighs and a last desperate duck-waddle it popped out before she had gone ten metres, dropping the stone to the grass. She was taken off the track and the next girl stood over the fallen stone. The dildo was inserted into her and she set off in turn.

Some girls moved slowly so as not to set the stone swinging and trying to maintain their grip, while others made frantic waddling dashes to make as much ground as possible even as the rod-like dildo was sliding out of them. Their faces screwed up with effort and their bottoms wobbled as they made their ungainly way round the track. Of course their natural reaction to vaginal stimulation did not help them keep a grip on the dildos and their thighs were soon wet with their juices.

When all twelve girls had taken their turn, a coloured peg was put in beside the track to mark how far they had gone. Then the next chain was brought on to have their go. In the end Violet team won with Cherry coming third, and the crowd enthusiastically applauded their efforts. The first points went up on the scoreboard.

The next event was the Tug of War, once again adapted to suit the nature of the competitors.

Two chains straddled the long heavy rope as it lay on the ground and faced away from each other. On either side of the plain middle section of the rope were affixed a dozen strings of transparent plastic balls, about the size of golf balls, with a wire core running though them. Each string was set about half a metre apart and there were six close-spaced balls on each string.

As the girls stood with legs apart the rope was lifted up and the strings of balls pushed up into their greased rectums until all had been swallowed. Now both teams carried the rope between their thighs, suspended from the plastic-coated wire ropes hanging out of their bulging anuses.

On command they leaned forward and took the strain, legs clenched about the rope to try to hold the balls inside them. At the command to heave they dug their toes into the ground and leaned further forward, trying to pull their opponents backwards over the line. Grunting and sweating and red-faced they strained, thighs bulging and buttocks clenched. Of course their anal rings could not resist much pressure. One by one balls began popping out of bottom holes as they lost their grip. Girls jerked forward a little further along their strings of rectal beads as they emerged from their hot tight confinement.

When a girl reached the end of her string and the last bead popped out of her rear she usually stumbled against the girl ahead of her, who then lost her grip as well. This precipitated a sudden collapse and you could hear the soft ripping pop of beads being torn from a dozen sweaty bottom holes as the rope was wrenched from their grasp and snaked away between their legs, leaving a few rope burns on their thighs.

Each team hauled against the others and then the two with the most wins had a deciding contest. This time Cherry Chain came second, losing out to Azure in the final pull.

The Caber Tossing was an individual event, which gave them time to rest after the exertion of the Tug of War. The object of tossing the caber was of course to see who could flip something about half the size of a telegraph pole end over end, and was normally played by large strong men and not slender naked slave girls. Naturally a uniquely Glen Lothy solution had been found.

The 'cabers' had been scaled down and made from wooden rods with a thick sheathing of painted foam rubber. For this event their wrists were cuffed before them so they could cup the ends of the cabers and balance them against their shoulders. But so as not to make it too easy their wrist cuffs were hooked to short bungee cords that ran between their legs and hooked onto anal plugs. As each girl ran forward and tried to toss the caber she had to stretch the cord to its limits, cutting painfully deep into her cleft.

Vanessa was proud to see Kashika manage a perfect toss of the caber, even if she did double up immediately afterwards with a yelp of pain clutching at her rope-burnt vulva. Cherry Chain came second once again.

The Log Haul was a timed team event. The log, freshly trimmed from that fateful tree Mike and Jennifer had used as a bridge to scale the fence, had to be pulled the length of the field by each team in turn. A dozen ropes spread out from a heavy ring screwed into one end of the log. The end of each rope divided into two short leather straps that linked in turn to broad buckled cuffs with studded inner faces. The straps went over the girls' shoulders and the cuffs went round their breasts, drawn tight until they ballooned out from their collars. The studs bit into their tender flesh, preventing the cuffs slipping off and in the process making them wince and bringing tears to their eyes. But they were Shiller girls and they accepted the discomfort as part of the challenge.

One by one the chains dragged the log across the field. They gasped and sobbed with effort, tears in their eyes, purple breasts bulging, stretched upwards by the tension of the cuffs and straps cutting into their shoulders. It was a test of their determination and endurance, all over in less than a minute. As she watched, Vanessa could feel their suffering but also knew the pain was something they bore happily and proudly.

To her delight Cherry Chain won by two seconds. By her side Jennifer ruffled her hair and cheered loudly.

The Hammer Throw by contrast was almost a comic event, as intended. The girls stood before a fan-shaped wedge marked out on the grass, crossed by arcs spaced a metre apart, and had to throw a long-handled foam-rubber hammer with a weighted head as far as they could. The sum totals of the distances thrown would determine the winning team. Naturally they were not allowed the use of their hands.

The crowd roared with laughter as the girls, with the hammers jutting out of their vaginas, attempted to spin round three times and then release the hammer in the right direction. Only chain girls with highly trained inner muscles had the slightest chance of managing such a feat of delicate coordination. Even then they fell over, tangled the hammer up with their legs or flipped it wildly to one side or the other of the target area. Just a few hammers, flung with a grunt of effort and twist of hips and toss of breasts, trailing droplets of girlish juices behind them, flew in the right direction.

This time sheer vaginal experience counted and Cherry Chain came third.

The last event was the Sword Relay. This was a twelve-lap race round the track for all four teams in which they had to pass on the Glen Lothy version of a batten. This was a short double-bladed foam-rubber sword crossed by a handle bar. Naturally they did not hold it in their hands, which were of course cuffed behind them.

The first four girls of each chain lined up at the starting line. Jutting from their vaginas were the blades of their individually coloured swords. The gun cracked and they dashed off, hips rolling and breasts heaving, pounding their way round the track to the cheers of the crowd.

As they came back round to the starting line the second girls in each chain were waiting doubled over with legs spread and braced wide, presenting the flushed and gaping gashes of their vulvas as targets. Their teammates pounded up, panting and gasping, rammed their hips into the waiting haunches and thrust with their sword battens, stabbing the blades deep into their slave sisters' clefts. The new girls clenched the blades inside them, stood straight and dashed off, the blades that had been inside their sisters now jutting out ahead of them, glistening wetly.

Round and round they went. After four laps Cherry was in third place but Kashika darted round nimble-footed, overtook the Jade Chain girl and made a perfect transfer to Lisa's waiting sexmouth. But they were still trailing behind the Azure Chain until their number ten made a clumsy transfer, bumping her sister off balance and wasting precious seconds stabbing away desperately trying to find her slot. On the last lap it was Yvonne, with her full breasts bouncing and heaving, holding off the challenge of the Azure number twelve. By a hard red nipple she breasted the winning tape first.

All eyes turned to the scoreboard to see the accumulated points. A cheer went up. Cherry Chain had won the games by a single point! In her delight Vanessa kissed Jennifer's knees then inner thighs and would have gone further but her smiling mistress pulled her firmly back by her leash.

A red-cheeked and exultant Cherry Chain, hastily towelled down, assembled in front of the Laird's podium. The Laird congratulated them all as he pinned winners' rosettes to their breasts, and they gave happy whimpers in return.

Vanessa expected the Laird to close the Games. Instead MacDonald and Mister Stewart carried a trestle hung with straps out in front of the podium and set it down.

'I have one final award to make,' the Laird announced. 'Bring forward Vanessa Nineteen White!'

MacDonald and Stewart strode up to a dazed Vanessa, took her by an arm each and led her over to the trestle. They laid her backwards along its padded top and strapped her down, with her legs bent back and splayed wide facing the podium. Her stomach fluttered as she felt a brief but delightful frisson of acute embarrassment. Fifty people could look right up her exposed groin. But she was a Shiller girl. This was what she lived for and she held herself proudly.

The Laird was standing over her smiling. He had a shining metal device about the size of a staple gun in his hand. 'For her efforts to ensure the continued safety and security of Glen Lothy and the company, by the order of our esteemed Director, and with my hearty endorsement, I award Vanessa Nineteen White a second gold ring.'

And he held up a tiny golden circlet, the twin of the one in her left labia minora. Vanessa gaped at it in wonder.

He bent between her legs. There was a moment of exquisite pain, and then the feel of cold metal slipping through her delicate right petal of flesh and closing tight. Dimly she was aware that the crowd was applauding as her heart thudded with pride. Now she was a two-ring girl.

Then the Cherry girls crowded round her, kissing her lips and breasts and newly pierced labia. Suddenly Kashika was straddling her, her soft warm loving pussy pressing into her own, their juices flowing together. Kashika's breasts were mashing against hers even as their lips met and melted together. And Vanessa kissed her back with equal passion even as her eyes filled with tears of joy. Life did not get any better than on this magical afternoon in the valley of the Girlflesh Castle.

nexus

The leading publisher of fetish and adult fiction

TELL US WHAT YOU THINK!

Readers' ideas and opinions matter to us so please take a few minutes to fill in the questionnaire below.

1. Sex: Are you male ☐ female ☐ a couple ☐?

2. Age: Under 21 ☐ 21–30 ☐ 31–40 ☐ 41–50 ☐ 51–60 ☐ over 60 ☐

3. Where do you buy your Nexus books from?
☐ A chain book shop. If so, which one(s)?
_____

☐ An independent book shop. If so, which one(s)?
_____

☐ A used book shop/charity shop
☐ Online book store. If so, which one(s)?
_____

4. How did you find out about Nexus books?
☐ Browsing in a book shop
☐ A review in a magazine
☐ Online
☐ Recommendation
☐ Other _____

5. In terms of settings, which do you prefer? (Tick as many as you like.)
☐ Down to earth and as realistic as possible
☐ Historical settings. If so, which period do you prefer?
_____

☐ Fantasy settings – barbarian worlds
☐ Completely escapist/surreal fantasy

- ☐ Institutional or secret academy
- ☐ Futuristic/sci fi
- ☐ Escapist but still believable
- ☐ Any settings you dislike?

_____

- ☐ Where would you like to see an adult novel set?

_____

6. In terms of storylines, would you prefer:

- ☐ Simple stories that concentrate on adult interests?
- ☐ More plot and character-driven stories with less explicit adult activity?
- ☐ We value your ideas, so give us your opinion of this book:

_____

_____

_____

7. In terms of your adult interests, what do you like to read about? (Tick as many as you like.)

- ☐ Traditional corporal punishment (CP)
- ☐ Modern corporal punishment
- ☐ Spanking
- ☐ Restraint/bondage
- ☐ Rope bondage
- ☐ Latex/rubber
- ☐ Leather
- ☐ Female domination and male submission
- ☐ Female domination and female submission
- ☐ Male domination and female submission
- ☐ Willing captivity
- ☐ Uniforms
- ☐ Lingerie/underwear/hosiery/footwear (boots and high heels)
- ☐ Sex rituals
- ☐ Vanilla sex
- ☐ Swinging
- ☐ Cross-dressing/TV

☐ Enforced feminisation
☐ Others – tell us what you don't see enough of in adult fiction:

_____

_____

_____

8. Would you prefer books with a more specialised approach to your interests, i.e. a novel specifically about uniforms? If so, which subject(s) would you like to read a Nexus novel about?

_____

_____

_____

9. Would you like to read true stories in Nexus books? For instance, the true story of a submissive woman, or a male slave? Tell us which true revelations you would most like to read about:

_____

_____

_____

10. What do you like best about Nexus books?

_____

_____

11. What do you like least about Nexus books?

_____

_____

12. Which are your favourite titles?

_____

_____

13. Who are your favourite authors?

_____

_____

14. Which covers do you prefer? Those featuring:
(Tick as many as you like.)

☐ Fetish outfits
☐ More nudity
☐ Two models
☐ Unusual models or settings
☐ Classic erotic photography
☐ More contemporary images and poses
☐ A blank/non-erotic cover
☐ What would your ideal cover look like?

_____

15. Describe your ideal Nexus novel in the space provided:

_____
_____
_____
_____

16. Which celebrity would feature in one of your Nexus-style fantasies? We'll post the best suggestions on our website – anonymously!

_____

THANKS FOR YOUR TIME

Now simply write the title of this book in the space below and cut out the questionnaire pages. Post to: Nexus, Marketing Dept., Thames Wharf Studios, Rainville Rd, London W6 9HA

Book title: _____

NEXUS NEW BOOKS

To be published in January 2009

WICKED OBSESSION
Ray Gordon

Eighteen-year-old Anne has always been jealous of her attractive and successful older sister, Haley. Feeling second best is something she has grown used to. But when a handsome young man rejects her advances and takes a shine to Haley instead, it is one humiliation too many. Seething with envy, Anne decides to take revenge the only way she knows how – by using her young body and sexual charms to destroy Haley's relationships. Before long behaving wickedly becomes an obsession and Anne relishes the rewards of her promiscuous behaviour. Prepared to go to any extreme to trump her sister, Anne makes plans to seduce Haley's future husband on the night before the wedding.

£7.99   ISBN 978 0 352 34508 0

To be published in February 2009

NEXUS CONFESSIONS: VOLUME 6
Various

Swinging, dogging, group sex, cross-dressing, spanking, female domination, corporal punishment, and extreme fetishes . . . *Nexus Confessions* explores the length and breadth of erotic obsession, real experience and sexual fantasy. This is an encyclopaedic collection of the bizarre, the extreme, the utterly inappropriate, the daring and the shocking experiences of ordinary men and women driven by their extraordinary desires. Collected by the world's leading publisher of fetish fiction, these are true stories and shameful confessions, never-before-told or published.

£7.99   ISBN 978 0 352 34509 7

If you would like more information about Nexus titles, please visit our website at www.nexus-books.co.uk, or send a large stamped addressed envelope to:
  Nexus, Thames Wharf Studios,
  Rainville Road, London W6 9HA

NEXUS BOOKLIST

Information is correct at time of printing. To avoid disappointment, check availability before ordering. Go to www.nexus-books.co.uk.

All books are priced at £6.99 unless another price is given.

NEXUS

NEXUS CONFESSIONS

NEXUS ENTHUSIAST

NEXUS NON FICTION

---------- ✂ ------------------------------

Please send me the books I have ticked above.

Name   ....

Address   ....

             ....

             ....

             .... Post code ....

Send to: **Virgin Books Cash Sales, Thames Wharf Studios, Rainville Road, London W6 9HA**

US customers: for prices and details of how to order books for delivery by mail, call 888-330-8477.

Please enclose a cheque or postal order, made payable to **Nexus Books Ltd**, to the value of the books you have ordered plus postage and packing costs as follows:
    UK and BFPO – £1.00 for the first book, 50p for each subsequent book.
    Overseas (including Republic of Ireland) – £2.00 for the first book, £1.00 for each subsequent book.

If you would prefer to pay by VISA, ACCESS/MASTERCARD, AMEX, DINERS CLUB or SWITCH, please write your card number and expiry date here:

....

Please allow up to 28 days for delivery.

Signature ....

Our privacy policy

We will not disclose information you supply us to any other parties. We will not disclose any information which identifies you personally to any person without your express consent.

From time to time we may send out information about Nexus books and special offers. Please tick here if you do *not* wish to receive Nexus information.   ☐

---------- ✂ ------------------------------